SHELL-SHOCK

ADELBERT SCHOLTZ

SHELL-SHOCK

A ROMATIC WAR STORY

RESOURCE *Publications* · Eugene, Oregon

SHELL-SHOCK
A Romantic War Story

Wipf & Stock
An Imprint of Wipf and Stock Publishers
199 W. 8th Ave., Suite 3
Eugene, OR 97401

www.wipfandstock.com

PAPERBACK ISBN: 978-1-6667-4670-9
HARDCOVER ISBN: 978-1-6667-4671-6
EBOOK ISBN: 978-1-6667-4672-3

READ THIS FIRST

This story is a work of fiction. Some of the characters mentioned in this book really lived, but most of the actions and words ascribed to them are nothing but fantasy. The other characters are purely the inventions of the author, although they may be partly modelled on real persons. If a photograph of a certain person appears in this book it may be assumed that that person existed. The places where this story unfolds are real places. There were really Luftwaffe units such as Kampsgeschwader (bomber wing) 26, 51, 54 and 200 but Kampfgeschwader 32 never existed.

Liberties were taken with the description of certain historical events to achieve a more dramatic effect, although care was taken to make this story as credible as possible.

A glossary of German words and expressions with their English equivalents is to be found at the end of the book. An explanation of the rank structure of the German Luftwaffe is also to be found as an appendix to this book.

PROLOGUE

Pretoria, Thursday, 14 August 1975

Nobody should ever try to convince me that any war is a great, glorious and glamorous series of heroic and Herculean events. It's not. It's rather a series of terrifying, traumatic and tragic experiences. And I can personally testify that this is the case since I contracted bad, ugly and serious shell shock during the Second World War and it took me a long time before I was able to shrug the effects off.

In hindsight, I realise that it was actually a silly, stupid, and sorry decision of mine to join the German "Luftwaffe" (Air Force) in 1936. Very stupid. It was taken on the spur of the moment and it was impossible, at that time, to foresee the consequences. Unfortunately, it's not possible to turn the clock back and I have to live with the emotional scars of my terrible, torturous and traumatic experiences.

But, on the other hand, I also found the love of my life in Germany – the gorgeous , glamorous and golden girl whom I married. I was also trained as a pilot and after the war I was able to create a new career as a pilot – for which I am grateful. After all, I fell in love with airplanes and flying from the start, although I love my wife much more.

It is a long story how it happened that I participated in the war on the German side and, therefore, it is necessary that I start at the beginning.

I, Karl Krause, am a German South African – or, a South African German, if you will. However, I grew up in the German village of Kroondal near Rustenburg. My grandparents were involved with the Hermannsburger Missiongesellschaft (Hermannsburg Missionary Society) and they settled down in the South African Republic (the old name of the province of Transvaal) during the nineteenth century. My grandfather – after whom I was named – farmed in the vicinity of Kroondal on behalf of the missionary station. During the South African War of 1899 to 1902, he helped to defend his adopted fatherland against the British imperialists and he was a bitter-ender who had to lay down arms in 1902 when the Peace Accord of Vereeniging was signed.

My grandmother, with two minor children, was forcibly taken to a concentration camp by British soldiers where she had to live in a tent, suffering bitter winter cold, summer heat, starvation, lack of medical care and humiliation by the "Tommys" who afforded her and the other inmates of the camp little privacy.

I was born during 1915 – shortly after the outbreak of the First World War. Because my father, Kurt Krause, was born in Germany before his parents emigrated to the Transvaal, he was interned with many other German-speaking people at Fort Napier in Natal. He was released after a few months with most other missionary staff, mainly because his parents and their children obtained Transvaal citizenship during the South Africn War, which automatically made them South African citizens when the Union of South Africa was created in 1910. My father was, therefore, not at home when I was born and he wasn't able to assist my mother, Käthe – also a German girl from the vicinity of Vryheid in Natal – during childbirth.

My brother, Konstantin, was born two years after me and my youngest brother, Konrad, was born shortly after the end of the war in 1919. Because the first names of all five members of our family started with a K and we have the family name of Krause, our neighbours often referred to us as the "K-Bande" (K Gang).

Since I wasn't particularly interested in mission work, I decided do pursue another career after school and, therefore, I joined the South African Police. My training took place in Pretoria during the depression year of 1933 and with that, I secured my occupational future – exactly at a time when many people were unemployed and doomed to poverty. It was my goal to become an officer in due course and to reach an important position in the

Police Force. At school, I was a leader and during my last school year, I was head boy of our high school and captain of the rugby team. In our church, I was the leader of the youth group. Therefore, I hoped to reach a senior position in the Police Force with my leadership qualities.

We got lots of physical exercise at the Police College and that was something I enjoyed. Since my high school days in Kroondal, I was a diligent athlete and the mile was my speciality – apart from rugby, which I also enjoyed. I often took my bicycle to explore the countryside.

Something else which I relished at the Police College, was the training in driving and maintenance of all sorts of motor vehicles. I found that I had a mechanical aptitude.

After my training as law-enforcement officer, I was deployed to the Free State town of Kroonstad. In other words, I progressed from Kroondal to Kroonstad. I joined a cycling club – and rapidly became the fastest cyclist in the whole of the Free State Province. It helped that I often had to visit the farms in the district with a Police bicycle to investigate complaints.

And then, a team had to be chosen for the 1936 Summer Olympic Games in Germany. Due to my German background, I was naturally very eager to participate in these Games and I made sure that I became very, very fit and strong by running a lot, riding my bicycle and training with weights.

During the trials to choose members for the South African team, I participated in the race over sixty miles and the speed tests over one mile and on both occasions, I came first. The man who came second and who also recorded excellent times, Eddie Edwards, was chosen to be my team mate for the cycling events.

The South African Olympiuc Committee, fortunately, took care of all the expenses regarding clothes and the passage on a ship. I was even to be outfitted with a new racing bicycle in Germany.

Because I grew up in an Afrikaans-speaking environment, my Afrikaans was, of course, flawless. I had to take it as a subject in school – together with English and German. I am, therefore, trilingual, because I am naturally also fluent in German, my mother tongue.

This story, which I am starting to write on my sixtieth birthday, is being done in Afrikaans for the benefit of my children and grandchildren who are mainly Afrikaans-speaking. I rely on my memory, but also on documents and history books that I have consulted, to write this story. This storymay, perhaps, also be translated into English by a benevolent publisher.

THE STORY OF KARL KRAUSE
(IN HIS OWN WORDS)

Berlin, Friday, 17 July 1936

There is still a fortnight to go before the Olympic Summer Games in Berlin start, but our South African team of 32 members, together with a few officials, have already arrived today. We were confined to a passenger liner for a fortnight and in that time, we could not participate in our respective sports to stay fit. I, though, did my best to keep my muscles strong by doing squats with my team mate Eddie Edwards on my shoulders and other exercises.

Our team already departed on 4 July from Cape Town with the passenger liner SS Usambara of the "Deutsche Ost-Afrika-Linie" (German East Africa Line).

We could, perhaps, also have travelled with a ship of the Union Castle Line, but that would have been rather cumbersome, because we would have had to transfer onto a ferry to the European mainland in Southampton before catching a train to Berlin. The Usambara took us directly to the harbor in Rotterdam in Holland and there we got onto a direct express train to Berlin, where we arrived the same afternoon.

The express train dropped us off at the Hauptbahnhof (main station) in Berlin and from there we were taken by bus to the Olympic Village at Elstal in Wustermark, thirty kilometers (that's eighteen miles) to the west of Berlin's city centre. We travelled initially through Berlin's main street, Unter den Linden. It was clear that that the street, a fortnight before the Games, already had a festive atmosphere with hundreds of red banners with the Nazi Swastika sign hanging from poles.

At the Olympic Village, we are housed in new buildings. Eddie and me get a double room – quite neat, but without luxuries.

Berlin, Saturday, 18 July 1936

The bicycles that I and Eddie have received are the latest German racing models. The two of us get into our cycling clothes directly after breakfast – which was served in a big central dining hall – and we took to the road. We, first of all, went to ride on the new Wilmersdorf-stadium, which is almost finished, to get the feeling of the place. This is where the speed tests are to be held – and not in the new Olympic Stadium where the athletic events are to take place.

Initially, we thought that the stadium would be directly adjacent to the Olympic Village, but when we made inquiries we were told that it is situated half-way back to the city centre. The ride there of about twenty kilometers – twelve miles – was good exercise.

After we have rested somewhat we try the cycling track and we enjoy it very much. The cycling surface is made of wood and it is pleasant to ride on. We enjoy loosening our stiff muscles after a fortnight on the ship. We are not the only cyclists and we conclude that team members of other countries also came to train here.

After half-an-hour of hard cycling, we get thirsty and we sit down on a bench next to the track to empty our water bottles. A young guy on his bicycle joins us and asks in broken English from which country's team we are. I immediately recognise his German accent and I answer in German.

"Hallo, I am Karl Krause of South Africa. This is my team mate, Eddie Edwards (and I point in his direction). Unfortunately, he cannot speak German and I will have to interpret for him, if necessary. Anyway, it's pleasant to meet you."

The man smiles broadly: "Ja, and I'm Sepp Schellenberg, a member of the German cycling team. And how did you acquire your good German? You speak a good High German, just like us Germans."

"It's because I *am* German."

Sepp offers his hand and we shake hands: "Good to meet you. Welcome to Berlin."

"Thanks. How many members are there in your German cycling team?"

"There are twelve of us."

"There are only the two of us. But I am sure that we will be just as good as you Germans, even if there are more of you that us."

"And what does a German, like you, do in the South African team?"

"My dad was born in Germany, but I entered the world in South Africa."

"I see. Let's see if you are as good as you say, right now. Let's do four rounds around the track and see who comes first."

"Our legs are tired after we have ridden here from the Olympic Village and we have already done a few rounds on this track."

"I have also ridden from the Olympic Village. My legs are also tired. But, let's give it a try."

"Oekee" (the way the Germans pronounce OK).

It seems that Sepp is a fraction better than me. After four rounds, he was merely a yard or so in front of me and three yards before Eddie.

When we halt to regain some breath, I declare: "You have an advantage because you know this track. We only tried it today for the first time."

"Let's try again tomorrow."

"Then it's Sunday. I would like to go to church. Let's do it during the afternoon."

"Will three o' clock suit you?"

"One hundred percent. And then we can also get used to the summer heat in these parts."

Berlin, Saturday, 25 July 1936

During the past week, Eddie and I competed against Sepp on four occasions. He was better then me on three occasions and I beat him once with more than three yards. Eddie was not quite able to beat us and he always came third.

This led to a friendship between me and Sepp – my first "real" German friend. We stopped addressing each other as "Sie" – the polite form of address in German – and we spontaneously starting calling each other "Du" (you), the informal way friends address each other.

While we were resting after this morning's informal race on a seat next to the track, Sepp says: "How do you feel about lunch tomorrow at my parents' place? Only you because your friend won't be able to take part in the conversations."

"Sounds oekee. How do I get there?"

"Let's meet each other just after breakfast at the dining hall and then we ride together to my parents' home in Dahlem, a suburb of Berlin. That will count as our daily exercise."

"May I attend church first?"

"If we get away early enough, we can attend church together with my parents at their church – and then we enjoy the visit at their home afterwards, before we return to the Olympic Village later during the afternoon."

"I look forward to that. All right, we take our breakfast early tomorrow, as soon as the dining hall opens."

Berlin, Sunday, 26 July 1936

Sepp and I are the first persons to order breakfast after the dining hall has opened. We need a little more that an hour to reach Sepp's family home. We are early enough to attend the "Gottesdienst" (divine service) with the Schellenberg family in their church. The family consists of the father, Sebastian, the mother, Sofia, elder brother Siegried, and younger sister Sonja.

After I have shaken hands with all of them, I remark: "Oh, you are clearly the 'S-Mannschaft' (S Team)?"

Father Sebastian: "How did you guess?"

Me: "Oh, I grew up in the K-Bande."

Father Sebastian gives a broad smile: "It is actually only Sepp who does not really fit into our team. He was named after his grandfather on his mother's side. His real name is Josef, but that is abbreviated to Sepp. So, your Krause family is, therefore, the 'K-Bande' there in your German village in Transvaal?"

During lunch I get to know the Schellenberg family better. Herr (Mister) Sebastian Schellenberg is a bank manager with the Dresdner Bank, "Frau" (Missus) Sofia Schellenberg is a "Hausfrau" (house wife), elder brother Siegfried is an "Oberleutnant" (Lieutenant) in the Luftwaffe and younger sister Sonja is studying English and German Literature at the Humboldt University in Berlin and she hopes to become a teacher some or other time.

Herr Sebastian and Oberleutnant Siegfried are both active members of the NSDAP ("Nationalsozialistische Deutsche Arbeiterpartei") – better known as the Nazi Party. They encourage me to buy the book in two volumes of the German "Führer" (Leader), Adolf Hitler, titled "Mein Kampf" (My Struggle), so that I can get acquainted with his philosophy of life.

According to these two men, it is the best thing that could have happened with Germany when Hitler took over the government in January 1933. The country has progressed at a fast pace since then and was able to shake off the consequences of the bad economic circumstances of the previous decade. Hitler refused that Germany continue to pay any more reparations to Great Britain, America and France to compensate them for the damages they had suffered during the Great War of 1914 to 1918. There is little unemployment and the Germans smile again after they had sunk into despair after the defeat of 1918.

Siegfried is especially enthusiastic about the fact the the German "Wehrmacht" (Defence Force) is growing rapidly and is supplied with the most modern hardware.

Siegfried: "After the Peace of Versailles of 1919, Germany was forbidden to have an effective military force and U-boats (submarines) and airplanes were strictly forbidden. Hitler didn't care for these restrictions. Germany has a number of U-boats presently, as well as an Air Force, of which I am a proud member."

Me: "What is your function in the Luftwaffe?"

Siegfried: "Oh, I am an instructor at the 'Luftkriegschule' (Air Warfare School) at the airfield of Berlin-Gatow, not far from here."

Me: "That sounds exciting. I have never flown in my life yet and in South Africa I never even got the chance to have a close look at an airplane."

Siegried: "Are you interested in visiting our 'Fliegerhorst' (air base)? There are many airplanes standing around."

Me: "Naturally!"

Sepp: "Let's borrow my dad's automobile and drive there later on. Vati (Daddy), is that in order?"

Father Sebastian: "As long as Siegfried drives. If he knows how to handle an aircraft in the air, he will surely be able to keep an automobile on the road."

After we have enjoyed coffee, Sepp, Sonja,, Siegried and me set off to the airfield, a few miles from their dwelling. At the gate, Siegfried shows his identity document as a member of the Luftwaffe and the guards salute him as we drive inside. After parking, we walk onto the great grass-covered plain where a few airplanes rest. Because it is a Sunday, the place is more or less deserted – except for the guards at the entrance.

Sepp: "You may touch them, if you want to."

Me: "Yes, please."

I fondle the wings, engines and propellers of a few machines standing around. Sonja follows my example.

Me: "How does it feel to take such a machine into the air?"

Sonja: "Some people become sick. They vomit. And then it's a marvelous dirty mess!"

Siegfried: "And then there are those who enjoy it tremendously. Like me. You feel free like a bird, up there in the sky. Then you look down on all the houses, trains, automobiles and small people down below. And then you feel superior."

Me: "I wonder – am I perhaps one of those people who will become sick or am I one of those who will enjoy it?"

Siegfried: "You took a voyage on a ship to Europe. Were you ever sea-sick?"

Me: "Never."

Siegried: "Then you ought to be able to take it easily."

Me: "What is the possibility that I can fly with you for a little while?"

Siegfried: "Not today. The airplanes you see around here don't have any fuel."

Me: "When can we do it?"

Siegfried: "Actually, never. We are not allowed to transport civilians in military aircraft, except in exceptional circumstances."

Me: "I'm not a civilian. I'm a member of the South African Police. For the past three-and-a-half years."

Siegfried: "Perhaps, perhaps, we can make a plan, after all. I see a fuel lorry over there. I am going to look for its keys and bring it to my personal airplane so that I can take on a bit of fuel for a short flight."

Sonja: "Yes, please! You can see that the man is extremely excited and very anxious to fly. His eyes sprakle just by touching a flying machine."

Siegrfried sprints away and half-an-hour later he drives the fuel lorry to a spot next to his personal airplane. It takes some time to tank enough fuel.

Me: "What type of airplane is this?"

Siegfried: "It's an Arado 66. It's a trainer we were using the last three years."

Siegfried: "I also went to the airport tower. Today, there are only three guys, amongst other an "Oberfeldwebel" (Flight Sergeant). I simply told him that I am taking a member of the Police up to do some reconnaissance from above before the Games start in a week's time."

Me: "Wonderful!"

Sonja: "And you didn't tell a single lie!"

Sepp: "Karl, 'Hals-und-Beinbruch'!" (break your neck and leg! – the German way of wishing somebody a pleasant outing).

Siegfried: "Here you have a flying helmet and flying goggles. Put this jacket on because it can become quite cold and windy up there."

Sepp helps me to get into the rear seat of the airplane after he has made sure that I was properly clothed for the biggest adventure in my life. I get strapped in. In front of me are a number of unfamiliar instruments of which I understand absolutely nothing.

It takes some time before we get moving and we progress across the uneven grass field. After two minutes the airplane lifts off and I look down. The surface of the earth is rushing away from me and soon I am able to look down on houses, roads and buildings, as well as forrests and lakes of which there seem to be quite a number around Berlin.

Siegfried turns around to look at me. I greet him with a huge smile and my thumb pointed to the sky. He looks ahead again and suddenly pulls the aeroplanbe steeply skywards so that we gain more height. We fly progressively slower as we loose speed, due to our "uphill" trajectory and it suddenly feels as if the airplane comes to a standstill. Mother earth down there is very far below us.

It feels as if the airplane suddenly starts to fall and she picks up speed as we dive down. Suddenly, the earth makes a summersault around me as Siegfried throws the aircraft into a corkscrew. That's jolly exciting. Suddenly, he pulls the aircraft upwards so that we fly vertically. Mother Earth is directly behind me. He draws a full circle and we fly upside down for a short moment before we return to a horizontal flight. I feel like cheering, singing hymns and to yodel – so exhiliarating this is.

After that, we fly over the Olympic Village and the new Olympic Stadium, a little distance further on. I also see the track where our cycling events are to take place. I assume that this is how I must do reconnaissance from the air as a Police official, as Siegfried has explained.

I don't know how long we have been playing up there in the air. But, for me, it was hopelessly too short. At last, the airfield comes into sight again and Siegfried places us gently onto firm terrain and we move to the spot where Sepp and Sonja are waiting. After the engine has been switched off and the propellor has stopped turning, Siegfried gets out and I follow his example.

Sonja: "You don't even look pale! How was it?"

Me: "Better as anything else that I have experienced in my life. I think I will never get enough of flying in my life. Siegfried, what is the possibility that I can get flying lessons from you?"

Siegfried: "For that, you will have to join the Luftwaffe. After you have received your basic training, you become a 'Fahnenjunker' (flight cadet) and receive training here at the Luftkriegschule. Later, you go to the 'Luftkriegakademie' (Air War Academy) before you are awarded your flying licence. Still later, you are to receive the rank of 'Leutnant' (Second Lieutenant)."

Me: "That's what I want to do!"

Siegfried: "You are a South African citizen. They won't take you. Afraid you're a spy."

Me: "My father was born in Germany. Maybe, that will help."

Siegfried: "Take your bike tomorrow morning very early and come here and then I will take you to the recruitment office. Perhaps, you may achieve something there."

Sepp: "Karl, have you forgotten about the Olympic Games?"

Me: "Of course not. But I can come and join in the meantime. That is, if they want me."

Siegfried: "Get me exactly at eight o'clock at the gate where we entered today. Will you be able to find the place again?"

Me: "As a Policeman, I have been taught not to get lost."

Berlin, Monday, 27 July 1936

Fortunately, I was able to get breakfast at six o' clock and shortly before eight o' clock I stop at the main gate of the Fliegerhorst Berlin-Gatow. Siegfried is already waiting there.

To the guards at the gate he declares that I'm his guest and I am allowed to enter. My bicycle is locked away in the gate office. At the recruitment office, I am introduced to "Hauptmann" (Captain) Werner Waldstein, the head of the office. Siegfried explains that this friend of his would like to be trained as a pilot of the Luftwaffe.

Waldstein: "You will have to undergo a selection process. You will have to be tested whether you will be able to operate as a pilot and whether you are officer material. Are you ready for that?"

Me: "Certainly."

Waldstein: "All right. Let's complete your application form right now. Ah, here it is. Allow me to dig my 'Tintenkuli' (fountain pen) out of my drawer. Right, here we are. First names and family name?"

Siegfried asks to be excused because he has to work. He salutes the Hauptmann and departs.

I supply all sorts of particulars, as requested.

"Date of birth?"

"21 February 1915."

"Place of birth?"

"Kronenthal (I translate the Afrikaans name to German)."

"Where is that? Never heard of the place."

"It's not far from Rustenburg."

"Did I hear you correctly? Rastenburg? Right, I'll write that down."

I smile somewhat, but I don't correct the man. I don't have the faintest idea where Rastenburg is situated, but if the

Hauptmannn thinks that's where I came from, then that is certainly in order.

"Name of father?"

"Kurt Krause."

"Place of birth of father?"

"Lüneburg."

"Name of mother?"

"Käthe Krause, born Meier."

"Place of birth of mother?"

"You may write Hermannsburg."

This information I give without hessitation because it is true, as far as I am concerned, although it is the Hermannsburg in Natal, South Africa, not in Germany.

"Highest academic achievement?"

"Abitur (Matriculation)."

"Present occupation?"

"Police official."

"Since when?"

"Since 1933."

"Place of employment?"

"Kroonstad." (This question comes so suddenly that I cannot think of anything else).

"Kronstadt? As far as I know, there a Kronstadt in Sweden, or maybe in Russia also. Where is this Kronstadt?"

"Somewhere south."

"All right, Kronstadt it is."

As present address of abode I supply the address of the Schellenberg family in Dahlem. That is where all postal items will have to be sent.

And so it continues. In the end, the Hauptmann declares: "Herr Krause, you are provisionally accepted as 'Offiziersanwärter' (officer candidate). Please write down your force number. The next intake is on Monday, 17 August, the day after the Olympic Games have ended. Are you, perhaps, going to watch any events during the Games?"

"Ja, I'm especially interested in the cycling events, but I'm also going to attend the opening ceremony."

"Unfortunately, I won't be able to get any leave to experience anything of the Games. Did the Police give you leave to go and watch the cycling events?"

"I received leave for the whole duration of the Games."

"Lucky devil."

Berlin, Saturday, 1 August 1936

Today, the opening ceremony of the Games takes place. All the athletes in the Olympic Village had an early breakfast and we were transported to the main venue, the Olympia Stadium, where we had to gather outside in our different national squads.

And then Adolf Hitler, the German Führer arrives. The German team becomes ecstatic when he leaves his special motor vehicle, together with a few other dignitaries. He waves at the athletes and enters the stadium. We can hear how the crowd inside the stadium cheers and roars as he appears.

And now, it's our turn to enter the stadium while a brass band provides some marching music. The team of Greece takes the lead, since Greece is the country where the ancient Olympic Games originated. The German team, as the hosts, are to form the rear-guard. The German team is by far the largest with more than four hundred sportsmen and -women. Each team has a leader who carries the national flag of that country.

As we pass the place where Herr Hitler sits in a special raised box, our leader lowers our national flag to honor the leader of our host country. All of us give the Nazi salute to greet Hitler by raising our right arms at an angle of 45 degrees. We go to our place on the field and we are to wait there till the end of the ceremony. We were told that almost four thousand athletes will participate, of which about 330 are women. There are to be more or less 130 events.

All eyes are suddenly raised towards the heavens as a big flying gas bag, a Zeppelin, the Hindenburg, glides over the stadium, towing the Olympic flag, consisting of a picture of a huge bell with the inscription "Ich rufe die Jugend der Welt" (I call the youth of the world). On the bell is a drawing of the German eagle on top of the five Olympic circles.

The chairman of the German Olympic Committee gives a speech in German, which I am, of course, able to follow. Thereafter, Hitler delivers the opening speech and he receives thunderous applause. Suddenly, I feel very good about my German ancestry. It is clear that these Germans are proud of their country, in spite of the fact that they suffered a humiliating defeat in 1918. I look forward to my training as an officer in their Luftwaffe.

An athlete with a torch appears and runs through a passage between the rows of athletes up to a large cauldron on top of a platform and lights the Olympic flame.

After this, Hitler leaves his seat of honor and walks over to the German team on the field to wish them luck. He is photgraphed where he poses next to a few German girls. The crowd evidently likes this and Hitler receives some more rupturous applause.

As Hitler and his entourage are leaving the stadium, a few dozen baskets containing hundreds or even thousands of pigeons are opened and the birds take to the air. To mark the official end of the opening ceremony, an artillery piece of the Army is fired. That scares the poop out the flying birds and I don't think that is something the organizers envisaged. The bird droppings rain out of the sky onto athletes and spectators alike, before the poor panicked birds disperse and disappear.

Eddie murmers: "This is how the Germans take revenge on the rest of the world for losing the war. We are defenceless, right now."

Berlin, Sunday, 2 August 1936

My friend Sepp invited me again to visit his folks for lunch today.

He added: "It is becoming time for us to rest our legs. Our first events are Wednesday and then we want to be in top condition. We must have a last light session on Monday and then we can be lazy on Tuesday before we must do our best on Wednesday."

And that is why I am again spending the day with the Schellenberg family. They all want to know what happened on Monday at the recruitment office.

Sepp hands me a letter that has arrived on Friday. The sender is some or other office of the Luftwaffe. It contains my call-up instructions to report at the Fliegerhorst Berlin-Gatow on Monday, 17 August 1936.

Herr Schellenberg asks: "And how will your parents in South Africa feel about the fact that you seek a career in the German armed forces?"

"I'm quite sure that they will welcome my decision. My grandfather fought the British during the South African War of 1899 to 1902 while my grandmother and her two children were held in a horrible concentration camp by the British Army. Germany and Great Britain were also enemies during the Great War and, therefore, my folks will certainly welcome my decision to become a member of the Luftwaffe."

Sonja remarks with a wide smile: "One of these days I will know two members of the Luftwaffe – my eldest brother and you."

We discuss the prospect of our teams. Sepp is adamant that the German team will be the best team. "During the Winter Games, in February, which were held at Garmisch-Partenkirchen, Germany came second. The top six countries were all Germanic or Aryan countries: Norway, Germany, Sweden, Finland, Switzerland and

Austria. That proves that we, the Aryan people, must be the master race. We are destined to rule the world. These Summer Games will confirm that."

Herr Schellenberg: "Karl, with your German ancestry, you are also a member of the master race. Your people in South Afrika, whose ancestors were Dutch and German, are destined to remain the masters of the black barbarian peoples on your continent."

Sonja: "The German culture is superior to anything any other country could produce, especially the British. We have the best actors, architects, authors, composers, musicians, playwrights and poets. I am also convinced that we have the best theologians and philosphers in the world. Our painters are only surpassed by our Dutch neighbours and the Italians."

Me: "How do you know that?"

Sonja: "I spent a whole year in Manchester after finishing Abitur at a sister of my mother who is married to an Englishman. That was before I started studying here in Berlin. I learnt to speak English just as well as the Englishmen themselves. And that is why I am studying English Literature, as well as German Literature."

Frau Sofia: "The Brits have nothing to compare to Bach, Beethoven or Brahms. Or Wagner. They even had to import a German composer, Georg Friedrich Händel, to teach them how to compose music. The English Royal Family is, actually, more German than English. King George the First was born in Germany from the House of Hannover. Queen Victoria's mother was a German princess and her husband and cousin, Albert, was a German prince. They spoke German with each other and her German was actually better that her English."

Sepp: "We have world-class scientists and engineers. Britain, certainly, doesn't have the talents our people have.
"Karl, one of these days, you will share in the glory of German culture and achievements."

Me: "I can't wait."

Berlin, Saturday, 8 August 1936

Sepp comes to my table during breakfast in the dining hall: "I have two tickets for the athletics events of today in the main stadium. Would you like to come with me?"

"Certainly. When are we leaving?"

"Directly after breakfast. We can take one of the busses that transports athletes to their venues."

During the day we enjoy a number of athletics numbers. When it's time for the final of the 4 X 100 meters relay for women, Sepp says: "Both German tems qualified for this final. There is an A-team and a B-team. Let's hope that both teams make it to the medal podium."

The girls, all of them superb athletes, get ready. To my surprise, I notice that Sepp's sister, Sonja, is running the last 100 meters for the B-team. Although both Sepp and me shouted our throats hoarse – together with the rest of the crowd – the B-team gets nowhere. Neither does the A-team. The Americans receive gold, Great Britain get silver and the bronze medals are given to the Canadians. Anyway, I am proud for my friend's sake that his sister also participated in the Olympics and that she was a member of the B-team that qualified for the finals. That is no mean feat.

Sepp: "I'm surprised and disappointed that the German A-team didn't do better. During the heats, they broke the Olympic record."

Berlin, Sunday, 16 August 1936

The Games are over. I feel quite satisfied with my acheivements. In the race over 100 kilometers, I came fifth – a mere seventeen seconds slower than my friend Sepp who got third place and the bronze medal. In the time test over one kilometre, I also came fifth, a matter of seconds behind the first three cyclists. I feel that I should have tried a little harder and that I would have, at least, conquored a bronze.

It is, however, no use crying over spillt milk. One cannot get the milk back into the bucket while it is seeping into the dirt. But I feel proud that I, after all, didn't do so badly. I also feel good about my friend Sepp, who managed the bronze in the road race. In the past, he was always a slightly better than me.

The whole world is duscussing the fact that Jesse Owens, a black American, was the most successful athlete during the Games. He won four gold medals for the 100 meters sprint, the long jump, the 200 meters sprint, and the 4×100-metre relay. Photos were taken of the disgusted Hitler who evidently didn't like the fact that a black "Nigger" and "Untermensch" (subhuman) was able to do better than white Aryan men.

After we have attended the closing ceremony this afternoon and returned to the Olympic Village, I go to our team manager:

"I know we are to catch the train to Rotterdam tomorrow morning early. I won't be going with you. I am staying behind."

"Why on earth? Don't you want to go home?"

"I have a job offer over here. You know that I speak German fluently and I will easily fit in here. I like this country and I simply couldn't resist the offer."

"OK. I can't restrain you or force you to get onto the train. It's your choice. But don't expect the South African Olympic

Committee to pay for your passage back to South Africa at a later stage."

Berlin, Monday, 17 August 1936

Last night, Siegfried Schellenberg fetched all my lugage from the Olympic Village with his father's automobile, to store everything (including my bicycle) at the Schellenberg home. Sonja made sure that the guest room is clean and neat. This morning Siegfried takes me with him to the Fliegerhorst Berlin-Gattow on his motorcycle where I am to be trained at the Luftkriegschule 2.

Siegfried: "Don't take notice of those other guys you may see marching around. They started in April as cadets on general training – the same type of training you will be receiving. Some of them will become pilots as time goes on. There are also those who will get onto all sorts of other courses – machine gunners, anti-aircraft artillery, radio operators, navigators, mechanics and the like. You applied to become a pilot.

"If you are rejected at a later stage, you may perhaps join one of these other courses. But – I think you will be accepted for pilot training. You have a stomach for flying, you are extremely fit and strong and I believe you're not colour blind or have any other defects or diseases or disorders or disabilities."

Me: "Thanks."

"And, remember, don't ever volunteer for anything. Stay as invisible as possible. It will become known that you are a Policeman, but don't talk about your experiences in that regard. It might become known that you are actually a South African Policeman and that will result in your immediate dismissal and deportation."

"Thanks. Fortunately, during my training as Policeman, I learnt to stay as invisible as possible and never to volunteer for anything. "

I report again at the recruitment office and I find a big crowd of young men, waiting to be processed. Exactly at eight o' clock two officials arrive with a table, two chairs and boxes filled with documents. After they have arranged everything, one of them barks: "All of you imbeciles! Get into a long queue!"

We oblige. I happen to be the fifth man in the row (again!).

We have to present our call-up papers and after it was noted that we are present and that we are who we are, we are directed to the quarter master's store. I am kitted out with overalls, a full uniform, boots, a steel helmet, bedding, a toilet kit, other items and writing materials. I gather that we will have to endure quite a number of lectures about the theory of flying and that we will have to take notes.

With my arms full of articles, I am directed to get a bed in one of the barracks – a brand-new group of buildings. We are to fill up the place from the back onwards.

Because I was the fifth man to be helped, I get a bed rather deep into the dormitory. I dump my new belongings on my bed. I try my new uniform on, put my civilian clothes in the steel locker next to my bed and get my bed ready. Fortunately, at the Police College in Pretoria I was taught how a military bed has to be made and I help the guys around me to get their things in order. They are grateful to have the help of a Policeman.

It suddenly strikes me that I will have to send a letter of resignation to Police Headquarters in Pretoria. It won't look good if I don't turn up at the end of my special leave to attend the Olympics. But how am I to get out of this place and find a post office? Heaven knows.

After all the men have received their kit and dumped everything on their beds, one of the officials who inspected our call-up papers, appears at the door at the far end of our dormitory: "All you filthy pieces of shit, get into your overalls. And then you get into a long row, in alphabetic order. Outside."

I hastily get rid of my uniform and put on my overalls. It takes a long time before we are able to assemble ourselves into a very long alphabetic line. I stand between Koch and Krüger. It appears that our group is distributed over eight dormitories, each with fifty men.

The same official reappears with a loud hailer: "You silly lot, you are not even able to form a straight line! A gang of kids in a third-rate Kindergarten annexed to a whorehouse will do better! Who of you lot knows how to march? You must have been taught that in the 'Hitler Jugend' (the Nazi yough movement)."

Everybody raises his hand.

The long line of men is, thereafter, arranged into three rows by this official and he divides us into four companies, each with one hundred men. I find myself in "Schülerkompanie" (student company) number 2. Other officials take control of the different companies.

Our official takes us to one side and shouts while we are standing at attention: "And now you do a right turn and march to the barber shops where your hair will be cut so that you can look like decent clean Aryans. And after that, you are to get into the communal bathrooms of your barracks where we will hold an inspection to see whether anyone of you is a Jew. Your male instruments will give you away if you are one of those horrible children of Abraham! Verstanden? (Do you understand?)"

Nobody answers.

The man gets red in his face: "You are to reply as a choir of queer boys, simultaneously, by shouting: 'Jawohl, Herr Oberfeldwebel!' Verstanden?"

A few mumble something. The individual who calls himself an Oberfeldwebel roars: "Do it all at the same time! Verstanden?"

All of us: "Jawohl, Herr Oberfeldwebel!"

I gather that an "Oberfeldwebel" must be something like a staff sergeant.

Afterwards, we assemble outside where we are addressed:

"All right, you silly, sorry, stupid lot. It is lunch time. You are to march like prospective Aryan soldiers of the Reich without mutilated sexual instruments or deformed reproductive organs to the soldiers' mess hall, where the Wehrmacht will fill you up with fodder."

After lunch, we assemble outside again, in our respective companies.

The Oberfeldwebel arrives and informs our company: "Please take note, those of you who have brains and ears, that my name is Oberfeldwebel Erich Erhardt. You may only speak in my presence if I give you permission to do so or if I address one of you. Verstanden?"

"Ja, Herr Oberfeldwebel!"

"And when you are in my presence, you stand at attention, while you stare at a spot exactly twenty centimeters above my head. Verstanden?"

"Ja, Herr Oberfeldwebel!"

An officer appears and he announces: "Herr Oberfeldwebel, thank you for getting these men organized. Give the order that they may stand at ease."

The order is given and we stand at ease.

The officer: "Men, thank you for volunteering to be trained as members of our glorious Luftwaffe. Only a few of you will make it to the pilot training course, but the rest of you will be trained to perform other essential functions, mostly as ground crew.

"My name is Hauptmann Wilhelm Wolters and I will be your company's chief instructor for the time being. The Oberfeldwebel will teach you to march properly and how to take part in parades. Other non-commissioned officers will give you physical exercises to make you fit and strong. We need men with guts in the Wehrmacht. If you cannot stomach all the exercise, we will employ you as pen pushers, store room clerks, wheel-barrow operators, inspectors of light bulbs, door hinge operators, broom handlers or something similar. But I suspect that most of you are fit and strong, otherwise you would not have applied to be trained as pilots and officers or for other responsible positions.

"Please remember that this base, the Fliegerhorst Berlin-Gatow, is the most important Luftwaffe base in the country. We have a reputation to uphold and, therefore, no monkey tricks or silly antics from your side will be tolerated. This base was an army training field during the nineteenth century and thereafter, but it was converted to a Luftwaffe base two years ago when the Luftwaffe was officially established. As you can see, all our buildings are new, clean and neat. You have to keep them that way.

"You have received writing paper, pens and pencils. You are to use those when you attend lectures on the organization, rules and traditions of the Wehrmacht. You will also get some basic lectures on the theory of flying machines heavier than air. You will be taught how to use radio equipment and how to read maps. And, most important of all, you will be instructed about the doctrines of National Socialism. You need that background to be of use to the Reich.

"Herr Oberfeldwebel, you may take over again."

At five o'clock, when most activities on the base come to a halt, Siegfried comes looking for me. Because I am in overalls, which is deemed to be military garb, I salute him. With a smile, he reciprocates.

"Karl, you are stuck at this base for at least three months before you will get any leave. When that time comes, you may come and visit us because you have nowhere else to stay during your leave."

"That's very generous of you."

"My parents feel sorry for you, because your folks are very far away."

"Thanks. May I ask you a big favor, please?"

"What is it?"

"I must write a letter of resignation to the South African Police, but it will be impossible for me to post it. I will write it tonight. Will you come and collect it tomorrow afternoon from me and post it?"

"No problem."

"And I will also write a letter to my parents, which you must also post for me. I don't want the military postal service at this time to know that my parents live in another country or that I am corresponding with the South African Police. Please."

"My pleasure."

Berlin, Tuesday, 18 August 1936

Siegfried awaits me at the entrance of our barracks. All the men who enter the building salute him, as we have been taught today.

Me: "Come inside with me and then I can hand you the letters that I have written. I don't have envelopes. Will you please be so friendly as to put them into envelopes, write these addresses on the envelopes and take them to the post office?"

Siegfried: "I knew that you wouldn't have any envelopes. Here is a packet. Use two of them now."

"Thanks a lot."

I insert my two letters to my parents and the Personnel Department of the Police in Pretoria in their respective envelopes, write the addresses and provide Siegried with enough money for postage stamps.

Siegfried: "I have something else for you."

With that he gives me a sealed envelope and adds: "If you want to respond to that, get it ready by tomorrow the same time."

"What is this?"

"It's a letter from my little sister."

I salute Siegfried as he walks away.

I am totally taken by surprise that Sonja has taken the trouble of writing to me. The last time I saw her, yesterday morning early before Siegfried delivered me to the air base, she gave no sign of being interested in me in any way. I, nevertheless, open the envelope as soon as I have reached my bed.

Sonja's letter is actually only a short note. She informs me that she hopes that I will be successful in my endeavour to become a Luftwaffe pilot and that she would like us to become pen palls. She found me an interesting person with my combined German and South African backgroud.

It suddenly strikes me that Sonja is, actually, an attractive and intelligent girl. I was so focussed on the Olympics and my prospective career in the Luftwaffe that I paid her little attention. During my school years I had some sort of a relationship with one of the girls in my class, but nothing came from it. While I was a Policeman in Kroonstad, my work and my bicycle training kept me so busy that I had very little time for a social life. The available female talent in Kroonstad also didn't really appeal to me.

And now, suddenly, here is an attractive athletic Aryan female who shows some interest in me. I mumble inaudibly to myself: "Karl Krause, you are a normal, virile member of the male species. You do need female companionship. Where will you ever get a better opportunity with this special speciman of the female species from a good family?"

Berlin, Tuesday, 1 September 1936

The news broke today that that Hitler has decided to send a contingent of soldiers to Spain, including a few squadrons of the Luftwaffe, to help the Spanish leader, General Franco, in his fight againt the Communist rebels. This German force was called the "Condor Legion" and the first soldiers arrived in Spain already towards the end of July.

My fellow cadets argue that it was about time that Germany started to flex her muscles by becoming involved in international affairs, especially since Soviet Russia started to help the Communist rebels in Spain.

Berlin, Friday, 13 November 1936

We are getting our first weekend pass today after three nonths of hard work and Siegried has promised to take me to his parents' home where I can enjoy my first free time since joining the Luftwaffe as a cadet.

I look forward to see Sonja again. We regularly wrote letters to each other, more or less once a week, and Siegfried willingly played the role of postman. I learned that Sonja is in her third year of studying German and English literature, that she is an active and avid athlete who excells in the 100m and 400m sprints, that she loves classical music and mountaineering and that she likes working with children.

I confided to her that I have made friends with Wolfgang Schenck, one of our group of prospective pilots. He grew up in Windhoek, the capital of South West Africa, the former German colony, and he speaks Afrikaans fluently, just like me. When his father, a farmer, died, he and his mother returned to Germany a few years ago. Since he was born under the German flag before the Great War, he could claim German citizenship and was, therefore, accepted into the Luftwaffe. He is about two years older than me.
I also look forward to see my old friend, Sepp, again. He is a final year student in electrical engineering.

We both arrive on Siegried's motorcycle at the Schellenberg home in our Luftwaffe uniforms – Siegfried as an officer and I as an ordinary cadet without a rank. I greet every member of the household by hand and Frau Sofia shows me again to the guest room.

Suddenly, I feel shy in the presence of Sonja. I find her very attractive with her blonde hair and blue eyes and athletic figure, but I don't know how to start a conversation with her. In addition, today is Friday, the thirteenth. According an old superstition, this is supposed to be a very unlucky day and, therefore, I keep my distance and my mouth shut.

During supper, I am requested to tell about my experiences the past three monthis. I tell about the Oberfeldwebel who is our marching instructore, the NCO's who give us physical training and the officers who instruct us about the Luftwaffe and its organisation.

Herr Sebastian: "Any experiences out of the ordinary?"

"Oh, yes. It happened twice that we saw the Führer when he got out of an airplane. We couldn't see much of him because he was rather far away and he was surrounded by other high ranking officers and Nazi officials. But, it was rather special to see him."

Siegfried: "I've also seen him quite often. He has his own private aircraft with which he visits other parts of the country. This aircraft, a Junkers Ju 52, is permanently stationed at our airfield. The Junkers is lovingly called 'Tante Ju' (Aunty Ju) because she is just as slow, ungainly, wrinkled and gentle as an old lady."

While we are drinking coffee after dinner, Siegfried comments: "All my colleagues at our base are overjoyed by the news that our aircraft, especially the bombers, are proving to be very valuable in combat, down there in Spain. The Communist rebels, who have the backing of Russia, don't have an answer for our Heinkels and Dorniers.

"Karl, if you want to become a bomber pilot, you will fly machines that have been tested in combat."

Berlin, Saturday, 14 November 1936

When Sepp suggested that the two of us take our bicycles and ride into the countryside, I was game immediately. I actually missed my racing bike while sweating and slogging at the Fliegerhorst, although there were enough opportunities to take part in sports and stay fit.

When I agreed with Sepp's suggestion, Sonja immediately announced that she would accompany us on her own racing bike. We didn't have the heart to tell her that we would have preferred to go without female company.

And now Sonja surprises me. She is just as fit and strong as me and Sepp and she has no trouble keeping up with us. We ride to Potsdam, a town to the south west of Berlin and from there on to Beelitz through wooded countryside. Sonja makes our day because she has brought some "Brötchen" (bread rolls) with cheese and ham along so that we can enjoy lunch under a big tree.

While I still feel nervous in her presence, I refrain from talking to her most of the time. It is, though, as if something inside me urges or pushes me to watch her the whole time. My eyes cannot get enough of her, although I hope that she doesn't find it rude of me to watch her whenever I get the opportunity. She is – in my eyes – the perfect example of womanhood: strong, fit, athletic, intelligent and good-looking. She also has a sunny, friendly and pleasant disposition. I am glad that we are pen palls.

Berlin, Sunday, 15 November 1936

The Schellenberg family attend church this Sunday morning and it is taken for granted that I accompany them. After all, I grew up on a missionary settlement and it may surely be assumed that I am a religious person.

It happens that I sit next to Sonja. How it happened is a mystery. Anyway, since I do not have my own hymn book with me, I am obliged to sing with Sonja from her hymn book. She has a beautiful soprano voice.

I find it, all of a sudden, impossible to concentrate on the pastor's sermon because I am far too conscious of the female body in close proximity to mine. If I wished, I could have touched her, but I do not dare something like that in church and not with her father sitting next to her on the other side. Moreover, her two brothers are also present and I don't know how protective they are regarding their little sister who isn't so little anymore.

I decide to stay away from her during the remaining part of the week-end because I don't want to make a fool of myself.

After lunch, Sonja confronts me: "Karl, am I correct in assuming that you have had English as a school subject and that you speak it fluently?"

"Yes, I had to take it. As a Policeman, I was supposed to serve English-speaking people in their own language and even to take down statements in English."

"Marvelous. From now on, you are going to speak English to me. As you know, I an studying English Literature at university. But I must get my ear to stay attuned to this language. I can read it without difficulty, but my ears must stay used to the sounds. Will you help me?"

"All right." Secretly I think that this is a tall order and I will stay out of Sonja's way. And besides, my English is not quite perfect and I am afraid to make silly mistakes within earshot of an expert of English Literature.

Sonja: "Wonderful. Can we start right away? What will we discuss? Let's talk about the pastor's sermon this morning."

Berlin, Monday, 16 November 1936

Siegfried delivers me this Monday morning to the doorstep of our barracks. I dare to ask him: "Does your sister have a boyfriend? Such a beautiful girl must, surely, have many admirers."

"She used to have one, but she grew tired of him and got rid of him. Why?"

"Oh, nothing. I just wanted to know."

Siegfried gives a sly smile before taking off again.

Berlin, Wednesday, 16 December 1936

We recruits get a few days off during the Christmas period and we have to report back on Monday, 4 January 1937. After four months at the Luftkriegschule, we have completed "Lehrgang 1" (the first part of the curriculum).

Siegfried collects me from our barracks: "Have you ever learnt how to ski?"

"No. Why?"

"We are going on a skiing outing to the Hochsauerland just after Christmas. There's already lots of snow on the hills."

"Who are 'we'?"

"Who do you think? The whole S-Mannschaft, as well as the one present member of the K-Bande."

"Oh. Thanks. But I don't know how to ski. We never got snow in the Transvaal."

"Then we will teach you. But, first of all, you are to spend Christmas with us."

"I actually had the idea of visiting Holland or Denmark. I wanted to see something of Europe."

"Nonsense. You cannot refuse such a friendly invitation. Do you have enough warm clothes for the snow?"

"I hope so."

"We will provie you with snow goggles, a helmet, gloves and skis."

Berlin, Monday, 21 December 1936

At Kroondal, we always celebrated "Heiligabend" (Christmas Eve) in true German style with a church service and celebrations at home around a Christmas tree where presents were distributed, while we pretended that Father Christmas left them somewhere to be found.

I suddenly find myself in a difficult situation. I ask Sepp after breakfast to accompany me to some shops in Dahlem where I could buy a few presents for my hosts.

"Karl, I would have loved to help you, but I can't. I am sure that Sonja will be willing to help you."

Sonja: "Yes, I will take you. Let's leave just after you have helped me to wash the dishes."

Herr Sebastian: "Take my automobile. Karl, I'm sure that you have learnt how to drive in the Police."

Me: "Yes, I have. But I don't have a valid German driver's licence yet. We are to get some training on vehicles only during January."

Sonja: "I will drive. Thanks, Vati."

We find some shops in Dahlem where I am able to buy small presents for the Schellenberg family.

Plettenberg, Saturday, 26 December 1936

The six of us arrive just after dark at our destination, the little town of Plettenberg in the Hochsauerland, a hilly part of Western Germany. We took the train from Berlin to Hagen and from there we travelled by bus to Plettenberg. We made use of public transport because the Schellenberg family car would have been too cramped with six adults. And, besides, Father Schellenberg was not sure whether it was safe to drive on snow-covered roads.

We arrive at our destination, a "Pension" (guest house) where three rooms were booked for us. I occupy the biggest bedroom with Siegfried and Sepp. I look forward to a week of sports in the presence of beautiful Sonja, although I promised myself that I won't take any liberties with her – especially not with the rest of her family around.

We continued with our weekly letters to each other and I decided that I really grew fond of this wonderful example of womanhood. I regard myself as a not-too-bad specimen of manhood, either, since I did rather well at the Olympics and one of these days I hope to be commissioned as an officer in the German Defence Force. I have already learnt that the Germans regard military officers to be the cream of society.

But the question remains: what are Sonja's intentions with me? Am I simply an interesting foreigner, or something more?

Berlin, Monday, 4 January 1937

It is night-time and I am lying in my bunk at the barracks at the Fliegerhorst Berlin-Gatow and I am thinking back about the most pleasant time that I have experienced in my life.

Due to the generosity of the Schellenberg family, I was able to learn to ski. The member of the S-Mannschaft who taught me mostly was Fräulein (Miss) Sonja Schellenberg. I often wonderd how it would be to kiss her marvelous mouth but I couldn't go as far as that. What would happen if she gave me a slap in the face for being so stupid or "frech" (cheeky)?

And while my companions are snoring, I review the time in Plettenberg in my memory. I am not able to erase the face of Sonja from my mind and it is very late before I drift off.

Tomorrow will be a repetition of today – footslogging, exercises and lectures. By this time we know how to handle most hand-held weapons and one of these days we will get driving lessons on Wehrmacht vehicles. That will be a piece of cake for me, I decide, because I was already taught at the Police College how to handle and fix all sorts of vehicles.

Berlin, Friday, 19 February 1937

The four companies of recruits or cadets are having a parade today. Our basic training has been completed and very soon the selection for the candidates for pilot training will take place. All the prospective pilots are feeling nervous because nobody knows who will be accepted. The uncertanty consumes me as well.

The salute at the parade is taken by "Generalleutnant" (Lieutenant General) Otto von Stülpnagel, Kommandant of the Luftkriegsakademie. He is assisted by Oberst Julius Schulz, commander of the Luftkriegsschule 2.

After the parade, Siegfried and Sonja wait for me at their family motor car. I introduce them to my friend from South West Africa, Wolfgang Schenck. He invites us to enjoy refreshments at a restaurant. We are to celebrate our promotion to the rank of Fahnenjunker, which is equivalent to that of a Unteroffizier (corporal).

Berlin, Monday, 22 February 1937

After a pleasant weekend with my adopted German family, the S-Mannschaft of Berlin-Dahlem, I return to the air base with Siegfried. Those who will be selected for pilot training are to receive two months of general aeronautical instruction.

The selection process starts with interviews with a selection board and a written exam about the stuff that we were taught during the previous six monthis. More or less half of the two hundred men who applied for pilot training, fail to satisfy the selection board and they are relegated to other types of training.

Those of us who satisfied the selection board are taken up in airplanes and subjected to aerobatics to make sure that they can handle that. I have already proved to myself and Siegfried six months ago that I am able to deal with an aircraft's antics. I am, nevertheless, taken up in a trainer called a Focke Wulf 44 Stieglitz and the pilot tries his best to make me sick. He doesn't succeed, of course. When I reach terra firma again I am all smiles – in contrast with some other men who look as if they are on the verge of tears or stumble out of the aircraft while carrying big paper bags into which they threw up while flying around.

Only about fifty men are selected for the flying course and we are ordered to move our belongings into the same dormitory. Wolfgang and I make sure that we occupy adjacent beds. We all are promoted to the rank of "Fahnenjunker-Unterfeldwebel" (Flight Cadet-Senior Corporal).

This is something that I can mention in my weekly letter to Sonja.

Berlin, Friday, 26 March 1937

By this time, it is taken for granted that I visit the Schellenberg residence during weekends when my training is interrupted. Today, I sit with my adopted family in church for the service of "Karfreitag" (Good Friday). We were given the whole Easter weekend off and I only have to report for duty again on Tuesday.

It so happens that Sonja sits next to me in church again and we both sing from her hymn book. I am again very conscious of her body. Suddenly, I feel that she has shifted her body nearer to mine. That is unexpected and I make sure that I shift a few centimeters away from her, so as not to offend her by pushing my body against hers.

During the afternoon, Sepp, Sonja and I go riding on our racing cycles again. We return just before dusk. I get great respect for Sonja's fitness and strength. She must be the dream girl of any man. I find that I really enjoy her company but I don't know how she feels about me. She is always friendly, polite and considerate, but she is too much of a lady to demonstrate anything more than an ordinary friendship towards me – not even when she practices her English on me. Besides, I never had a sister and, therefore, I never learnt to understand or to deal with the so-called weaker sex (although Sonja seems just as strong as any man).

Berlin, Monday, 19 April 1937

The two months of studying general aeronautical subjects are over and our group is ready to start with the elementary flying course at the Luftkriegschule today. We assemble in our lecture hall and we are told to have a look at the list of instructors on the notice board to see which pupil is assigned to which instructor. We are also told to proceed to the quarter master's store to collect our flying gear – goggles, flying helmets, flying jackets and so forth.

We are also promoted to the rank of "Fahnenjunker-Feldwebel" (Flight Cadet-Sergeant). That means that we are getting a slight pay rise.

We congregate at the notice board and to my surprise I find that my instructor is none other than Oberleutnant Siegfried Schellenberg. That cannot be a coincidence and I am sure that my friend must have pulled a few strings to get me attached to him.

There is much news for my next letter to Sonja.

Berlin, Tuesday, 1 June 1937

A very important event takes place today – my first solo flight, which marks the end of "Lehrgang II", the second part of our training course. Siegfried has trained me carefully and patiently on a Focke Wulf 44 Stieglitz, his new trainer. By this time, I have taken control of the aircraft on many occasions with Siegfried as supervisor. But today is different. I am doing a solo flight, all on my own.

After I have completed a flight of almost an hour and have returned to Mother Earth, Siegfried takes me to the officers' mess for a cup of coffee.

"Look, my friend, you are almost ready to proceed to bigger aircraft. In a month's time, after you have completed 150 hours in the air, you will be ready to receive your 'Luftwaffenflug-zeugführerschein' (Luftwaffe pilot's license) and your 'Flugzeug-führerabzeichen', also called a 'Pilotenschein' (pilot's badge). That will happen at a grand parade."

"I can't wait."

"And then some more training is to start. You will be taught to do formation flying, together with other aircraft in a 'Kette' (flight) or a 'Staffel' (squadron). And then you will be posted to some or other station elsewhere, depending on which type of aircraft you would like to fly – twin-engine bombers, dive bombers, fighters, transport planes, reconnaissance planes or whatever. What would you like to do?"

"As far as I am concerned, the backbone of the Luftwaffe is its bomber force. They carry the biggest punch. That has been proven in Spain with the Condor Legion. Fighters only have to shoot down enemy planes, but bombers are supposed to inflict much more damage on the enemy. That's where I would like to go."

"In that case, you will be sent to Lechfeld, south of Augsburg, in the southern parts of the country. And, if I may give you some advice: keep a personal log book of all your flights – apart from the log book of each aircraft that you fly. That will ensure that you compile a complete record of everything you do in the air. Note down the date, your task and destination, the hours in the air, weather conditions and anything else noteworthy. I've been doing that since I got my pilot's wings."

"Thanks for this grand idea."

"But, one of these days you will depart for Lechfeld. Then it won't be so easy to come and visit us anymore. You won't have a family to take care of you over there."

"I think I will be able to take care of myself. That's what I did when I was a policeman."

"And what will happen to Sonja when you are so far away?"

"I don't know. Why are you so concerned about her?"

"She will miss you terribly."

"I will miss all of you when I am over there. You almost feel like family. You always made me feel welcome and you took care of me. I will be in your debt for the rest of my life."

"But how will you miss Sonja?"

I stay silent. I cannot divulge to my friend how I really feel. As time marched along, she occupied a bigger and bigger part of my heart and I decided that she was the woman I would have liked to make my wife. But she never gave any indication that I was anything but a good family friend and I didn't want to spoil that type of relationship by imposing myself on her. And besides, at the moment I am only a lowly "Fähnrich" (Ensign) and there is no way that I am in a position to think of an engagement or even marriage.

Siegfried sees my hesitation: "My friend, it is clear as daylight that you are totally in love with my sister. The way you look at her gives you away. The way you try to avoid her when in our company shows clearly that you don't want us to see how you really feel. Am I correct?"

I cannot avoid this direct question and I mumble: "Ja."

"Then, my friend, I also have good news for you. My sister is also head over heels in love with you. She's crazy about you, but she had the good sense not to behave in a stupid way by showing her affection too directly. That's why she sits next to you in church. That's why she accompanies you and Sepp when you go riding your bicycles. That's why she asked you to become a pen pal. That's why she asked you to help her with her English. And you were too bloody blooming blind to notice all that!"

I stare in bewilderment at my friend and instructor and I cannot produce a single sound with my vocal cords. I catch myself with my mouth agape.

"What are you going to do about this state of affairs? Are you going to break my little sister's heart by keeping your distance? Or by disappearing from her life?"

"I'll think of something."

"You'd better think of something very quickly, before you are transferred to Lechfeld or somewhere else."

"Will you be able to organize a pass for me this Friday?"

"I'll see what I can do."

Berlin, Saturday, 5 June 1937

It is a mystery how it came about that only Sonja and I go riding into the countryside this Saturday. Sepp complained that he was too busy with his academic work to go riding and, therefore, I and my dream girl set off on our own.

We ride in silence – or, almost total silence. We say only the most necessary things. When we reach our turning point, Sonja points to a big tree under which we can rest. From her rucksack, she takes our lunch. We consume it in silence. We both look in different directions.

At last, Sonja says: " Look here Karl Krause, I always thought that you were an intelligent guy, but I don't know anymore. You seem to be the most stupid, dim-witted, slow and retarded man on the whole of God's earth."

"Why do you say that?"

"Any other man with red blood cells in his veins and arteries and male hormones pumping through his body would have taken advantage of a situation like this."

"Taken advantage of what?"

"To make advances."

"Advances to what?"

"See, you are really an idiot. Any other girl would have given up on you."

"What do you mean?"

"Any normal man with normal urges and normal needs would have gotten me in a grip and would have given me a kiss."

"Oh, is that what you want?"

"Hell! Are you totally blind? Must I apply to have you committed to a madhouse? What's wrong with you?"

I don't answer and suddenly I cannot control myself anymore. I get Sonja in a strong grip and press my lips against hers.

She starts laughing and I release her: " Look here, Herr Krause, let me show you how you must kiss a girl properly. Relax, and let me be your instructor."

After thirty minutes of training in this regard, I regain my breath: "Sonja, will you please forgive me for not telling you how much I have already loved you before this. I was too afraid to offend you by opening my heart to you, but now the ice is broken. I think about you almost every moment of the day. Your lovely face is the last thing I see in my mind before I go to sleep at night. I dream about you. I love flying. I enjoy flying very much. But nothing of that sort can compare to the wonderful kisses you have just taught me. May we have some more practice? Can we continue our lesson? Please?"

"Only for a few minutes. Remember, we have to be back at home before dinner time."

Berlin, Thursday, 25 June 1937

During the last few months we received instruction in aerodynamics, aeronautical engineering, elementary navigation, meteorology, flying procedures and training in the reception of Morse – apart from more flying time.

Our aircraft have received other markings. The Swastika remains on the tail fin, but big black crosses are painted against the sides of the fuselage, as well as on top of and on the bottom of each wing. That is to distinguish Luftwaffe aircraft from aircraft of any other air force. The Royal Air Force and the French Air Force both have circular multi-coloured markings to identify their airplanes as British or French.

Our group of fifty new pilots were divided into five "Staffeln" (squadrons) to practice formation flying. Wolfgang and I ask to be assigned to the same Staffel.

Berlin, Friday, 9 July 1937

Today is a red-letter day in my life. A parade is to be held where we receive our pilot's wings and our pilot's licences after a year's training. We are also promoted to the rank of "Oberfähnrich" (Senior Ensign) – which is on the same level as a Stabsfeldwebel or Sergeant Major. That means another slight pay increase.

We assemble with our steel helmets and carbines. We present arms while the Kommandant of the Luftkriegsakademie, General von Stülpnagel inspects us.

Afterwards, there is a reception in the officers' mess and everybody is entitled to invite a guest. My guest is, of course, my wonderful girlfriend, Sonja Schellenberg. Some of my friends are openly envious of me for having such a beautiful woman as my companion.

I cannot but be proud of my pilot's wings, as well as my new rank as Oberfähnrich after having completed Lehrgang III. There is still much training to be done before I am ready to be assigned to an active air unit and become an officer.

Our group is to disperse to different flying schools. I am to say farewell to my friend Wolfgang Schenck, who is to be trained as a fighter pilot. I am dispatched to the "Große Kampffliegerschule Lechfeld" (Big Bomber School, Lechfeld) with the strength of a "Kampfgeschwader" (Bomber Wing).

Kufstein, Wednesday, 14 July 1937

The six of us – that's me, Sonja, Siegfried, Anja (Siegfried's girlfriend), Sepp and Katja (Sepp's girlfriend) – are having breakfast in the garden of our Pension in Kufstein. We arrived yesterday by train. Kufstein is situated on the border between Germany and Austria and the village is surrounded by beautiful mountains.

This is my first opportunity of experiencing something of Germany outside of Berlin, apart from our expedition to the Hochsauerland. The next part of my training as bomber pilot at Lechfeld is to start during August. I am, therefore, free for more than three weeks. Siegfried also has a break because the next intake of recruits at the Fliegerhorst Berlin-Gatow is to take place during the middle of August.

Sepp, Sonja, Anja and Katja are all students and their lectures only start towards the end of August. Sepp has already received his diploma as electrical engineer, but he wants to do some post-graduate work before joining the Navy as nautical engineer.

All our parents agreed on this holiday on the condition that the three girls occupy one bedroom and the men sleep in another bedroom. That is to prevent us from doing something silly, stupid or naughty. During our train journey here, we have already decided that nothing is going to stop us from being silly, stupid or naughty. We will draw lots and the couple who draws the unlucky straw is to give the other two couples the opportunity of using a bedroom each in private for bed gymnastics – or whatever we choose to do during that time.

Last night, it was the opportunity of Sepp and Katja to wander the streets of Kufstein while Sonja and I occupied the girl's bedroom for more than an hour. We both decided that we enjoy being silly, stupid and naughty and I wonder what my prudish folks at the missionary settlement in the Transvaal would say if they knew.

Tonight, it will be Sonja's and my turn to explore the streets of Kufstein after dinner to give the other two couples some private time together.

While we are having breakfast in the garden, I seem to hear Afrikaans spoken by two couples at the table next to ours. I listen a little better.

I hear one of the men say: "Stem julle saam? Dis pragtig hier. (Do you agree? It's beautiful here.)"

Before any of the other can answer, I quip: "Jaaa, ek stem beslis saam! (Yeees, I really agree!)"

Sonja: "What did you say? I didn't understand."

Me: "My girl, I spoke Afrikaans to our neighbours."

I get up and walk over to the other table: "Hallo! I am Karl Krause of Kroondal, near Rustenburg. Also from Kroonstad. What are you guys doing here, so far from home?"

They all look surprised at my Afrikaans. One of the men says: "Hi! Nice to meet a fellow Afrikaner. I am Willie Scholtz, and this is my wife Annemarie."

We shake hands.

The other man, evidently a twin brother of the first speaker, replies: "And I am David Scholtz. This is my wife, Josephine."

We also shake hands.

David: "And what on earth is a guy from Kroondal or Kroonstad doing in Germany? We are also from the Free State and we are studying in Berlin. I want to become a medical specialist and my brother wants to become a scientist. My wife is a teacher and my sister-in-law works for a bank."

Willie: "And we are on our honeymoon. We got married the other day."

Me: "Congratulations. I am also from Berlin, but one of these days I am to settle in the vicinity of Augsburg. I and my friend over there (and I point to Siegfried) are Luftwaffe pilots. The other four of us are all students, some of them probably at the same university as you two guys."

David: "How in heaven's name did you manage to join the Luftwaffe, seeing that you are a South African from Kroonstad?"

Me: "That's a long story. I suggest that the ten of us go for a long hike through the fields and the mountains and then we can get better acquainted. I would like to hear your stories."

Kufstein, Tuesday, 20 July 1937

We made friends with the Scholtz twins and their new wives. The conversations are mostly conducted in German, but when I speak Afrikaans to my new friends, the others seem to understand some of it since Afrikaans (and Dutch) is somehow related to "Plattdeutsch" (the German dialect spoken in some parts of Northern Germany). We undertook four hiking expeditions through the mountains together while discussing the political situation in Europe. We all agreed that the Führer was spending much money on rebuilding Germany's armed forces in an effort to revenge the disaster of 1918 when Germany was totally humiliated at the end of the Great War.

Yesterday, David exclaimed: "It suddenly dawns on me that I must have met you, Karl, at the opening ceremony of the Olympic Games! The four of us attended the ceremony and afterwards we went to the South African squad to wish you luck."

Me: "I seem to remember something of the sort. Were you also subjected to the aerial bombardment when the pigeons got a fright from the gun shot?"

But tonight, we are in a festive mood. We sit in a restaurant in Kufstein and order dinner. I leave my seat next to Sonja and proceed to the "Kellermeister" (cellar master) and order three bottles of "Sekt" (sparkling wine) for our table, which has to be delivered at the same time as our plates of food.

When the order is executed, the other nine occupants of our table suddenly get frowns on their foreheads for this extravange and David Scholtz asks: "Is one of you celebrating a birthday or something important?"

I get onto my feet again: "Yes, you guessed correctly. Let's fill our glasses with this golden fluid and then I have an important announcement to make."

The bottles are opened and each one's glass is filled.

"Meine geehrte Damen und Herren! (my honorable ladies and gentlemen!) I indeed have an important announcement to make. Sonja, here (and I place my left hand on her shoulder), is a very obedient girl. I have given her a very important order today and she complied. We Germans use to say: 'Befehl ist Befehl' (an order is an order). That's how it works in the Luftwaffe and the rest of the Wehrmacht. I simply informed this gorgeous girl that we are going to get engaged to be married. She realised that she had no choice whatsoever in the matter and she agreed to do as ordered. So – as of today we are inofficially engaged. An official engagement party will be held in Berlin at a later stage after I have informed her parents of my decision."

Siegfried: "What will happen if my father forbids you to marry his daughter?"

Sonja: "Then we just run away. Easy."

Sepp: "Before you can do that, I will lock you into your bedroom and hide the key. Your food will be delivered through the window."

Sonja: "I have already spoken to Vati. Inofficially, of course. He likes Karl and he will welcome him as his son-in-law."

Me: "So, you have conspired behind my back? Have you?"

Sonja: "When I set my eyes on you for the first time, before the start of the Olympic Games, I already knew that this day would come."

Siegfried: "I don't know whose job it really is, but I want to propose a toast on the future Herr and Frau Krause."

We all take a sip after we have bumped our glasses against each other.

Sepp: "Let's celebrate something else that is due to happen soon. Fähnrich Karl Krause is to become Leutnant Krause of the Luftwaffe. One of these days!"

Another round follows with glasses lifted and sips taken.

20 July 1937

Sonja: "I will always remember this date, the twentieth of July, as a special date."

Berlin, Sunday, 1 August 1937

After our holiday in Tyrol, I briefly returned to Berlin. While Siegfried and Sepp are taking their girlfriends home, I ask Herr Sebastian and Frau Sofia Schellenberg whether Sonja and I could have a chat with them.

Sonja's father starts the conversation: "When are you two getting engaged? That is – officially? Or don't you have such an intention?"

Sonja: "Vati, thank you for making it easy for Karl. He is sometimes clumsy and shy."

Me: "Herr Schellenberg, I indeed thank you for making it easy for me. You are, no doubt, aware of the fact that I and this beautiful, wonderful, colorful and playful daughter of yours are very much in love with each other. I cannot imagine myself ever having an interest in any other woman. We plan to marry as soon as I have received my commission as Leutnant and that ought to be either during December or January. We will become engaged officially whenever I get my first pass from the Kampffliegerschule where I must report shortly."

"But my daughter hasn't completed her studies yet. She still has another year to go."

"Vati, there are no rules against married women studying at the university. And as soon as Karl gets a permanent posting I will look for a position as teacher in the vicinity."

Frau Sofia: "So, that's settled, then."

Lechfeld, Tuesday, 3 August 1937

It is certainly not pleasant to be so far from Sonja. I arrived at the Luftwaffe base of Lechfeld yesterday; more specifically at the Große Kampffliegerschule Lechfeld, also known as the Kampffliegerschule 3. It is situated about 20 kilometers south of the Bavarian town of Augsburg. I arrived with a group of about one hundred other pilots from different parts of the country where they had received their initial flying training.

And now the one hundred of us are sitting in a lecture hall where the "Kommodore" (commander) of the Kampffliegerschule addresses us.

Oberst Erhard Krüger welcomes all of us and stresses the fact that we are the elite of the Luftwaffe and, therefore, the elite of the whole Wehrmacht: "There is no other officer training course so difficult and demanding as this one that you will now be subjected to. To fly a bomber requires more skill than flying a fighter, a transport plane or a dive bomber. You will be the leader of a crew of four or five members. You must help the observer to place your load of bombs at exactly the correct spot, otherwise you will have wasted valuable time, valuable bombs and valuable fuel.

"This school was established two years ago, just after the Luftwaffe came into being. This field was used by the 'Luftstreitkräfte' (air combat units) of the German Army during the Great War. Therefore, we have to uphold the traditions of those heroes. I am sure that your conduct will reflect your Germanic spirit.

"As you, no doubt, know – we have the strength of a regular Geschwader with about 100 aircraft. We are divided into a headquarters' Staffel and three 'Gruppen' (Groups), each consisting of three Staffeln. Every Staffel (squadron) of our ten Staffeln has about ten aircraft each.

"Please go to the notice board where you will see into which Staffel each one of you is placed and who your instructor is to be.

"Initially, you will fly with your instructors and later, when your crew members have also received their training, you are to fly with them. In total, you will be required to fly more than 160 hours during the five months at this school. You will, of course, also receive lectures on various subjects.

"I want to introduce you to the three commanders of our Gruppen. The one at the far left is Oberstleutnant (Lieutenant Colonel) Hans von Wussow. He commands the first Gruppe. Next to him is Oberstleutnant Hans Steinweg of the second Gruppe and here, next to me. is Major Josef Segschneider, the Gruppenkommandeur (Group Commander) of Gruppe Three.

"I thank you, gentlemen."

We leave the lecture room in an orderly fashion and proceed to the notice board. I notice that I am assigned to Staffel 6, which is the third Staffel of the Second Gruppe. My instructor is Leutnant Werner Baumbach. He is to teach me how to fly the Heinkel He 111 bomber.

Lechfeld, Wednesday, 4 August 1937

Leutnant Werner Baumbach is taking me up in a Heinkel He 111 bomber today – the biggest bomber in the Luftwaffe arsenal. He indicates that he only graduated on this aircraft during the first part of this year. He does not have much experience of being an instructor. I find him, though, a pleasant chap with a wide grin and I feel safe in his presence. By this time, I have flown all the trainer types of the Luftwaffe and I am confident that all will be well.

While we are strolling to our aircraft, Baumbach points to some single-engine aircraft on the field: "Those are our newest fighters, Model 109 of the Bayrische Flugzeugwerke (Bavarian Aircraft Works). It is called the Bf 109. It is being tested here because the Bayrische Flugzeugwerke is situated nearby and they test their prototypes here. Their chief engineer, Willi Messerschmitt, is a genius."

We roll to the end of the long runway in our Heinkel after I was made familiar with all the dials, switches, levers, sights, handles and grips.

Me: "This thing's nose is totally made of glass. Won't this glass shatter when we pick up speed?"

Baumbach: "It's reinforced glass within a strong frame. You'll be oekee enough."

` "How long can this thing stay in the air?"

4 August 1937

"Easily five hours or more."
"How far can she fly?"
"She has a range of more than 2 300 kilometers."
"Does she have a toilet?"
"You take your steel helmet along."

Berlin, Tuesday, 21 December 1937

Our passing out parade as fully fledged bomber pilots took place yesterday. On the same occasion we all received our promotions to the rank of Leutnant. I was posted to Lüneburg for my fist operational unit.

Today, Sonja is to become Frau Krause officially when we are to get married at the "Standesamt" (registry office). A church service for the religious solemnisation of our marriage is to take place tomorrow.

Sonja and her family organized everything and I was informed by letter about the progress. It was impossible to get away from Lechfeld and I had to be satisfied with whatever they did. Since it wasn't possible to get any leave since August we could not get engaged officially. We rush, therefore, straightaway into holy matrimony without an official engagement.

Berlin, Wednesday, 22 December 1937

The service in the church today is a military affair. I have invited a squad of my fellow new bomber pilots who live in or near Berlin, to be my guard of honor in their uniforms at the church. Siegfried, who was recently promoted to Hauptmann, is my best man. He is als wearing his uniform. Sonja's bridesmaid is Anja, Siegfried's fiancee.

Unfortunately, my parents can't be present. Kroondal in South Africa is just too far away for them to travel to these parts. They have, nevertheless, sent their best wishes by means of a telegramme.

Sonja is beautiful in her bride's gown. The church, which was built more than six centuries ago, is filled with flowers and beautiful music emanates from the organ. Sepp and Katja are to sing a duet at the end of the service.

My new parents-in-law are clothed in their best clothes and they look like the important people they are.

This is my first opportunity of wearing my new uniform as Leutnant. I am proud of my pilot's badge on the left breast pocket of my jacket, as well as the new rank insignia on my shoulder straps and on my jacket's collars.

Vati Sebastian has organized a dinner at a local hotel for our wedding reception. During the dinner, Vati Sebastian and Siegfried talk to me in earnest.

Vati Sebastian: "Your new wife still has one semester left before she can call herself a qualified language teacher. I suppose that you would like her to work near to you. Lüneburg is a fairly large town and there will certainly be a school where she will be able to get a job."

Me: "That is something that we have already discussed. I am glad that we think along the same lines. And we also have agreed to wait some time before we start a family. We want to establish our careers before we get to that."

Vati Sebastian: "A wise decision."

Siegfried: "Have you made sure that you have the correct recipe to increase your numbers at a later stage?"

Later, Sonja introduces me to her cousin, "Sturmbann-führer" (Major) Walter Schellen-berg in his SS uniform. We start chatting and I learn that cousin Walter is part of the "Sicherheitsdienst" (Security Service) or SD of the SS, the "Schützstaffel" (Protection Squadron), which used to be Hitler's body guards but which has developed into a separate organisation, the political police of the Nazi Party.
I find him an attractive and friendly man who has a law degree from the University of Bonn.

Something about him, though, makes me uneasy and I decide to steer clear of him in future.

He tells us: "Since it's my business to look at security matters, I know that you, Karl, are actually a South African citizen, albeit of German descent. For the sake of my dear cousin, Sonja (and he points at her), we will keep that information under the blankets (he says this whith a sly smile).

"I gather that you are committed to the struggle of Germany to become a world power and I support you in that endeavour. Congratulations with your officer's rank and your pilot's badge.

"If you ever need a favour you may contact me. I will also gladly help your beautiful new wife."

I feel a few drops of sweat running down my spine.

Lüneburg, Monday, 3 January 1938

Lüneburg! The city where my father was born. That is where I report this first Monday of the New Year. I was given my first posting as a bomber pilot to the Second Gruppe of Kampfgeschwader 257. The Fliegerhorst, which was established about two years ago, is still brand-new. It is situated about four kilometers east of the town and about 45 kilometers south of Hamburg, the biggest German port city.

Right at this moment, I am not quite in the mood to fly a Heinkel 111 bomber because my honeymoon with Super Sonja was far too short. We spent ten days, including Christmas and New Year, in the coastal village of Katwijk-aan-Zee in Holland where we stayed in a Pension overlooking the North Sea. I was able to travel over the international frontier with my South African passport.

And now, I am again the property of the Luftwaffe. Siegfried told me before the time that I was fortunate to get into this outfit, because it has a famous Geschwaderkommodore, Oberst Wolfram Freiherr (Baron) von Richthofen. He was an air ace during the Great War and served in the same Staffel as his more famous cousin, Manfred Freiherr von Richthofen, better known as the "Red Baron" due to his red Fokker Triplane with which he scored many victories. Manfred was succeeded as commander of that Staffel after his death by Hermann Göring, the present Commender-in-Chief of the Luftwaffe.

I report at the headquarters of the Second Gruppe of KG 257. The Gruppenkommandeur introduces himself to me: "Welcome, Herr Leutnant. I am Major Simon von Busche. You will be a member of the fifth Staffel of the Geschwader, which is also the second Staffel under my command. Let me take you to Hauptmann Ulrich Schwartz, your 'Staffelkapitän' (Squadron Captain)."

We find the Hauptmann at his desk in one of the hangars on the north side of the Fliegerhorst. It appears that Hauptmann Schwartz has the wrong family name. "Schwartz" in German means "black". He is, though, anything but black with his blonde hair, rosy cheeks and blue eyes.

Schwartz: "Ah, Herr Leutnant, I am glad that you are here. Take today off to get your things organized. Tomorrow I will show you to your brand-new Heinkel bomber and introduce you to your new crew members. Your task will be to build your crew into a smooth-running team. It is important that each man knows exactly what is expected of him and what he can expect from the others."

Me: "Herr Hauptmann, thank you. That is exactly how I was trained at Lechfeld."

"Have you already met our Geschwaderkommodore?"

"Not yet."

"Do it today."

After the Hauptmann has shown me around in the hangar and introduced me some of his staff, I take off to the central adminstrative block where I ask a clerk at a desk where I could find Oberst von Richthofen.

When I reach the Geschwaderkommodore's office, I am told by his secretary that I will have to wait. There is a meeting going on in his office. Fortunately, there is a chair on which I can sit and wait. I engage the secretary, an Unteroffizier, in conversation and I ask him what type of person the Oberst is.

"Very Prussian, very Prussian. Stiff and strict with discipline. His word cannot be questioned. He hates Fat Hermann Göring, who is a boorish Bavarian playboy."

I smile at this indiscretion of a lowly Unteroffizier to belittle the Commender-in-Chief of the Luftwaffe likes this.

After thirty minutes, the door of the inner office opens and a few officers emerge. The Unteroffizier indicates that I may enter.

I enter the inner office, stand at attention, salute and announce: "Herr Oberst, Leutnant Karl Krause reports for duty."

I am invited to sit down and the Oberst questions me about my training and my ancestry.

I divulge that my father was born in these parts.

"Did he fight during the Great War?"

I cannot evade the question and I cannot lie: "No."

"How did he manage that?"

"He was interned."

"Why?"

"Because he was born in Germany."

"That cannot be a reason why the Kaiser's Government would have interned him. Really!"

"He wasn't interned by die Kaiser's Government."

"Who did it then?"

"The South African Government."

"What the hell was he doing in South Africa?"

"Doing missioanary work for the Hermannsburg Missionary Society."

"Ah! That explains it. So – you are actually a German South African? Of are you rather a South African German?"

"Both, perhaps."

"But, you are a South African citizen?"

"Correct."

"Then how on earth did you manage to join the Luftwaffe?"

"I completed an application form."

"Yes, of course. When was that?"

"Directly before the start of the Olympic Games in August, thirty-six."

"Why at that time?"

"I competed in the Olympic Games. And that is how I came to Germany."

"As a member of the South African team?"

"Correct."

"In which sport?"

"I was a member of the cycling team."

"Any medals?"

"Unfortunately not. But I came fifth on two occasions."

"You know, I am supposed to report you to the "Gestapo" (Geheime Staatspolizei – Secret State Police). They will certainly deport you, throw you out of the country."

"That cannot be done."

"And why not?"

"Because I am married to an Aryan German woman. And my father was born in this country. Here at Lüneburg."

"When did your father move to South Africa?"

"During the 1890's. As a child, he accompanied his parents who were missionaries. My grandfather fought during the Boer War on the side of the commandos of Präsident Paul Kruger, also known here in Germany as Ohm Krüger."

"Oh, he fought against the British?"

"Correct."

"Well, well. I don't think I can report and deport the grandson of a Boer warrior, who fought against the Brits. Herr Leutnant, I welcome you as a member of our Geschwader. I am sure that you will be the only member of our Geschwader who has ever competed in the Olympics, even for a foreign country. I won't report you to the Gestapo."

"Thank you, Herr Oberst. My loyalty is totally with Germany. My grandfather's enemie are also my enemies."

"But we are not at war with Great Brittain. They're not our enemies."

"Everybody expects war to break out, sooner or later."

"Let's wait and see. One last point. Make sure that you destroy your South African passport. It could bring you into trouble. Use your Luftwaffe membership card to apply for a German passport. That's much safer."

"Thank you, Herr Oberst."

Lüneburg, Tuesday, 4 January 1938

We experience a snow storm and no flying is possible today. I, nevertheless, get to know my crew. We get into my Heinkel and each of them sits at his station.

My observer, navigator and nose gunner, who sits slightly in front of me, is Leutnant Franz Feierabend. His job is to guide me to the target and again back to our base. When we reach the target, he is to guide me so that I can drop our bombs at the right moment. He also mans the nose gun, a 20 millimetre canon, in case we are attacked by enemy fighters from the front. We both occupy seats in the "Gewächshaus" (greenhouse), the glass-enclosed cabin of the Heinkel.

My Funker (radio operator) and side gunner is Feldwebel (sergeant) Gerhard Gärtner. He has to keep us in contact with our base and other aircraft accompnaying us, as well as manning one of the 7,9 millimetre machine guns on each side of the fuselage.

The gunner manning the dorsal turret is Hauptgefreiter (lance corporal) Heinz Huber. He has a twin 7.9 millimetre machine gun at his disposal. The belly gunner, who lies on his stomach to shoot at fighters attacking us from below, is Gefreiter (Private, First Class) Johannes Jössel – the youngest member of my crew.

After I have inspected each man at his position, we retreat to our hangar where it is warmer. Franz Feierabend remarks: "I have noticed that our names follow the alphabet from F to K: Feierabend, Gärtner, Huber, Jössel and Krause. I propose that we call ourselves the F-K Mannschaft."

Me: "I don't think that will work. People will easily transform that into FKK, which is the abbreviation for 'Freikörperkultur' (free body culture – the German nudist movement). We don't want to be known as the FKK-Mannschaft, or do you? We are certainly not going fly around without clothes. It's too cold up there and I don't wish to get frozen. Anyway, it's against Luftwaffe regulations."

Lüneburg, Thursday, 6 January 1938

The weather has cleared and I and my team get into the air for the first time. Because Werner Baumbach has instructed me properly at Lechfeld I feel confident behind the controls of this brand-new Heinkel.

We are supposed to fly at least every day, except weekends. I feel totally at home, here high in the sky. This is exactly what I wanted to do since Siegfried has taken me up in his trainer in August 1936. I can't say that I am sorry for leaving the South African Police Force and joining the German Luftwaffe.

And, of course, the Luftwaffe made it possible to get married to superb and stupendous Sonja!

Lüneburg, Thursday, 3 February 1938

All officers are ordered to attend dinner in the officers' mess tonight with full uniform.

When we are all seated, each with a wine glass in front of him and two bottles of Port Wine on each table, Oberst Wolfram von Richthofen calls for silence: "Meine Herren, it is my duty as a German soldier to propose a toast to the Commender-in-Chief of our Luftwaffe. Please pour a generous tot of Port wine into your glasses and then we all stand at attention with the glasses in our right hands."

We do as ordered.

"As I said, it is my duty to propose a toast on the health of the Commender-in-Chief of the Luftwaffe. The Führer has announced that he is be promoted to the rank of Generalfeldmarshall (Field Marshall), with effect from tomorrow. Since many of us will be gone for the weekend tomorrow night, this is the best opportunity to drink this toast. Therefore, to the Commender-in-Chief of the Luftwaffe!"

All of us: "The Commender-in-Chief!"

With this ceremony completed, we start dinner.

Hauptmann Ullrich Schwartz, my Staffelkapitän, remarks: "Have you guys noticed that the Oberst never mentioned the name of our Commender-in-Chief? He only mentioned the position held by that man."

We all nod in acknowledgement.

Schwartz: "It is an open secret that our Oberst cannot stand Hermann Göring. He served under him during the Great War when Göring succeeded his cousin, Manfred, as Staffelkapitän. Our Oberst accusses Göring of being lazy and cowardly. As he said, it was his duty to propose a toast and he could not shirk this duty, but he could not bring himself to mention the hated man's name."

One of my fellow-Leutnants declares: "He is only the second Field Marshall appointed by the Führer. The first one was Generalfeldmarschall Werner von Blomberg, but he was forced to resign a fortnight ago because it came to light that his new wife had posed for dirty pictures before their marriage."

Another man opines: "I bet that it was Göring who engineered von Blomberg's downfall. That, anyway, opened the way for his pal Hitler to declare himself Head of the Wehrmacht."

Schwartz: "Göring is seen by the members of the aristocracy, such as von Blomberg and our Oberst, who is a Freiherr and a Prussian, as an uncouth and uncivilized commoner from Bavaria. Göring is aware of this attitude and that's why he influenced his crony, Hitler, to make him the only Generalfeldmarshall in the Wehrmacht. I bet he wanted von Blomberg's job for himself, but Hitler took the chance to make himself Head of the Wehrmacht – although he was merely a Gefreiter during the Great War. What does the man know about military matters?"

Me: "Please don't utter those sentiments outside of our circle, because you may get into serious trouble!"

Schwartz: "Men, whether we like it or not, but we have no choice. We are all under the command of Herr Generalfeldmarschall Hermann Göring and we will have to obey his commands and directives. We may sometimes disagree, but we will have no choice in the matter."

We finish the wine left in our bottles and glasses.

Berlin, Tuesday, 1 March 1938

The biggest parade in the history of Berlin is taking place today. Thousands upon thousands of Luftwaffe men are assembled. I can't count them all – of course – but I am sure that up to a hundred thousand men are taking part, almost half of the manpower of the Luftwaffe. Today is designated "Tag der Luftwaffe" (Luftwaffe Day).

A large number of us stand in long rows along both sides of the Wilhelmstraße (Wilhelm Street) in front of the 'Luftfahrtministerium' (Ministry of Air Transport), the headquarters of the Luftwaffe where the OKL (Oberkommando der Luftwaffe – High Command of the Luftwaffe) is situated. A brass band plays and a long column of marching men is following the band. All soldiers in the parade are in full uniform with steel helmets.

I'm impressed by such an organisation and such a parade, although it is extremely boring to stand at attention the whole time. At the Luftkriegschule we also had parades, but this one is certainly the grandest, best organized and biggest display of Germany's military power that was ever held.

I have a good view of the important people in front of the building of the Luftfahrtministerium. There are generals of the Army and Luftwaffe, an admiral or two of the Kriegsmarine (German Navy) as well as big shots of the SS.

But all the attention is focussed on the Commender-in-Chief of the Luftwaffe, Generalfeldmarshall Hermann Göring, who takes the salute. He is clothed in his full Field Marshall's outfit, together with a wide cloak and his Field Marshall's baton, which he holds up in a salute. It is clear that he staged this whole show to glorify himself. Only the Führer is more important. His rival, the chief of the SS, Reichsführer Heinrich Himmler, is one of the guests of honor, but he must have gotten the message that Fat Hermann is his superior, although his rank of Reichsführer, which he held since 1934, was deemed to be the equivalent of a Field Marshall, which would have made him Fat Hermann's senior on paper.

The man next to me mumbles: "I don't see the Führer. Where is Hitler today?"

The worst thing about this whole boring parade is that there won't be any opportunity of seeing Sonja, although I am in Berlin most of the day.

Lüneburg, Monday, 11 April 1938

There is much excitement in the officers' mess. Units of the German Army crossed into Austria about five weeks ago and annexed the country without any resistance. Yesterday, a referendum was held and the Austrians voted overwhelmingly for "Anschluss" (joining) with Germany.

During dinner, Oberst von Richthofen asks for a moment of silence:

"My fellow officers, we are experiencing historical moments. The German Reich has just been expanded without shedding a single drop of blood. Our Austrian friends and relatives have chosen to throw in their lot with ours. We share a common history, language and culture and we belong together.

"I have ordered that each of you is to receive a tot of Schnapps. After that has been served, I will propose a toast on our enlarged Wehrmacht, because the Austrian 'Bundesheer' (Army of the Federation) becomes part of the Wehrmacht as of today."

After the Schnapps has been served and the toast drank, my fellow officers start singing. And I join in heartily.

Hauptmann Ullrich Schwartz, my Staffelkapitän, sighs: "Let's hope that the standard of their pilots is the same as ours. I'm afraid we will have to retrain the lot of them."

Berlin, Friday, 15 April 1938

It has been possible to visit Sonja in Berlin every second weekend from Lüneburg by train. Being a very junior officer, it was expected of me to remain at the base every second weekend to do duty. Fortunately, I was able to get away for Easter and only a skeleton staff was left at the base.

After having attended church this morning, we are having lunch in the Schellenberg family home. Sonja informs everybody: "I wanted to keep this news under wraps until Karl came. I got a telegram yesterday that I was appointed as a teacher at the Bernhard-Riemann-Gymnasium at Scharnebeck."

Vati Sebastian: "Now, where on earth is Scharnebeck?"

Sonja: "Vati, yes, Scharnebeck certainly is on this Earth. I can assure you of that. It's not on the Moon or Mars or somewhere else."

Vati Sebastian: "Well, where then? Somewhere in Germany?"

Sonja: "It's a small town, east of Lüneburg, almost a suburb. It's on the banks of the Elbe."

Me: "And how far from the Fliegerhorst?"

Sonja: "Almost next to it. I may get lodgings somewhere directly next to the Fliegerhorst."

Me: "I have heard rumors that the Luftwaffe is planning to erect married quarters at our base. If that happens, Frau Krause can move in there with Leutnant Krause. Then we won't have to pay rent somewhere."

Lüneburg, Monday, 22 August 1938

Frau "Lehrerin" (teacher) Sonja Krause started her career as language teacher today. Her father and I helped her yesterday to move into her lodgings in the home of two elderly ladies, both spinsters, nearby.

After my working day has come to an end, I take my racing bike and ride the few hundred meters to her lodgings.

I knock on the front door and one of the ladies opens: "Yes?"

Me: "Good afternoon. Is Sonja here?"

"We don't allow men to visit the ladies who live here."

"I'm her husband, in case you didn't know that she is married. I helped her yesterday to get settled here."

"In that case, we will allow you into he drawing room, but not into her bedroom. We disapprove of what goes on behind closed doors when men and women are together."

My eyes turn to the heavens. I think: "Heavens! This won't work if Sonja is to stay here any longer. I can't smuggle her into the officers' quarters, either. What next?"

I manage to utter: " All right, we will use your drawing room, if that won't inconvenience you too much."

When Sonja enters the drawing room, I dare not greet her as I would have liked because both sisters are still present. I tell my wife: "Get your walking shoes. Let's enjoy this lovely summer weather outside."

When we are out of earshot of the two spinsters, I tell Sonja what I have been told and I add: "One can only guess what has happened in the lives of your two landladies. They must be very unhappy old maids, frustrated, angry, disappointed and utterly bitter because no man ever showed any interest in one of them."

"Don't be so hard on them. You don't know their history."

"All right. But it won't work for you to stay there. I will have to think of something else."

" Yes. But it will only be possible to leave at the end of next month because I will have to give a full month's notice before I can leave."

"I will willingly pay for that time, but you are to move out as soon as possible, as soon as something better has been found."

We carry on in silence while holding hands as we walk. There are woods and forests in the vicinity and we disappear from the road into the forest, between the age-old trees.

Later, while walking back, Sonja tells me about her first day at school. She is mostly responsible for English but she also does a little bit of German Poetry with her pupils. She adds: "Siegfried thinks we're preparing for war. Yet again. It will be worse this time because we and our enemies will be able to bomb each other from the air. During the Great War that possibility didn't really exist, although a few Zeppelins bombed London without causing any real damage."

"He's certainly correct. You will be quite safe here because the British and French bombers will target our military installations, factories, harbours and train stations. We will do the same. Here, you will be far away from all those. Our Fliegerhorst may be attacked, but you will be out of the way."

"And if you get a place in the planned married quarters – what then?"

"Yes. Of course. That can become dangerous."

"My friend Sieglinde also suggested that I join the 'Abwehr' (the Wehrmacht's Intelligence Service) with my knowledge of English. They meed people who know English to listen to radio messages or to interrogate possible British prisoners of war."

"How do you feel about that?"

"Perhaps over a year. I first want to get some teaching experience and be near to you."

We say good-night to each other a little distance away from Sonja's lodgings, far from the prying eyes of the two old maids.

Lüneburg, Thursday, 1 September 1938

Through the help of Franz Feierabend, my navigator and observer, I've been able to get better lodgings for Sonja. Franz has an uncle and aunt living quite nearby and through his good services I was able to rent a room for my dear wife.

After a day's work at the Fliegerhorst, I help Sonja to pack all her belongings in her room at the old ladies' residence. I do this under the watchful eyes of the ladies because they reluctantly allowed me to enter Sonja's room.

I got permission from the Oberleutnant in charge of the vehicle pool to use a staff motor to move Sonja's things. The rent at the Feierabend home is even less than the two old ladies charged.

We find Herr and Frau Feierabend a pleasant couple.

Herr Feierabend: "You are welcome to visit your dear wife as often as you like, but not later than ten o' clock at night, because that's our bed-time. Then we would like the house to be quiet. How about a cup of coffee before you start to arrange everything in your wife's room?"

Me: "Thanks a lot."

Frau Feierabend arranged cups, saucers and a kettle. We are treated with "Keks" (cookies).

Frau Feierabend: "You Luftwaffe people are heroes in our eyes. You are a symbol that Germany has regained her self-respect."

Me: "Thanks."

Frau Feierabend: "But is it necessary to create so many bangs? We can tolerate the engine noises of your bombers, but is it really necessary to make us think that war has already broken out?"

Me: "It is necessary that we get lots of training to bomb a target successfully. There are different ways of delivering a bomb from the air. We must know how to do it accurately from high up, but also when we attack only a hundred meters above ground level. And then we also have to be proficient in dive-bombing. We dive from a great height, straight down at the target and at the last moment we release our bombs before we shoot up into the air again. That is the most accurate way of bombing."

Herr Feierabend: "What do you use for target practice? We cannot see from here where you drop your bombs."

Me: "We have a huge field a little distance away from here. Our ground staff mark a certain spot on this field with whitewash and then we dig holes and craters on that spot with our bombs. I think we are are rather good at it, by this time."

Berlin, Friday, 23 December 1938

My brother-in-law, Siegfried, was married yesterday to Anja, his girlfriend of a number of years. After the service in church today, a dinner is being held at a local hotel.

The occasion is a military affair, of course. I attend in my best Luftwaffe uniform and Sepp appears in his uniform as a Fähnrich zur See of the Kriegsmarine. He is receiving training as an officer in the Navy's technical service at the shipyard in Wilhelmshaven, north of Bremen. His job will be to oversee the electrical installations of U-boats.

During the dinner, I get the opportunity to chat with my two brothers-in-law.

Sepp asks: "Is Sonja satisfied to live on a Fliegerhorst with you?"

Me: "Yes, certainly. It's a huge improvement over her lodgings with two old ladies who frown upon married life and all that goes with it. She also stayed with a pleasant couple for a few months. Our married quarters consist of prefab buildings, which are not really luxurious, but we live comfortably enough. We have one bedroom, a living room, a kitchen and a bathroom. For us, it's quite adequate."

Sepp: "Siegfried, where are you going to live with Anja?"

Siegfried: "Anja only agreed to get married to me if I didn't serve in a combat unit of the Luftwaffe, such as bombers or fighters. It had to be a transport unit that has its headquarters here in Berlin. I am transferring to "Kampfgeschwader zur besonderen Verwendung 172" (Combat Wing with Specialized Duties 172) at Berlin-Tempelhof."

Me: "That doesn't tell me anything about its function."

Siegfried: "We will be flying around in Aunty Ju, that slow, clumsy, dependable and ubiquitous transport plane, the Junkers 52.

I will be nothing but a glorified lorry driver, but I did that to please Anja."

Me: "What will you deliver all around the place?"

Siegfried: "Anything you can imagine. Rations, machine guns, bomb crates, 'Fallschirmjäger' (paratroopers), generals, medical supplies, anything. Although we will be based here in Berlin, I will visit every obscure airfield somewhere in this country to download something or to pick up important folk."
Sepp: "Does that satisfy Anja?"

Siegfried: "She is more than happy that I don't fly fighters or bombers. According to her, they are prone to be shot down."

Me: "I think I prefer my Heinkel. She's much faster. And more elegant. And also, much better armed. I think I'm safer in a Heinkel."

Lüneburg, Monday, 1 May 1939

Suddenly, I am no longer a member of Kampfgeschwader 257, based at Lüneburg. The whole Luftwaffe has been reorganized. As of today, almost all units receive new numbers and many units are divided into two or more units with the increased influx of new pilots and other flying personnel, as well as the increased production of new aircraft.

Kampsgeschwader 257 ceased to exist at midnight, last night. It's headquarters Staffel was expanded to become a whole new Kampfgeschwader with the number of KG 26. My promotion becomes effective today and I am now an Oberleutnant and Staffelkapitän in Number One Gruppe of the Geschwader. This position is usually held by a Hauptmann, but due to the rapid growth of the Luftwaffe, there are not enough men with this rank to lead all the new squadrons.

Our Geschwaderkommodore is Oberst Hans Siburg, a former "Seeflieger" (naval pilot) of the "Kaiserliche Marine" (Imperial Navy) of the Great War who joined the Luftwaffe after its inception. He succeeds Oberst von Richthofen who became a major general.

While Sonja and I are having our dinner in our makeshift home, she smiles: "You may congratulate me."

"All right. Congratulations, with whatever. If I may, I will seal my congratulations with a kiss of at least five minutes and a wrestling match on our bed afterwards. The living room carpet will also do. I want to try some new wrestling grips, if you will allow me."

"Aren't you going to ask me why I have to be congratulated?"

"I needn't ask. I already know that you are the most intelligent, good-looking, superlative and marvelous woman in the whole of Germany who is married to a Luftwaffe pilot who also competed in the Olympics. I congratulate myself every day for having you in my life. And you may congratulate me on the excellent taste I have in women, as well as on my promotion today."

"We can have our wresteling match later, as you call it. But there is something important that we have to discuss, first of all."

"Yes?"

"I have tendered my resignation at the Gymnasium today. I leave the teaching profession at the end of this month."

"Don't tell me that you are planning to help in the population growth of the Greater German Reich?"

"Perhaps later. Not now. No, I have a new job offer. At the Abwehr. As an expert of the English language."

"Are you going to teach the spies of our country about English poetry and prose? Shakespeare and Shelley? William Wordsworh and Viginia Woolf?"

"No, stupid. They have extremely advanced and sensitive radio equipment. We can listen to the radio conversations the British Air Force pilots are having with their headquarters. With a husband and a brother who are both Luftwaffe pilots, I have picked up a lot of aercraft jargon over time. I think I will be able to understand the chatter of those British pilots."

"And then you hope to pick up some of their secrets?"

"Exactly."

"When do you start?"

"The first of July."

"And then you will have to go and live in Berlin with Vati and Mutti and work at the Abwehr Headquarters?"

"Exactly."

"I will miss you. May I come and visit you at your workplace?"

"Don't think so. But you may, of course, visit me at the Schellenberg house. Anyway, it seems as if war is inevitable. Your squadron will be moving all over the place as the war progresses and we push our enemies further and further away. We will be separated for most of the time, anyway."

"Then we will have to make the most of our time while it is still peaceful in the world. I think I will improve on my offer to give you a congratulatory kiss of five minutes. I'll make it *six* minutes."

Lüneburg and North Sea, Monday, 3 July 1939

Leutnant Erich von Ehrenstein, one of the new pilots assigned to my Staffel, does not seem to be quite on standard. Last Friday, I practised formation flying with the members of my Staffel and he seemed to struggle to keep his place. Therefore, I decied to take him on a training flight, together with two other planes to give von Ehrenstein some more training. We don't take any crew members along and I occupy the navigator's seat in von Ehrenstein's Heinkel.

When we start up, I ask: "Are you ready? Is everything oekee?"

"Jawohl, Herr Oberleutnant."

We fly out onto the North Sea where there will be less air traffic and we reach the coast just north of Cuxhaven. The other two planes fly in front of us on both sides and von Ehrenstein has to fly just below and just behind them. Under my watchful eye, he seems to have mastered the art of keeping his position, even when the formation makes turns or increase altitude.

When we turn back to reach land again, I notice a surfaced U-boat on the water, below us.

Suddenly, one of the engines of the Heinkel cuts out.

I ask: "Can you see what's the matter?"

Before von Ehrenstein can answer, the other engine also starts stuttering and cuts out a few seconds later.

Von Ehrenstein: "We're out of fuel. The ground crew never topped her up!"

"You bloody fool! It's your responsibility as pilot to check up on that before we flew off!"

While we are losing height, I order: "Now you do a soft landing on the sea. And, for heaven's sake, don't lower your wheels, otherwise we will cartwheel upon impact! Take her down near that U-boat, if you can."

Von Ehrenstein looks terrified: "I'll… I'll try."

Two minutes later, we manage to land safely on the water, a hundred metres from the surfaced U-Boat. The other two planes circle around us, but they are powerless to help.

As the Heinkel slowly sinks into the water, we leave the cockpit through the upper hatch and slide down onto the port wing. Both of us have donned our life vests to stay afloat. Our comrades in the other two planes have, no doubt, radioed for help. Or, perhaps, they contacted the U-boat.

Just as the Heinkel is about to disappear beneath the waves, we jump into the water to get away. We have already seen that a life raft has been launched from the U-boat.

A few minutes later, the life raft reaches us. A Leutnant zur See (naval Ensign) is in command of three other seamen and he asks: "Hallo! Are there only the two of you?"

Me: "Yes, just the two of us."

We are being pulled from the water and given seats on the raft. The four crew members row back to the U-boat.

The officer introduces himself: "I'm Leutnant zur See Stefan Strauss, first watch officer of U-30. We are on our way back to Wilhelmhaven, where we can deliver you the day after tomorrow."

After we have been taken aboard, we are welcommed by the captain, Kapitänleutnant (naval Lieutenant) Fritz-Julius Lemp, and we are given dry clothes and a mug of warm tea each. The U-boat dives again and I start chatting with the friendly officer who rescued us: "I can't quite place your German accent. From which part of the country do you come from?'

"My folks live in Bremen, where I'm married. And where do you come from? Your accent, also, doesn't sound familiar."

"My folks live in Berlin. That's where my wife is waiting for me."

"You certainly don't speak like the people in Berlin. If I may say so, your accent betrays some Afrikaans from South Africa."

I gulp and swallow.

"Aaah, I see, you've given yourself away."
Strauss switches over to Afrikaans: "From which part of South Africa do you hail? If I may betray myself: I come from Walvis Bay. But keep that under wraps, because I'm not supposed to be a member of the Kriegsmarine with my South African passport."

I respond in Afrikaans: "Well, well. I grew up in the vicinity of Rustenburg in the Transvaal. But my parents are German. I also hold a South African passport and I'm also not supposed to be part of the Luftwaffe."

Berlin, Saturday, 15 July 1939

It was possible to take my racing bike with me on the train to Berlin to see Sonja back at her parents' home. We agreed on the phone the day before yesterday that we would go cycling out into the countryside today.

I haven't seen my parents-in-law for some time and during breakfast I was required to tell them everything about the Staffel I am commanding, as well as my narrow escape a few days ago.

The summer heat makes us sweat as we head south on our bikes. At our turning point, we take a breather under a big tree in a forest. Sonja produces the usual Brötchen with cheese and ham.

Sonja: "The Brits are preparing for war. They expect it any time now."

Me: "How do you know?"

"In case you haven't heard: I happen to work for the Abwehr. I am actually some sort of a spy, if you want to know. My job is to listen to the conversations of the fucking Royal Air Force pilots with their units. I am part of a big team and we monitor various bases of the Royal Air Force. My job is to eavesdrop mainly on RAF Marham in Norfolk, East Anglia. They are busy practicing to bomb Berlin, Bremen, Braunschweig and other big cities."

"But we don't plan to start any war soon."

"Don't be a bloody fool. Why is the Wehrmacht being expanded at such a breakneck speed? I am not privy to all secrets, but I can assure you, we can expect something damn big, very big, very soon."

"Are you allowed to tell me all this?"

"Of course not. But nobody can overhear us where we are now. You are to keep your bloody mouth shut, otherwise both of us are in deep shit."

Silently, I decide that I don't like the place where my wife is working. That must be where she picked up her uncivilized language.

"You may also never mention to anybody that I am working at the Abwehr. Just say that I have a job as a civilian in the Wehrmacht in an administrative post."

"Did they give you a rank?"

"No, I'm a bloody civvie. No fucking rank. Not yet."

Berlin, Sunday, 16 July 1939

We are having lunch in the Schellenberg home. Siegfried wants to know where Sonja works and she tells him that she simply has a desk job in a building on the Tirpitzufer (Tirpitz Embankment) in Berlin. Nothing glamorous.

While we are taking a stroll through the streets of Dahlem after lunch, Sonja says: "I'm going to tell you who my boss is and what we are doing."

"You already told me a lot yesterday."

"Yes. But you have the right to know that my boss is Vizeadmiral (Vice Admiral) Wilhelm Canaris. He's the head of the Abwehr. Somehow or other, he has noticed me and had a private conversation with me on Friday."

"Hell's bells!"

"Yes. He wants me to be his interpreter when he has confidential interviews with the bloody ambassadors of Great Britain and America."

"Hell's bells, again."

"That's when I am not eavesdropping on the fucking British pilots. Canaris will meet these ambassadors somewhere secretly. Perhaps even in Switzerland. For that, he has organized a diplomatic passport for me. On my married name. He was grand enough to include your name on that passport as a dependent."

"Hell. You are really deep into this cloak and dagger stuff!"

"Damned deep, detestably deep. I'm stuck in the stinking shit…"

I decide again that I don't like the fact that my dear, civilized, and respectable wife has learnt to use dirty language at her secret workplace. I hear this type of language on a daily basis in the Luftwaffe and I expect that that is also the case with the other branches of the Wehrmacht. But to hear beautiful Sonja talk like that is too much to accept.

"Something else. Canaris knows everything about the two of us. Although I am employed as Fräulein Schellenberg, he knows that I'm actually Frau Krause. He knows, of course, that I have spent a whole year in Manchester and that I can speak English as well as any Tommy and that I know the country fairly well. That's why he chose me as his interpreter. He is also impressed by the fact that I am an Olympic athlete. He knows that you are actually a South African citizen who managed to become a member of the Luftwaffe, quite illegally. He is, however, convinced of your loyalty to Germany and he won't make waves in the soup of shit and piss. He knows about your participation in the Olympics and that you were a member of the South African Police. He also knows that my father and my one brother are members of the Nazi Party, but that the two of us, as well as Sepp, are not quite enthusiastic about Hitler's policies."

"Well, well. Does he know of our holiday at Kufstein and how we practised bed gymnastics there?"

"He didn't mention anything of the sort, but I wouldn't be surprised if he knew – not that it would bother him. I've heard a rumour that he has a secret affair with a dirty Jewish girl somewhere in sucking Switzerland."

"You stay out of his bed! Do you get that?"

"You needn't worry."

Berlin, Saturday, 29 July 1939

The Krauses go cycling again today. We need the time together, all on our own because we don't see enough of each other. At our turning point, we disappear into a forest where we can consume our lunch of bread rolls with ham and cheese.

Sonja confides in me: "I was with the admiral in a hotel room in Potsdam on Wednesday."

"Did he take any liberties with you there? I will shoot the guy if he tries anything with you. I will even crash my Heinkel into his office to show him who's boss."

"No, Karl. Relax. I was merely his interpreter when he had a secret conversation with the British ambassador and the British military attaché. They also had a secretary with them who took notes of what we were telling them. The secretary seems to be from MI5. There were five people in that hotel room. That is, if I counted correctly. All of us kept our clothes on during the whole murky meeting."

"And what did you discuss?"

"Highly secret stuff."

"And you may not talk about it?"

"If I am caught that I tell you anything I will be in a huge hole filled with stinking shit and yellow fluid. You also. But, anyway, Canaris discussed the coming war with the Brits."

"Which coming war?"

"Hitler wants to invade Poland six weeks from now. Canaris doesn't want war and he asked the Brits to put pressure on Hitler to desist from such a foolish venture because that will only bring about a repetition of the Great War of 1914 to 1918, which ended in a dirty disaster for us."

"I don't agree with Canaris. I am sure that we will be able to run over the British beer drinkers and the French frog eaters this time. We are much better prepared than last time. In 1914 we got into the war without really preparing for it, almost by accident. This time it's different. We have a superb, specialised and well-trained Luftwaffe."

"Karl, please promise me you will be careful. Don't take unnecessary chances. I can't lose you and neither can Germany afford to lose somebody like you."

"My training is of the best in the world. I'm sure that I'll be able to take care of myself. And I don't want you to become a young widow. But, if you ever take another man after my death I will come and haunt at your wedding to scare him off."

Lüneburg, Monday, 31 July 1939

After breakfast I convene a meeting of all the members of my Staffel in our hangar – the eleven flight crews and the ground staff.

"Men, thank you for listening to me. I have a horrible feeling that we will be at war one of these days. I can't say why I feel that way, but something just tells me that we have to be ready. I talked to a number of my colleagues and they feel the same. If that time comes, we must be a solid unit. Every member knows by this time what is expected of him and he knows where he fits in. We must rely on each other. I think that you are all a wonderful lot as I have gotten to know you.

"We must make sure that every one of our eleven aircraft is serviceable. We hear far too often of aircraft that have been written off due to accidents. That is because the flying crews and the ground crews have been negligent. We had a nasty incident three weeks ago because a pilot didn't check his fuel level before take-off. He has been scolded by a board of inquiry. When I was in the Police, we held a so-called first parade every time before we drove off in a vehicle. We had to check the tyres, the level of water in the cooler, the battery acid, the quantity of fuel in the tank, whether the mirrors were in the right positions and whether the lights were working.

"We must do something like that here. Every time before a pilot takes off, he must follow a check list that I will draw up. Everything on his plane must be in perfect working order before he takes to the skies.

"Any questions?"

One of the pilots, Leutnant "Kuli" Kuhlmann: "Must we do that in an emergency? When we have to get away when the siren goes off, there won't be any time to check everything. We must trust our ground crews."

Me: "Your check list must have been performed as soon as the ground crew has completed their tasks. And, ground crew, that alo means that you cannot be lax. The pilots will check up on you. The same goes for our Funkers. They must check the serviceability of their radio sets on a daily basis. Before any plane takes off, the guns on the aircraft have to be checked. We cannot afford jammed guns and dirty guns when war comes and we are being attacked by enemy fighters.

"Anybody else?"

Leutnant Hansen: "We haven't been taught about check lists during our training."

"That's a mistake. We must do better than that. Which one of you is fond of accidents? (I look around.) Nobody? Oekee, then we prevent accidents by being careful and looking a little better after our aircraft.

"Something else: should the time come that one of our planes is attacked and the crew have to bail out, they will have to rely on their parachutes. I want to organize a few parachute jumps for all air crews later this week. That could save lives. I know, you have received some training in this regard, but we must stay in tip-top condition.

"Any other questions?"

Nobody replies.

"One last thought: Do you see that heraldic sign on our airplanes? It shows a lion with a poisonous tail. Our motto says we are the 'footsteps of the Lion'. That's what we are. We are part of the Lion Geschwader. Don't ever forget that. Do you all agree?"

All of them smile and shake their heads up and down.
"Dismiss."

Berlin, Saturday, 26 August 1939

Sonja: "My dear husband, this is most probably the last occasion we have of being on our own. The bombs are due to start exploding next Friday."

Me: "You and your Admiral ought to know, of course."

"Of course. Our Admiral took me along to Berne on Tuesday where he met the British Ambassador to Switzerland to inform him of Hitler's intentions, with the hope of averting a war."

"What did the ambassador say?"

"He was actually quite rude. He told Canaris straight to his face that he was wasting his time. That's the ambassador's time. His government was quite clear on the topic of war. If a single German soldier steps with the toe of his left boot over the Polish border, Britain will declare war and also request other Commonwealth countries to do the same. A boot on the right foot will, likwise, serve as a *casus belli*. He is also sure that France will follow."

"So, the die is cast?"

"Yes. We are in for some rough times. May I tell you a secret?"

"You are divulging secrets by the dozen. Another one won't make any difference."

"Canaris doesn't like Hitler and he has tried in the past to get rid of the fucking Führer. That's what he told the ambassador – in confidence. He failed. Fortunately, Hitler doesn't know of this and Canaris hasn't landed on his arse in a concentration camp. Not yet."

"What will happen to you if he gets caught?"

"Shit knows."

"Is it so bad?"

"Please remember, I am a confidante of Canaris. I may also become a target."

"Let's pray that you stay safe. Is your Admiral going to turn traitor during the war?"

"No. Certainly not. He is too much of a German, even if he has an Italian or Greek family name. He only dislikes Hitler and the Nazis, but he will support our war effort wholehartedly if war breaks out. His efforts up to now were only to try to avert war, nothing else. But he is fiercely anti-Communstic and he doesn't trust the Russians one bit, although that poor sod of a Ribbentrop, the foreign minister, has concluded a non-aggression pact with Molotov, the Russian foreign minister."

"My dear, if you are ever to fall into enemy hands with all this knowledge they will torture you to press all the info out of you. But, anyway, how are we going to keep contact when war breaks out? All our leave will certainly be cancelled."

"I am allowed to use a safe telephone. I will phone you at your Staffel, which has its own extention line. Then we speak in code. If you want to give me numbers, don't rush all of it off at once. Say for instance: 'I have six holes in my socks. I need twelve new pairs of socks. My two shoes are dirty and I will have to get somebody to clean them.'Then I will know that you meant 6122 or something like that. If you are moving to a new air base, give me the name in code. Something like this: 'Do you remember our holiday in Bad Godesberg?' or: "How is your aunt in Hamburg?" Then I will know that you will be moving there. And if you have a telephone number there, you supply it to me in that manner. Or, when you want to tell me of a date, do it this way: 'Please tell your cousin Dora that I hope her birthday on the first of July will be pleasant and that I send my congratulations.'"

"Will it be safe to phone me?"

"Our telephone lines at the Abwehr Headquarters are totally safe. Bloody crafty Canaris made sure."

"It might also happen that we move to a base in a conquered country. What then?"

"Then you write me a regular letter to my parents' address and supply me with your details by means of our code. There's a possibility that your letters may be intercepted and censored and therefore you cannot be too direct."

"I like the fact that my wife is a clever spy."

"I hope you will also like the bread rolls that this spy has brought along. Ham and cheese and I have also put in some tomato and mustard. After that, you can do with me whatever you like. But only you. I'm not a Mata Hari."

While we are returning home, Sonja tells me: "You remember my cousin Walter? That SS guy who was at our wedding?"

"Jip."

"Canaris told me that he and Walter are supposed to be quite good friends. Walter is a 'Standartenführer' (SS Colonel) nowadays and head of the foreign section of the Sicherheitsdienst of the SS. They often meet to swop information because both are in the intelligence business. Walter has, for instance, a spy ring in Paris. His misstress, the well-known fashion designer Coco Chanell, is the secret head of this gang of spies."

"You do have an enterprising cousin!"

"That's what my Admiral told me in confidence. When they had a recent meeting, Canaris asked him whether he and a new employee of him, a certain Sonja Schellenberg, were somehow related. Walter confirmed that we are cousins. That's why Canaris has chosen me to be his interpreter – apart from my other sterling qualities."

"That explains how you got Canaris' favour so easily."

"And Canaris also indicated that we wants to use me sometimes as a go-between him and that fucking wily Walter."

"You cousin actually gives me the creeps. I don't know why, but I don't trust him – even if he's family."

"I feel the same. I never trusted those Nazi big shits, I mean shots."

"Why?"

"Most of them are of the lower classes, without any education. Walter, with his law degree, is an exception. I also cannot understand why they hate the Jews so much. After all, Jesus and his disciples were Jews. Back in 1933 a bunch of Nazi rowdies started burning books from libraries because those books were written by Jews. One of these days, they will start burning Bibles, because the authors of the various parts of the Bible were also Jews."

Sonja gives a sigh and I put my arm over her shoulders as we walk along.

Lüneburg, Friday, 1 September 1939

Oberst Hans Siburg hastily calls a meeting of all Staffel commanders: "Meine Herren, you must, surely, have heard the news. Germany has invaded Poland and our men are making rapid progress. Our Geschwader has not been tasked with participating in the campaign to overrun Poland, but we have other tasks.

"Everybody expects that Great Britain and France will declare war against us very soon. Our job is to intimidate them beforehand. All our aircraft are to take part in sorties over the North Sea. Staffel 3 of Oberleutnant Krause will have to do the most daring part, by doing reconaissance over the Thames Estuary about eighty kilometers east of the City of London. Dart in and out of their airspace and take some photos through your glass domes. We would like to know what type of defences they have at that spot. But – don't violate the airspace of the Netherlands and Belgium. They are neutral.

"All the other Staffeln are to fly out over our North Sea coast in the direction of the east coast of England – within sight of the land. We want you to be seen. But don't stray into alien airspace.

"Be ready within the next hour. Go and brief your crews and then we scramble. Any questions?"

Me: "Herr Oberst, I made plans for the week-end. Can I go ahead with those plans?"

"Herr Oberleutnant, what the hell do you think? Put those ideas out of your head, once and for all times to come. We are in a war situation, in case you haven't heard. All leave has been cancelled. With immediate effect."

All of us run out of the conference room and I ask Oberfeldwebel Hans Holgers, my most senior Oberfeldwebel in charge of the ground crews, to assemble all the men in our hangar. I need them there within ten minutes.

All my men dumped the jobs with which they were busy. I ask: "How many of our planes are serviceable?"

Oberfeldwebel Holgers: "All of them, expect for one. The hinges to the entry hatch are broken."

"Thanks. Men, Germany is, yet again, in a state of war. You must have heard the news over the radio. All leave is cancelled and we are to fly out within the next hour. All air crews, you stay behind after this meeting so that we can discuss our target. All the other men, go and make sure that every one of our eleven serviceable Heinkels is ready. And if I say 'ready', then I mean 'ready' in all respects: fuel, ammo, tyre pressure, everything."

Oberfeldwebel Holgers: "What type of bombs must we fit?"

"None. We are going on a reconaissance flight. Nothing more. Arm the machine guns, just in case."

At nine-thirty all eleven available planes in my squadron are starting up and we move out onto the landing strip after all of us have worked through my check-list. My aircraft is in front. I talk to the control tower and tell them that we are ready and that our engines are warmed up. An Unteroffizier with a green flag appears and waves me on. I pull open all the throttles and we gather speed with both engines roaring at full revolutions. Our first wartime sortie!

When we are in the air and I have retracted the wheels, I start talking to my crew over the intercom: "Werner, is your camera loaded?"

"Herr Oberleutnant, yes. I have two extra rolls of film."

"Do you have your maps ready? Is your compass still working?"

"Jip. Keep going at 282 degrees."

"Bernard, is your radio working all right?"

"Five out of five, Herr Oberleutnant."
"Keep radio silence but listen to the British wavelengths."
"Herr Oberleutnant, will do."

"Have you tested both your MG's (Maschinengewehr – machine gun) on both sides?"

"Done."

"Franz, is your MG oekee?"

Franz does not answer and shoots three rounds with his gun.

"Monkey, how's your gun?"

Monkey is the man lying on his stomach under the belly of our Heinkel. He also shoots three rounds. He got his nickname because he is a smallish man who easily fits into the machine gun pit on the belly of the bomber.

We fly over Wilhelmshaven and reach the North Sea coast a little later on. About ninety minutes later we approach the British coast from the east.

Over the radio I announce: "Follow me at three thousand meters. Keep your cameras ready, We want high-quality pictures. Keep radio silence."

It is clear that we have caught the Brits napping. There is no reaction from their side. Bernard informs me over the intercom that he hasn't picked up any unusual chatter over the frequencies used by the Royal Air Force. We fly directly over the Thames Estuary and make a wide turn to the north before we turn back again.

We get back to Lüneburg five hours after we have taken off. Werner rushes off to have his films developed at our photographic section and I report back to Oberst Siburg.

After all the other squadrons have returned, our Geschwaderkommodore calls another confernece of squadron commanders.

He concludes the conference: "Meine Herren, we have demonstrated that we are ready for war. We can do what we are called upon to do. We can be proud of our Luftwaffe. It's a great organisation. I am not divulging any military secrets if I tell you what our strength is at this moment.

"Right now, we have nine Jagdgeschwader (fighter wings), mostly equipped with the Messerschmitt Bf 109E, four Zerstörergeschwader (destroyer wings), equipped with the Messer-schmitt Bf 110 heavy fighter, eleven Kampfgeschwader, equipped mainly with the Heinkel He 111 and the Dornier Do 17Z, and four Sturzkampfgeschwader (dive bomber wings), primarily armed with the Junkers Ju 87B Stuka. We have about 4 200 operational aircraft: 1 190 bombers, 360 dive bombers, 790 fighters, 430 heavy fighters, 490 heavy transport planes and a large number of trainers and light transport planes.

"In comparison, we estimate that the RAF has 3 700 planes at this moment, 500 less than we have. The French Air Force only has around 1 500 aircraft of which most are old and of dubious quality. I predict that the French won't pose any real threat to our Luftwaffe or our Army.

"Our manpower is impressive. Our strength is 373,000 men, of which 208,000 are flying troops, 107,000 men are in the Flack Corps and 58,000 men in the Signals Corps.

"As you can see, we are a force to be reckoned with. We can be sure that we will teach our enemies a lesson they will never forget."

Lüneburg, Friday, 22 September 1939

Sonja phones me during lunch time.

Me: "Have you been able to make many sales over the phone? Found any new customers for your services as a teacher of English?"

Sonja: "You will never guess how many people would like to know English better. I play recordings of conversations to my present customers and explain to them what everything means."

"Wonderful. Anyway, I met an old friend of mine from Schleswig yesterday. He turned up at our place unexpectedly. I hope that he will tell me all the news from Schleswig."

"Do I know your friend?"

"I would like to introduce him to you, some or other time, perhaps on Monday. His name is Kurt Gebhardt and he is twenty-six years old. His nickname is simply KG."

Schleswig, Monday, 25 September 1939

KG 26 arrived this morning at the air base of Schleswig. It is about seven kilometers south west of the town of Schleswig, right in the most northern part of Germany, near the border with Denmark. The Baltic Sea is nearby and it is easy to reach the North Sea to the west. The big naval base of Kiel is about thirty kilometers to the south east. I suppose that the fighters stationed at this base will be used to protect Kiel.

The past three weeks were rather uneventful. We continued with patrols over the North Sea, without seeing anything worthwhile.

We have a new Geschwaderkommodore: Oberst Robert Fuchs. Oberst Siburg has been promoted to Generalmajor and given a new command.

I wonder when Sonja will be able to phone me here. Since she sometimes works night shift, it may happen that she phones during the evening.

Schleswig, Tuesday, 26 September 1939

My Staffel takes off for our first operational flight from our new base at Schleswig. It is much easier to reach the North Sea from here and we have the task of seeking and destroying enemy ships. Britain is very dependent upon imported food supplies from her former colonies. During the previous war, the U-boats of the Kaiserliche Marine almost got the Brits to the point of starvation by sinking large numbers of freighters. Now, the Luftwaffe also has this role, together with our newest U-boats.

We fly high along the eastern coast of England. My observer, Werner, is the first to see a nice fat, juicy target: an aircraft carrier! I call the rest of my Staffel's pilots: "Männer, our target lies at two o'clock. Dive-bomb her! Follow me!"

The aircraft carrier has seen us and starts shooting at us with her ack-ack guns. Little clouds explode in our direction, but they are far from accurate and we pick up speed as we dive down at an angle of sixty degrees. This is the first time that we encounter a target on the ocean.

While I dive down, the heavy flack causes much air turbulence and that interferes with my aim through my visor. I notice, though, that our bombs splash all around the carrier and I gather that we must have, at least, caused some damage. I announce our success over the radio to our Fliegerhorst while we fly back.

I feel in one of the pockets of my flying suit to make sure that my Bible is still there. That is something that I always take along on a flight since my days at the Kampffliegerschule. I silently send up a prayer to say thanks that we survived the attack on the aircraft carrier and that we were able to inflict some damage on our enemies.

Schleswig, Thursday, 28 September 1939

Oberst Fuchs calls me to his office: "Krause, did your Staffel really damage that aircraft carrier the day before yesterday?"

Me: "Herr Oberst, that is what we saw. And Herr Josef Goebbels, our minister of propaganda, announced it on the radio the same night. So, it must have happened."

"If your Staffel had really damaged that aircraft carrier you would have gotten at least the Iron Cross, First Class. The carrier that you attacked is called the HMS Ark Royal."

"Herr Oberst, I am sure that, at least, some of our bombs must have hurt her."

"The only damage you caused was that some of her airplanes and crew on her flight deck got splashed wet with sea water. Winston Churchill went onto the radio to set the record straight. Our propaganda on account of your radio message blew up in our faces because the Ark Royal is, according to Churchill, totally unscathed. He even offered to let the American naval attaché fly out to see for himself that the ship is undamaged. Sorry."

I salute and leave the office while I mumble: "Karl Krause, your chances of becoming famous are blown!"

Schleswig, Saturday, 30 September 1939

My squadron flew out every day since our scrap with the aircraft carrier to look for shipping along Britain's east coast. Only today, we found two coastal freighters. My crews were more careful this time and we sank both of them.

We feel that we are starting to earn our keep.

During the late afternoon, Sonja's phone call comes through. I tell her: "We have been hunting ducks on a big pond this Saturday. We got two rather young ones of them."

Sonja: "That sounds nice. Have you plucked all their feathers?"

"Unfortunately, they were too far away on the water and we could not reach them. So we actually lost them. I think their families are also feeling the loss. But it was fun, anyway. And what are you doing?'

"Listening to my radio. It gets boring. The same programmes over and over. Nothing to get excited about. Too much idle chatter. The same stuff all the time."

"How often do you see your cousin, Herr 'W'?"

"We spoke only last week. I had to deliver some bread to him from Herr 'C'."

"Please tell him I send my kindest regards."

Sonja gives a nervous chuckle.

Schleswig, Tuesday, 10 October 1939

Oberst Fuchs converses with a few squadron leaders during dinner: "You may have heard the news that the campaign in Poland is over. The Polish military leaders threw in the towel. They simply could not hold out against our overweight."

I venture to respond: "Herr Oberst, that is indeed welcome news. Do you perhaps agree that most of the Luftwaffe units that have taken part in that campaign will return and help us against France and Great Britain?"

"Most certainly. I predict that we will make mincemeat of the French, especially when our forces along the borders are strengthened. A few French units tried to break through our Westwall the other day, the line of fortifications along our border with France. They succeeded at one spot, but our boys retaliated soon afterwards and the French hastily withdrew, too afraid to put up a real fight."

Schleswig, Tuesday, 17 October 1939

I have never seen something of this sort – a whole armada of bombers, filling the sky all around us. The whole of our Geschwader, consisting of about ninety bombers, as well as two other similar units, have been tasked to attack Scapa Flow in the Orkneys, one of the main naval bases of the British where they keep their battleships.

Although we expected that our attack would be a surprise it seems as if the Brits were prepared for us. They throw as much flack in our direction as they possibly can and I suspect that they have hit more than one of our bombers.

Our bombs rain down from a great height because the heavy flack makes it impossible to do dive bombing. I instruct my observer, Werner, to direct my aim to a large cruiser lying at anchor in the bay. I follow his instructions carefully and at the right moment, I release my external load of bombs, weighing 3 000 kilograms.

The Heinkel shoots up in the air as the heavy load of the stack of bombs is no longer attached to her. We follow the stream of bombers that turns east to get over the North Sea again.

Monkey, ou belly gunner, declares: "Our guys have a great talent to hit the water. We really caused huge, enormous splashes. Ha-ha!"

Back at Schleswig, our Oberst, who also participated in the raid, discusses the photographic evidence of the success of the raid: "I can merely see one single ship that has been hit. The rest of them are unharmed. Men, our bombing techniques have to improve. We start training in this regard again tomorrow!"

Later, at dinner, our air intelligence officer informs us that the only casualty of the raid was HMS Iron Duke, an old battleship that was built in 1912. She was decommissioned after the previous war and now only serves as a training ship.

Schleswig, Saturday, 28 October 1939

Our Staffel has been ordered to do reconnaissance of the docks at Glasgow and the estuary of the Clyde on the western side of Scotland. The whole Staffel flies high over the North Sea and crosses the Scottish coast south of Edinburgh.

It is easy to recognise Glasgow, an industrial city with all its smoke. I recognise the river Clyde curling through the city and the docks where freighters are moored. My observer, Werner, takes photos. We follow the course of the Clyde until we reach the wide estuary called the Firth of Clyde. We photgraph ships lying at anchor there.

We take another route to fly back and we pass north of Edinburgh.

Suddenly, Franz, my dorsal gunner cries out: "Fighters at eleven o'clock!"

Through my rear mirror I can see a whole squadron of fighter planes diving down upon us. There are at least ten of them. Franz starts shooting with his machine gun.

Franz cries: "A hit! There is smoke pouring from the engine of one of them!"

I take evasive action, as do all the other members of my squadron. When I turn sharply to port, Monkey shouts: "I think I nicked one of them!"

Werner, my observer who also mans the forward gun, starts shooting as a fighter roars past us. I can see that it is a Spitfire, the newest fighter of the Royal Air Force. Werner groans, because he is unable to hit the fighter that disappears. In order to stay out of the sights of the fighters I weave my Heinkel to and fro.

And then Werner cries: "Ach, nein!"

Me: "What's that?"

"A Spitfire has put one of ours on fire. One of her engines is smoking. I see flames. That must be Leutnant Fritz Engels."

There is nothing we can do to help the crew of Engels. Two minutes later, Monkey informs us: "They got out. I see four parachutes. One of them couldn't make it. But the Heinkel is crashing somewhere, just north of Edinburgh."

As I fly back, I suddenly feel tired. The excitement that rushed through me, kept me alert and I handled the situation almost automatically, as I have been trained to do. The danger is over because the fighters have left us. They are certainly very satisfied with their "kill". But I'm exhausted and only will power keeps me going to set our Heinkel safely down at Schleswig.

The fatigue I feel is not the same fatigue I felt after a road race of 100 kilometers on my bike. Although my legs were hurting after such an event, I always felt great. In contrast, my present exhaustion is accompanied by á feeling of misery, even pessimism.

Directly after we have landed, I call upon my crew to inspect our plane. We find three holes in the port wing, but no important points have been damaged.

"Werner, will you get the Oberfeldwebel to have these holes patched?"

I report to the Oberst and he sighs in response: "Krause, your Staffel has reached the distinction of being the first unit to have lost an aircraft over the British Isles. Fortunately, those four men got out with their parachutes. They will sit in a prisoner of war cage for the duration. Sorry for them."

I salute and leave while I tell myself: "Karl Krause, you are getting famous for all the wrong reasons!"

Schleswig, Monday, 20 November 1939

Another dangerous task awaits our Geschader. Instead of bombs, we are given sea mines. These have to be dropped by means of parachutes over the Thames Estuary to disrupt shipping to and from the Tilbury Docks near London.

We don't encounter any serious problems and we all return safely. It is expected that a few ships will be sunk by our mines. They have been laid haphazzerdly and it will be difficult to avoid them. We are also told that two U-boats have laid mines last night as well.

I tell myself: "Krause, if any ships are being sunk by those mines, nobody will know who to credit for that. Nobody will know who planted a certain mine. Another lost chance to become famous…"

It feels terrible without my Sonja.

Schleswig, Thursday, 7 December 1939

Before we flew off this morning, I told the flight crews of my Staffel: "We have acquired a rather negative reputation. We have only two small freighters to our credit. Nothing more. We totally missed a huge, fat, gigantic aircraft carrier. We couldn't hit anything at Scapa Flow. We were the first outfit to lose an aircraft over the British Isles.

"But – we have a great chance today. I have a set of photos taken four hours ago of the situation on the Firth of Forth. Taken by our friends of Staffel Number Two at dawn. As you may perhaps know, the Forth is the river that has an estuary just north of Edinburgh. There are a number of ships lying at anchor there – most probably waiting to join a convoy to America or Canada or somewhere. What do you guys want to do about that?"

My crews exclaim all at the same time:

"We bomb them!"

"We sink them!"

"They're just waiting for us!"

Me: "I heard you. We are to get ready. Immediately! Get your kit and then we start up and roll out. I will see to it that our aircraft are bombed up. And remember your check lists before your start up."

We take to the skies and more than two hours later we see the Scottish coast. There are indeed at least a dozen ships lying at anchor in the Firth of Forth.

I call over the radio: "We dive down in four flights of three aircraft abreast. Each one chooses a target on the side on which he is flying. And then we turn north after we have delivered our bombs!"

We dive down from five thousand meters. I am not surprised that a few shots are aimed at us by ack-ack guns, but their aim is poor and we fly undisturbed down at an angle of sixty degrees. I see a tanker in my visor and at the last moment I press the button on my joy stick to release my bombs. Werner is shooting with his gun at the same ship in the hope of causing some more damage.

Five seconds later, Monkey yells: "Bulls eye! Congrats, Captain!"

All twelve our aircraft throw down their bombs and we turn to the north. After two minutes I order a turn of 180 degrees and we fly over the scene of devastation again. Werner, my observer, comments: "Five ships have been hit. Two of them are already sinking!"

We climb again to gain height and after two more hours we touch Mother Earth at Schleswig again. All our observers scramble to the photographic section to have their films developed.

An hour later, our Geschwaderkommodore congratulates me: "Well done, Krause! We can confirm: five ships sunk or seriously damaged. Well done!"

I wishI could tell Sonja of this.

Schleswig, Saturday, 23 December 1939

All of us at the Fliegerhorst Schleswig hope that Christmas will bring some respite from our involvement in the war. This time of the year, after all, is supposed to be a time of peace and goodwill. I am dead tired of flying almost non-stop, looking for enemy ships on an empty North Sea. Many flying hours were wasted on fruitless searches. We all agree that this state of affairs is due to the fact that Britain has started to assemble all freighters and tankers into convoys and that these convoys mainly use ports on the western side of the British Isles, such as Glasgow, Liverpool and Cardiff, to be as far away from us as possible.

After I have made my report to our Geschwaderkommodore about this day's sortie, I retire to my bunk in the officers' quarters. A Gefreiter approaches me, salutes, and hands me an envelope. I return the salute and he disappears.

On the outside of the envelope is written in Sonja's handwriting: "Oberleutnant Karl Krause, I./KG 26."

How on earth did this guy get this letter? I want to ask him but he is already gone. I open the envelope with shaking fingers, in the hope that it doesn't contain bad news. There is a single blank sheet of paper with the letterhead of the Hotel Adler in Schleswig.

That must be where Sonja is staying! Somehow or other she has contrived to get leave from her duties in Berlin and travelled to Schleswig to see me!

I run to the office of my Geschwaderkommodore and ask whether he has any tasks for my Staffel for the rest of the weekend. He has none.

"Will it be in order if I take one of our Geschwader's motor vehicles so that I and a few of my men can go and celebrate Heiligabend by attending a church in Schleswig tomorrow night?"

"Do as you wish. Report back on Sunday morning early to hear whether there is anything waiting for you. If not, you may take that day off as well."

I salute with a straight face after having told a little lie and I go to the vehicle pool where I draw a small truck after having signed for the vehicle. As destination I simply note: "Schleswig."

It is fairly easy to find the Hotel Adler because the letterhead contains the address. At the reception desk I ask: "Do you have a Frau Krause as guest here?"

The elderly clerk behind the desk: "We are not at liberty to divulge that type of information. It's confidential."

"But Frau Krause is my wife. I am Oberleutnant Krause of the Luftwaffe."

"How do I know that? Any proof of identity?"

I produce my Luftwaffe identity card after thinking that this fool must have noticed my uniform and rank insignia.

The clerk: "I am sorry, but we don't have a Frau Krause here."

"But then you must have a Fräulein Schellenberg here. She is actually Frau Krause."

"I am not allowed to say anything in that regard."

I throw my arms up in despair and I almost want to threaten the man with arrest or assault or murder for being so obstinate. At that moment, Sonja descends the stairs and comes to my aid by embracing me in front of the startled clerk.

Sonja: "Let's go for a walk. I saw your vehicle parking outside and you getting out."

We leave the hotel and walk away from the town centre into the suburbs, while Sonja grabs my left arm.

"What on earth are you doing here?"

"Looking for you."

"How did you get here?"

She smiles mischievously: "With a fucking train."

"How did you manage that?"

"My bloody Admiral gave me a job."

"Yes?"

"I came back from Denmark this afternoon."

"And what did you do there?"

"I had to meet one of our Abwehr agents there."

"About what?"

"Hell, Karl, you are inquisitive! You are only interested in my job. You haven't asked me how I am or how my family is doing. Shame and shit on you!"

Silently, I curse the place where my civilized wife has picked up this vocabulary.

"I'm sorry. I was so overwhlemed by your sudden presence that I just wanted to know how you got here. Anyway, how are the Schellenberg family members and my dear darling wife doing?"

"Well, we are healthy and doing well. Siegfried is flying a bloody transport plane while Anja is staying with us in Berlin. Sepp is still working in Wilhelmshaven, busy building U-boats. Katja dropped him and he seems to feel very bad and sad and mad about it. He's a Leutnant zur See now. My dad is still working at the bank and my mom plays housewife. And how are you?"

"Almost dead. Working my arse off with very little to show for all my toils."

I tell Sonja about some important sorties that my Staffel has undertaken and she listens with attention.

"But how are you? What are you doing?"

"Thinking about you every day."

"The same with me. When is this war going to end so that we can resume a normal quiet married life?"

"Not soon. First of all, we are going to invade Denmark and Norway. And then it will be the turn of Holland, Belgium, Luxemburg and France. And still later, it might be Britain."

"Why Norway?"

"More than one reason. Number one: the Brits and the French are planning to occupy that crappy country to deny it to us and so that they can control the railroad from Sweden carrying iron ore for us. They also want access to Finland to help the Finns in their fight against the Russians. Number two: we need all the Norwegian harbours as U-boat bases with easy access to the Atlantic.

"There are also rumours that our scientists want to acquire an installation where heavy water is purportedly being produced. Don't ask me what heavy water is, but it is reportedly necessary for the development of super weapons with which we can wipe the Brits from the face of the earth."

"How do you know all that? Did your Admiral tell you?"

"I'm not listening to the idle chatter of British pilots with their bases anymore. We get very little real information from that. There are other girls who can do it just as well. My job nowadays is that of courier. With my dirty diplomatic passport, I have visited Switzerland, Italy and Denmark where I had to deliver messages to agents or to receive confidential reports from them. Often only by means of the spoken word. Canaris doesn't want to leave a paper trail for my cousin Walter to follow. Although they are seemingly on a friendly footing with each other, they are actually deadly enemies. Walter wants my Admiral's job and he is looking for evidence to discredit him in the eyes of Hitler."

"Your cousin seems to be a very ambitious man."

"Certainly. He was recently promoted to the rank of 'Oberführer' (Senior Colonel) in the SD of the SS. Still in control of the foreign branch of the SD."

"And your Admiral?"

"He is to be promoted to full Admiral, with effect from the beginning of next month. He seems to enjoy the confidence of Hitler – at least for now. If Hitler finds out about the double game he is playing it will be tickets for him, and me and many others.

With all his contacts all over the place, he knows exactly what is going on and what Hitler's plans are."

"And you know a lot, as well?"

"Naturally. That's why I wanted us to go for a walk. Walter's immediate boss, 'Gruppenführer' (Lieutenant General of the SS) Ernst Kaltenbrunner, had secret microphones installed in every humping hotel room and every known bloody brothel so that his agents can pick up any information about enemies of the Reich spoken in those rooms."

"Thanks for that warning. But here, in the open air, there are no microphones?"

"Of course not. And that is why I can tell you that we are going to invade Denmark and Norway one of these days. You will receive orders very soon to participate in those campaigns. And, of course, you stay silent about what you know now, otherwise both of us will land with our stinking asses in a cockass concentration camp – or even worse."

"It's cold outside and it may be snowing very soon. Are we going to spend the whole night here outside?"

"Of course not, you silly stupid son-of-a-bitch. I booked a double room in the hotel for both of us and you are to spend the night with me."

"Will that idiotic clerk at the hotel allow me to share your room with you?"

"He can't touch me. I intimidated him with my Abwehr identity card. I told him that he mustn't divulge any information about me to anybody, nobody whatsoever."

"Oh, that's why he would't admit to me that you were staying in the hotel. I almost banged his head against the wall for being so obstinate."

"Poor man. He was only obeying orders. My obsessive orders."

"I only have to go back to my base on Sunday morning."

"Then we can whisper into each other's ears while we are having a few wrestling matches, as you call them. Kaltenbrunner will only hear our grunts and growls."

"I got permission from my Oberst to attend church on Heiligabend. You may come with me, if you like."

Schleswig, Thursday, 22 February 1940

Very little happened between Christmas and today. But, suddenly, our luck is reversed. I am flying with my Staffel over the North Sea, in the vicinity of the Dogger bank, a shallow area in the North Sea. Werner, my observer, exclaims: "Destroyers ahead!"

He takes out his binoculars and confirms: "A tasty tempting target waiting for us!"

I order my Staffel to go in for a low-level attack. We fly through a few low-level clouds, which obscure our targets at times. But suddenly we are upon a flotilla of five or six destroyers. To my pilots, I radio: "Spread out! Hit as many as possible!"

At the right moment, Werner indicates that I must release our bombs and I do so. My Heinkel shoots up in the air, suddenly freed from a heavy load.

As we fly onwards to get out of range of any guns on the destroyers, I hear jubilation from one of my pilots: "We hit one of them! She is broken in two! She is sinking!"

While we fly back, I silently ask myself: "Karl Krause, will this victory secure you an Iron Cross or even promotion?"

After we have landed and handed our planes to the ground crews, I march to the office of Oberst Fuchs to deliver my report.

After I have saluted, but before I can utter a word, my commander yells: "Krause, you and your bloody Staffel! You will certainly face a court martial, very, very soon!"

All the blood drains from my face and I feel dizzy. I expected a hero's welcome after having eliminated an enemy warship. But not this reprimand!

Fuchs carries on: "If you think that you are a blinking hero, think again. You and your lousy Staffel have just sunk two German destroyers! The Leberecht Maass and the Max Schultz. The Führer was immediately informed of this incident and he is furious. He's spitting sparks and steaming saliva. He's blowing toxic fumes. He ordered a full inquiry. Until that is dealt with, you and your Staffel are grounded. Dismiss!"

It's useless to argue with the Oberst and I leave after having saluted him again.

I call the air crews of my Staffel together and I give them the news.

Leutnant Heini Hermann, my wing man: "Those destroyers were not supposed to be there! We had the fullest right to expect British destroyers at that spot."

Leutnant Ferdinand Fölscher: "Visibility was very bad. It was impossible to see the Kriegsmarine flag on any of those ships…"

Leutnant Gerd Gröblitz sits with his face in his hands and sobs: "My elder brother is – or was – an Oberleutnant zur See on the Leberecht Maass. I may perhaps be the guy who killed him with my bombs… Our father will never forgive me!"

Schleswig, Wednesday, 14 March 1940

During the time of our grounding, I had some chance of getting enough sleep, although it was a fitful sleep, filled with nasty nightmares. How could I and my whole Staffel be so stupid as to sink two of our own ships? I suddenly got time to do something about my fitness and I undertook daily runs to get some exercise.

All of us were required to face a board of enquiry yesterday and the day before that. Every crew member was extensively questionned about what he saw on that fateful day over the Dogger Bank.

We were ordered to appear in full uniform in the mess hall at eleven, this morning. The chairman of the board of inquiry, 'Konteradmiral' (Rear Admiral) Eberhardt Eckstein, calls for silence and starts to read the verdict of the board.

I hold my breath and my heart starts beating faster. I wish that Sonja was here to hold my shaking hand.

The Admiral declares that the real culprit in the whole saga was the Kriegsmarine itself. They failed to inform the Luftwaffe of the operation of six destroyers off the coast of Scotland, knowing full well that Luftwaffe bombers flew daily sorties over the North Sea. The Max Schultz did not sink as a result of our bombs. She rushed to rescue the survivors of the Leberecht Maass and then she struck a British mine, which caused her to sink almost immediately, with all hands lost. Only sixty survivors of the Leberacht Mass could be saved by the other destroyers.

The Staffelkapitän (that's me) and the members of Staffel 3./KG 26 are reprimanded for not being more careful and by failing to notice the Kriegsmarine standards on the sterns of the six destroyers. Our grounding is, nevertheless, to be lifted and we may, yet again, take part in operations.

I feel grateful and relieved. I might have ended up in prison or a concentration camp as a saboteur of the Third Reich's war effort, although I have to kiss good-bye my chances of getting an Iron Cross or a promotion soon.

Schleswig, Thursday, 15 March 1940

An interview was granted with Oberst Fuchs in his office.

"Herr Oberst, thank you for your time. I held a meeting with all my flying crews. We are greatly relieved that we have been cleared of gross misconduct and that we are allowed to fly again."

"I hope you keep your eyes open next time when you attack any warships."

"You may be sure that we will do just that. But I have a proposal, which will certainly not involve warships of the Kriegsmarine."

"How so?"

"My Staffel wants to attack Scapa Flow again. We can be absolutely sure that only ships of the Royal Navy will be lying at anchor there. Does it have your approval? When can we go out?"

"Not so fast. I will have to get approval from the OKL first. We don't know if your plans will perhaps interfere with anything those big shots have in mind. Come back tomorrow morning."

Schleswig, Saturday, 16 March 1940

My plan won approval from the OKL. My Staffel is strengthened with four extra planes from another Staffel of KG 26 and we fly out long before dawn with a force of fifteen bombers. I divided them into three flights of five aircraft each.

During the briefing of the pilots, I told them that if the first Kette was to encounter very heavy flack while attacking from the east with the rising sun behind us, the other planes had to attack another target instead: the Hatston airfield of the Fleet Air Arm, directly to the north of Scapa Flow. I hoped to cause as much damage as possible with one blow and to restore the pride of my Staffel.

We fly low over the North Sea to avoid detection. A few sea miles from Scapa Flow we suddenly increase height and try a dive-bombing attack on the ships we see there.

As my first Kette swings out to sea after the attack, Werner reports: "I see smoke pouring out of that cruiser. Another ship seems to have been hit."

The Brits seem to have woken up early this Saturday morning and the ack-ack guns get going with full fury after my Kette has left the scene. I advise the other ten planes to attack the alternative target.

As we fly back, one of the pilots of the other two waves reports over the radio: "We managed to dump all our bombs on that air base. I'm sure we've done lots of damage."

Schleswig, Sunday, 17 March 1940

Oberst Fuchs holds a meeting with all the pilots who have taken part in yesterday's operation.

"Männer, I am relieved that all of you returned safely yesterday. Your efforts were not totally wasted. Our intelligence service, which monitors radio traffic, has ascertained that you have severely damaged the heavy cruiser, HMS Norfolk. She did not sink, though, and can be patched up. You also damaged HMS Iron Duke, that ancient decommissioned battleship that is being used as a training ship. We also damaged her slightly on our previous raid over there.

"Those of you who have attacked the airfield wasted a lot of expensive bombs. According to radio reports picked up by our intelligence people, about 120 high explosives and over 500 incendiary bombs were dropped in all. Merely eight craters were made in the airfield at Hatston, some 800 meters from the hangers, and one bomb fell near a bomb store. No other damage was done."

"Anyway, I will recommend that the Iron Cross, Second Class, be awarded to the Staffelkapitän, Oberleutnant Krause. He devised this operation and his Kette put an important ship out of commission, at least for a few months."

Schleswig, Tuesday, 9 April 1940

After we have been briefed last night, we start early this morning to support the invasion of Norway. Our Geschwader is to attack coastal batteries near Kristiansand at the southern tip of Norway and also along the Oslo Fjord. Our Gruppe has to fly as a unit, just as the other two groups.

We see a fleet, led by a heavy cruiser of the Kriegsmarine, sailing up the Oslo Fjord. This time, we know not to attack our own ships. To help our Kriegsmarine, we bomb the old fortress on the island of Drøbak. There are various large guns, dating from the Great War. As far as we know, they have never been fired in anger before today. My Staffel succeeds in neutralising most of the guns and their crews with our bombs and machine guns.

The most southern gun on the island, nevertheless, keeps firing and hits our cruiser. She immediately takes on water and many crew members and soldiers on her decks jumpo into the water. The rest of the fleet turns around, too afraid to confront that single heavy gun.

Our bombs have been used up and we have to return home to prepare for another sortie before it gets dark.

After our last sortie, we are called for a debriefing conference with our Oberst. He has important news: "Männer, thank you for your sterling service today. Our Geschwader has lost only three planes. We have neutralized most of our targets in Norway and our Army units are landing at various spots along the Norwegian coast. We hope to take Oslo tomorrow after that heavy gun at Drøbak has been silenced.

"We also invaded Denmark. The Danes surrendered after only six hours. They hardly put up a fight.

"We are to support the Kriegsmarine and our Army to take Norway in as little time as possible. We believe the Brits and the French will interfere and we will have to get rid of them, as well."

Our Gruppenkommandeur, Hauptmann Detlef Drohmbach, asks: "What the hell do we want to do with Norway and Denmark, anyway?"

Oberst Fuchs: "We can cover the North Sea and the Atlantic so much better from there and sink enemy ships. There will be U-boat bases for us at Norwegian harbors. We need the harbor of Narvik to secure the import of Swedish iron ore for our steel factories. And, perhaps, we can recruit some of these Scandinavians to volunteer for our 'Waffen-SS' (Armed SS) units. That will help a lot."

Schleswig, Wednesday, 10 April 1940

Our Gruppe is to make yet another attack on Scapa Flow to disrupt potential British Naval reinforcements to Scandinavia. This is the third time that I participate in an attack on this major base of the Royal Navy, but we were told that other units also had a crack at the Royal Navy ships at this base in the recent past.

Our intelligence is outdated, though, and we find almost no ships there. There is only one conclusion possible: we are too late to prevent a British effort to disrupt our campaign in Norway.

We return home with our torpedoes still attached to our fuselages.

Schleswig, Thursday, 11 April 1940

Our whole Geschwader is to move tomorrow morning first thing to the Aalborg Air Base, near the most northern tip of Denmark. Our ground crews are to follow by road. At Aalborg we'll be able to cover the Kattegat to the east, the Skagerrak to the north and the North Sea to the west.

We are also informed that a flotilla of British destroyers and other craft have entered the fjord leading to the port city of Narvik in northern Norway to retake the port from our troops who have previously landed there.

While the members of my Staffel are getting ready for the move, I hastily write a note to Sonja at her parent's address, which I plan to mail to her tonight:

11 April 1940

My Darling,

We are healthy and well. They promised us some Danish eels from tomorrow and that will make life much easier – and hopefully more difficult for our friends from Gross Brandenburg.

My friend Karl-Gustav (who is 26) promised to visit me on tomorrow. He wants to show me something up north.

Hope you are well. A flying visit by you will be most welcome.

Love and kisses, X X X X

Aalborg, Friday, 12 April 1940

Fortunately, our soldiets captured the intact airfield a few kilometers north west of the Danish town of Aalborg. When we land there we can immediately refuel with the captured stocks.

After refuelling we immediately set off to throw some bombs on British forces landing in the vicinity of Trondheim, a port city in Central Norway. We can only do one sortie with the loads of bombs we brought from Schleswig and we will have to wait for the rest of our Gruppe to catch up with us by road, together with our loads of bombs.

We would have liked to intervene at Narvik as well, but that remote spot is out of reach for us.

Aalborg, Tuesday, 16 April 1940

Our Gruppe is fully operational again. At last.

Our Gruppe attacks the British Tommys and French Frogs near Trondheim in three waves today, with my Staffel forming the third wave. Two aircraft of my Staffel get hit by anti-aircraft fire from the British warships and the crews bail out by parachute.

We do two more sorties today and we lose two more aircraft, one of which crashes into the side of a mountain after being shot at by a British Hurricane fighter. We believe that there were no survivors. My two rear gunners achieve their first confirmed kill of a British fighter that spirals down into the sea after the pilot has received a direct bullet, although we also claim an unconfirmed kill over Scotland a few weeks ago.

Aalborg, Wednesday, 17 April 1940

There is no time to mourn the loss of one of my crews. The war is picking up speed and I just have to catch up.

Our Gruppe continues to hammer the Brits while they try to take Trondheim from our troops. According to messages we receive, they are attacking from the north and the south of Trondheim.

During our second sortie, we spot a naval force near Stavanger, south of Trondheim, although it is rather foggy and visibility is bad. It seems that these ships are shelling a target on land – presumably some of our troops. I immediately give the order to attack. All remaining seven aircraft of my Staffel concentrate their efforts on the biggest ship, a heavy cruiser, and we manage to hit her at the stern.

After our third sortie, just before dusk, we fly over the sea again and we see the cruiser limping home, escorted by a destroyer. She lists and her stern is considerably lower in the water.

During our debriefing that evening, we are informed that we hit the heavy cruiser, HMS Suffolk, a sister ship of HMS Norfolk, the ship we damaged a month ago. She is slowly sailing home to Scapa Flow. I volunteer to go after her again with my Staffel to put her out of her agony and misery and despondency, but I am told that our efforts are in greater need at Trondheim.

Aalborg, Saturday, 27 April 1940

Bad weather and bad visibility stopped us from flying out every day during the past ten days, but we, nevertheless, helped our troops in Trondheim to expel the British and French forces from these shores. We had a go at the retreating Tommys for a last time today before they were taken away by the Royal Navy.

We try to unload some bombs onto the naval force but the combined flak from all the ships makes it impossible to do anything worthwhile. We generously donate our loads of bombs to the last few ungrateful British soldiers still on solid soil.

After dinner, the phone in my Staffel's hangar rings. I hear immediately that it's Sonja's voice on the other side.

"May I speak to Herr Karlson, please?"

"Speaking."

"Herr Karlson, this is Frau Berg of Schellenhausen Fisheries. We ordered some Danish eels from you and they tasted wonderful. How long will your stocks last? When will you be moving on?"

"My dear lady, that is very difficult to say. I think I will have to move somewhat northwards to replenish my stocks. But how about some Norwegian hering? I have a contact who used to live in Trondheim who will be able to help me. Perhaps tomorrow or the day after that. Anyway, how is your health nowadays?"

"I get lots of movement, lots of running around. That keeps me fit. And you?"

"It is difficult to sleep in these times. I also have to run around a lot. There are so many vehicle noises that disrupt my sleep. But I and my team have managed to catch a large fish. Or, we almost caught him because he did get away, although I believe he was in a sorry state."

"That's good to hear. Please make sure of those Norwegian herings."

Trondheim, Tuesday, 30 April 1940

The remaining 24 aircraft of Gruppe I of KG 26 arrived yesterday at the Værnes airfield near Trondheim in Central Norway – despite lots of fog along the way. The airfield is at the far end of a fjord, while the port city of Trondheim is a few kilometers to the west and nearer to the North Sea. Elements of the Kriegsmarine, including a flotilla U-boats, immediately made themselves at home in the harbour after the enemy had left. Our task will be to aid our men who are cornered at Narvik in the north.

Flying today is out of the question, due to foul weather. A Feldwebel approaches me and hands me an envelope after having saluted. I respond. My name is written on the envelope – in Sonja's handwriting. I manage to ask the Feldwebel how he got this and he answers that a lady in the street just asked him to deliver it to the Staffelkapitän of the third Staffel of I./KG 26.

Inside the envelope there is a single blank sheet of paper – just as last time. On it is the letterhead of the Thon Hotel Nidaros. At the control tower of the airfield I find a map of the city and I manage to find the street in which the hotel is situated.

I quickly see that everything at my Staffel is under control and I go to our Gruppenkommandeur with the request that I need a vehicle to go to town to buy some items of a personal nature.

"Go, but be back as soon as the weather clears. We have to start flying again."

Fortunately, the Norwegians left their vehicles for us and I procure the keys of a staff car. I drive to town on the road along the edge of the fjord and I find the hotel. When I park the vehicle I press the hooter a few times in the hope of drawing Sonja's attention. I get out and stand next to the parked car.

Sonja must have noticed me and about five minutes later she appears at the hotel's entrance. I rush to her and we grab each other.

"Come inside. It isn't necessary to take a walk. The Gestapo or die SD hasn't had an opportunity of planting microphones anywhere here. Come up to my room and get out of the cold."

This hotel seems to be a grand institution built of stone and it has five stories. Sonja has booked a heated double room that overlooks a park. We sit down on a sofa.

Me: "I need at least a dozen photos of you to remind me of you when I am far away from you."

"I'm staying here for a few days. In that time, we can do something about that. I also want a few more photos of you."

"But what are you doing here? How long have you been here?"

"I arrived yesterday, just after the last Brits were ejected. I have to deliver messages to some of our agents here and hear their reports. They rendered us invaluable help in the past, especially while the Brits were trying to get a foothold here."

"The Brits have not yet left Norway completely. As soon as the weather clears we will have to bomb the Royal Navy ships and troops who have pushed our poor men up against the Swedish border, near Narvik."

"Those fucking Brits up there outnumber our men four to one. It's no wonder that our men are so hard pressed. We lost a few bloody destroyers that were holed up at the end of the fjord. A superior force cornered them there and they were powerless with all their ammo and fuel used up. Their crews scuttled the ships to prevent them from being captured. The sailors of our sunken ships joined the parachute troops and mountain troops who have previously taken Narvik, but they all had to retreat into the mountains when the British assault almost overpowered them."

I ask: "And how do you know all this?"

"My job is intelligence, in case you haven't heard. I was in Narvik a few days ago and our agents kept me up-to-date. Anyway, tell me, how you are doing? And what are you doing?"

"Thinking about you every day, most of the time. My fondest wish is to spend every day with you. And my second wish is that our Wehrmacht will end this war as soon as possible."

"The end may perhaps be not so far off. We can expect our troops to swarm into Holland, Belgium, Luxemburg and France in less than a fortnight's time. We hope to overpower France within a few weeks. The British military leaders also guess that we will attack soon, but they don't know what to expect. And I know that they are poorly prepared to repell us once we have crossed the Channel."

"How on earth did you get to know all this?"

"I visited southern England a fortnight ago. With a forged British passport and forged British pounds. I travelled via Spain and Portugal. And then I got reports from a few agents about possible fortifications and other preparations along the coast. There are almost none. I also went to look for myself."

"What name did they give you on that false passport? Certainly not your own name?"

"You won't believe it, but according to my forged passport I am an English woman called Elizabeth Rose Taylor, born in Birmingham in 1916. Anyway, my year in Birmingham and my studies in Berlin helped me to speak English perfectly."

"Well, well. It seems as if our Wehrmacht is on a winning spree. This esteemed member of the Luftwaffe (and I press my index finger against my chest) has to reaffirm an old conquest: this wonderful woman sitting next to me!"

Since the weather gives no sign of clearing I decide to stay for the night.

During dinner I tell Sonja: "It's amazing how you are able to predict what will happen. You predicted that we would take Denmark and Norway – and we did!"

"I can also predict that you will make love to me before you say good-buy later on."

"You really do have a prophetic gift."

Trondheim, Friday, 10 May 1940

We hear the news that our troops are at this moment invading the Netherlands, Belgium, Luxemburg and France. All resistance crumbles and the French soldiers and British Tommys are on the run – just as Sonja has predicted.

We are too far away to give our boys over there any aid. Our job to keep the pressure on those Brits and Frenchies who are still clinging to Narvik and the nearby Harstad.

Trondheim, Wednesday, 15 May 1940

Our Gruppe has been able to fly a number or sorties against the British and French soldiers who are making life difficult for our men in the mountains above Narvik. There are also a few Norwegian battalions fighting the Germans, in spite of the fact that their comrades have given up the fight in southern and central Norway.

Last night was one of those days when the weather permitted us to fly, although it is still rather foggy and visibility isn't optimal. A rather bright moon made flying possible.

The German units outside Narvik informed us that a number of British soldiers were being embarked on three troop ships from the harbour of the island of Harstad, north west of Narvik. We dive down in successive waves upon the harbour inside a shallow fjord. The troop ships are armed with a few flack guns and their inexperienced crews try to shoot us down, but with no real effect.

One of the three troop ships gets badly damaged and she sinks. I don't know what happened to all the soldiers already on that ship, but I suspect that many of them won't make it to France or Britain.

Trondheim, Friday, 7 June 1940

Although it is supposed to be summer, the weather is often unfriendly and it was impossible to fly half of he time. Today, we are ordered to do a last sortie over Narvik to look for any surviving British soldiers and ships taking them on board.

We don't find any British soldiers or ships and we turn out to sea in an effort to find British ships somewhere.

And then we witness the end of a proud important ship of the Roayl Navy. An aircraft carrier has accidently stumbled against two of our battleships, the Gneisenau and the Sharnhorst. We see the smoke from their huge guns from afar and we are just in time to see how the aircraft carrier and two destroyers are disappearing into the cold water while their crews try to get away on life rafts.

Trondheim, Monday, 10 June 1940

Today, we get the news that the battles of Narvik are something of the past and the Wehrmacht is in full control of Norway since yesterday. The last units of the Norwegian Army, that have given our troops a real hard time with their stubborn and heroic defence, surrendered. It took us two whole months to subdue these hardy Vikings, the inhabitants of a small country with twenty times less people than Germany.

Today is our first day of rest and relaxation in a long time. We wash our clothes, write letters, take lengthy showers, explore the countryside and listen to the radio. We also learn that the aircraft carrier that our battleships had sunk yesterday, was the HMS Glorious.

We all agree that our sudden idyllic holiday in beautiful Norway will soon be at an end. We will certainly be called upon to join the fight in the south. For that, we need reinforcements because the whole Geschwader has lost forty aircraft out of a full hundred and ten at the start of the Norwegian campaign – ten of them due to accidents. Fortunately, crews that bailed out of damaged aircraft and were captured could be freed again when we took control of the country and they are available to fly again. We hope that the new aircraft we are due to receive will be improved versions of our Heinkels.

Trondheim, Thursday, 13 June 1940

Our promised reinforcements start to arrive today. Four brand-new Heinkels land on our air base, destined for my Staffel. We are almost at full strength again.

I call a meeting of all the air crews after the new boys have been given an opportunity to make themselves at home: "Männer, let's welcome our new arrivals. May I ask each of you new boys to stand up and tell us something about yourself – name, home town, married or single, where you have received your training and how many flying hours you have logged."

The twenty new men do as requested.

"And now, men, you will have to become as proficient as possible. I will ask the Kriegsmarine to tow a delerict raft out to sea so that we can use that for target practice with dummy bombs. Each of the four new crews will practice under the watchfull eyes of four of our senior pilots, me included. I will tell you later about some of the failures of our Staffel, due to bad aiming and over-eagerness. For instance, we almost had the distinction of being the first Staffel to have sunk an aircraft carrier shortly after the war had started – but only almost, not quite. That is, anyway, a story for another day. The point is, though, that bad aiming cannot be tolerated.

"I will also require of each new crew to become familiar with the check list that I have devised. That list contains all the items that have to be checked before you start up. That check list has prevented this Staffel of losing a single aircraft due to accidents."

Trondheim, Monday, 24 June 1940

Our whole Geschwader is standing on parade today. We are being inspected by the "Fliegerführer Norwegen" (Flying commander, Norway) and Commanding General of "Luftflotte" (Air Fleet) 5, Generaloberst (Colonel General) Erhard Milch a former chief manager of the German Airline, Deutsche Lufthansa.

All pilots in the Geschwader who took part in the Norwegian campaign are to receive the Iron Cross, First Class, and the other member of air crews are to receive the Iron Cross, Second Class. Milch praises our efforts in driving out the British and French invaders and securing Norway for the Wehrmacht.

He also reminds us that an armistice was signed with France, the day before yesterday. That means that we can concentrate all our efforts on subduing Great Britain and the Luftwaffe is to play an essential role in that campaign.

24 June 1940

We also receive a new Geschwaderkommodore today, a nobleman to wit: Oberstleutnant (Lieutenant Colonel) Karl Freiherr (Baron) von Wechmar.

Stavanger, Thursday, 1 August 1940

We moved again, this time to Stavanger-Sandnes, near the port city of Stavanger in southwestern Norway. There are three Luftwaffe bases on the Stavanger-peninsula: Stavanger Sola, the main base with the headquarters of "Fliegerkorps" (Flying Corps) X, Stavanger-Forus and Stavanger-Sandness.

Stavanger lies almost directly on the coast and is the nearest spot on the European mainland to Scotland. For that reason, the three Luftwaffe bases house a large number of units – bombers, fighters, transport planes, anti-aircraft artillery and other service units.

Our Gruppe is not yet at full strength and we have 29 serviceable planes, instead of 36. My Third Staffel, though, is almost at full strength with eleven planes with crews. I had no opportunity of informing Sonja about my whereabouts and, therefore, she probably won't be able to reach me here.

Our Geschwaderkommodore holds a meeting with all the pilots: "Men, this base, as well as the other two Luftwaffe bases here at Stavanger, have been bombed by die RAF on various times during April and again during July, but we were able to drive them away – although they managed to destroy a number of our aircraft on the ground. No other airfield in Norway has suffered so many air attacks than Sandnes where we are based. Fortunately, they have not returned since.

"This tells me that they have lost the initiative. Now is the time for u to take the initiative and take the war to the British Isles. Our Kampdgeschwader's members are specialists in anti-shipping operations. And that is exactly what OKL expects of us to keep on doing. May God be with you all. Heil Hitler!"

While I walk away from this conference, I ask myself: "Karl Krause, what has happened to you? What the hell are you doing in this remote spot in a strange country where you are not really welcome? You joined the Luftwaffe because you wanted to fly. And now you are flying, day and night. You are so used to flying that it has become a tiresome chore with no pleasure anymore. You are actually dead-tired. You must stay on the look-out for enemy fighters every time you take to the sky. And your job is to destroy – ships, cargoes and people. It's impossible to calculate how many deaths you have caused, but it must be hundreds of fellow-human beings whom you have never seen in your life before. You were brought up on a missionary station where the Gospel of love, forgiveness and charity was preached. And now you thrive on hate and bloodshed and destruction. The Oberstleutnant blessed us with his wish that God be with us. Where does God fit in with this madness? On whose side is God really? Or is He disgusted with all of us on both sides? Yes, what has become of you? Are you satisfied with your life?"

At this moment I get tears in my eyes and the strongest wish I have at this moment is just to embrace my superlative Sonja and hear her velvet voice.

Stavanger, Tuesday, 13 August 1940

Oberstleutnant von Wechmar: "Men, a busy time lies ahead of us. It is the task of the Luftwaffe to soften up the defenses of the Brits before we can invade their island. We have to secure air superiority and, therefore, our task as bombers will be to put as many airfields in Scotland out of action as possible. We can expect stiff defense from anti-aircraft batteries and fighter squadrons and losses on our side will be inevitable. But, if we can hit as many airfields as possible, put them out of operation and destroy as many planes as we can on the ground, we will reach our goal of air superiority.

"Most of you are experienced pilots and I know that the Führer and the Reich can rely on you to deliver the desired results. The commander-in-chief of the Luftwaffe, Reichsmarschall (Marshall of the Reich) Hermann Göring, has ordered that today to be called 'Tag des Adlers' (Day of the Eagle), the day on which the Luftwaffe Eagle takes to the sky to bomb and shoot the Royal Air Force into oblivion. May God be with us all! Heil Hitler!"

Stavanger, Tuesday, 27 August 1940

The Geschwaderkommodore of KG 26: "Männer, we are to stop bombing airfields in Scotland, although we haven't yet reached our goal of securing air superiority. The RAF bombed Berlin last night and the Führer ordered Reichsmarshall Göring to direct the Luftwaffe that London has to be attacked in retalliation. Our target, therefore, has changed.

"We are to take off as a whole Geschwader from eleven tonight onwards and our task will be to drop bombs on the docks at Tilbury in the Thames. If we hit some civilian targets, then so be it. The RAF did not only hit military targets in their raid over Berlin and there were also civilian casualties. If they can do it, we can also do it. They have to be taught the lesson that we won't allow this nonsense.

"Each Staffelkapitän is to see to it that every available Heinkel is ready. The Headquarters Staffel will lead the way, followed by the first Gruppe, the second Gruppe and the third Gruppe. Each Gruppe is to try to follow the squadrons in front of them, but make sure about your own navigation in any case. You will recognise London by the Thames flowing through the city."

I brief my flying crews and the ground crews: "Meine Herren, it is already late in the afternoon. Make sure that every Heinkel is fully functional and bombed up. High explosives in the first six planes and incendiary bombs in the rest. When we depart at eleven tonight, it won't be totally dark because it is still summer over here. Over London it will be dark because there we will be further away from the North Pole with its perpetual summer sunshine, although a crescent moon will rise around one o' clock tomorrow morning, providing us with a little bit of illumination."

North Sea and London, Wednesday, 28 August 1940

We are approaching London almost from due north. There will be no time to linger over the target because London is on the outside edge of our range. We have to be very careful with our fuel stocks if we want to return to Stavanger safely.

Although it was slightly dusk when we took off it grew totally dark on our way to England. It's not difficult to find London in the dark because the place is already on fire. Thick clouds of smoke hang over the city, illuminated by huge flames. Bombs are exploding with huge flashes. Previous waves of bombers have already caused heaps of damage. All of a sudden, I hear our machines guns whine and whir and whistle as they send off their bullets against a swarm of fighters on our tails. I can see more than one Heinkel that was hit and is losing height as smoke is pouring from one of its engines. My four machine gunners shoot and shoot. Each has a thousand machine gun rounds available and they do not seem to be stingy in delivering these rounds onto the fighters.

Suddenly the fighters are gone. Searchlights illuminate a few planes and they start to manoevre to slip out of the beams of light.

I dare not look at the searchlights because that will affect my night vision. The flack picks up as we approach the city. There are clouds and puffs of smoke all around us as the gunners down below try to take us out. I see two Heinkels receiving direct hits and falling from the sky. The tail of one of them is blown off and the other one has lost a wing. There is absolutely nothing one can do to avoid an anti-aircraft bomb exploding beneath or next to a plane.

At last, my Staffel reaches a spot where our target is sighted. We can see bombs exploding on the ground and in the water of the Thames from a previous wave of bombers. We do high-level bombing because we cannot dare to do dive-bombing and lose height. The higher we fly the less chances there are to be hit by flack. Directly after we have downloaded our bomb loads upon a city in agony we turn around and try to reach more height to get away from the heavy flack.

It takes more than half-an-hour to reach the English coast over Yorkshire again. Suddenly I cannot keep my hands still any more. They are shaking and trembling. My legs do the same. Werner, my navigator and observer, asks: "What's the matter with you?"

"Don't know. My hands won't obey my brain anymore. Can you please hand me a handkerchief? My eyes can't see properly because of all the sweat on my face that interferes with my eyesight."

"Here."

Two minutes later our Funker, Bernard, comes to my aid with a flask of Schnapps. I take a mouth full and swallow the burning stuff down my throat.

"Hell, Bernard, this juice just gave me more tears in my eyes!"

"No wonder it's called fire water."

For the first time since I joined the Luftwaffe I feel sick while flying.

Some time later, Werner pours me a cup of strong black coffee from a hot water flask to keep me awake because the Schapps tends to make me drowsy. It will be a catastrophe and a calamity and a crisis if I were to fall asleep.

We land safely at Stavanger at dawn. Fortunately, my Staffel hasn't suffered any casualties, although I suspect that more than one plane must sport a few bullet holes. I feel in one of the pockets of my flying jacket to make sure that I still have my Bible with me. I murmur a prayer of thanks that I am still in one piece.

I stumble to the headquarters of our Geschwader where I find our Kommodore who looks awful with blood-shot eyes: "Had some fun? Krause, are you and your men ready for another outing and some sports and fun tonight? We will be having a go at Newcastle-upon-Tyne."

Beauvais, Friday, 27 September 1940

What is left of our Geschwader arrived at the French airfield of Beauvais yesterday. It is a former airfield of the French Air Force, north of Paris, which the Luftwaffe has taken over after the armistice with France.

The past four weeks went by as if in a blur. If I try to think back, I can only remember flack, attacks by Spitfires, Hurricanes and Beaufighters, exploding bombs, Heinkels and Dorniers falling from the sky, machine gun fire, some more flack and how dog tired I was. There was little time for sleep. Fortunately, we kept the Brits so busy over their own airspace that they couldn't sleep either and didn't find the time to send their bombers to harass us at Stavanger. They bombed Berlin, Hamburg, Bremen and other important cities, though, on various occasions.

We often heard the Fürher's furious voice over the radio, screaming revenge and calling all possible curses upon Winston Churchill, the British Prime Minister, and the chief of Bomber Command of the Royal Air Force, Air Marshall Sir Charles Portal, for having the audacity to bomb Berlin.

During the past four weeks, KG 26 bashed Newcastle-upon-Tyne, Edinburgh, Glasgow, Manchester and London. In the process we lost thirty-nine more Heinkels. A number of air crews could bale out when their bombers were fatally hit, but the rest were killed upon impact with British soil or the sea. My Staffel lost four aircraft during this time and we are again down to eight.

To supplement the squadrons already in France and to help us to reach London so much easier, we were shifted to Beauvais. It is a smallish city with a Gothic cathedral. The airfield is situated almost directly on the northeastern edge of the town.

During our stay at Stavanger there was no opportunity of letting Sonja know where I was and I had no news of her. During the little time afforded us to get settled, and to integrate new air crews with their aircraft into our Geschwader, I hastily wrote the following note on a typewriter:

26 September 1940

My Darling,
Do you remember the wonderful 3 days we spent in France? Unfortunately, I had to leave the train at Beauvais while you travel led on. Has Karl ever found out aboutour little affair? I hope to see you again on 24/10.
Please congratulate your Cousin Martin with his birthday on 13 October. I believe he will be 35 on that day. Or is it 36?
Keep safe and don't ~~frget~~ forget me,
KG
      PS   26 kisses X X X ….

I seal the envelope and walk over to one of the transport squadrons. I happen to find a pilot who is to fly to Cologne later the day and I ask him to post my letter over there. I give him money for a postage stamp.

Beauvais, Tuesday, 8 October 1940

It is shortly after breakfast after a busy night. All I want to do is to sleep a few hours before we take to the skies again.

A Gefreiter stops me: "Herr Oberleutnant, there is a telephone call for you. Come with me."

He takes me to an office where I find a telephone taken off its hook and waiting to be spoken into. It can only be Sonja after I have given her the number by means of our code in my letter.

"Hallo. This is Oberleutnant Krause."

Sonja's voice on the other side: "Herr Oberleutnant, this is Frau Schellenhausen. I'm phoning on behalf of your neighbour, Fräulein Sonnenschein. She just wanted to inform you that she is well and that she enjoys her work. She also would like to know how your are doing."

"Please tell her that I am still in one piece, although I am suffering from a bout of insomnia. I also have another problem. My neighbour shot four of my twelve pigeons the other day."

"Why did he do that?"

"He complained about their droppings on his roof. But, on the other hand, I don't like the barking of his bulldog and I want to shoot that animal in retaliation. I have been able to buy two new replacements, but these poor inexperienced birds also got shot."

"Your insomnia in these circumstances may be understandable. But, please, don't drown your sorrows with the contents of a wine bottle."

"I prefer Schnapps or French cognac."

Beauvais, Sunday, 13 October 1940

Extreme weather has stopped air operations over France, the Channel and Southern England. I utilise the opportunity to catch up on some sleep. I am rudely woken when somebody shakes my shoulder. With a curse on my lips, I open my eyes – ready to chase my tormentor away.

It is Siegfried, my brother-in-law. My foul mood improves immediately.

"What are you doing here?"

"Paying you a visit."

"Yes, I can see that. But what brought you to this place?"

"My airplane."

"But why?"

"To see you."

"Flying all the way from wherever, just to see me?"

"I actually had to deliver a bunch of big shots to this place and take them back to Berlin afterwards."

"So, you are still playing taxi driver?"

"Sort of. Actually, bus driver would be a better description."

I call upon my orderly to make us some coffee and we catch up on our respective experiences since the war started. He also keeps me up to date regarding the Schellenberg family. Sonja is still working at the same place and Anja has had a baby, a little girl.

Me: "When are you flying back?"

Siegfried: "The day after tomorrow, weather permitting. It was hazardous to fly here in this foul weather, but the mission of those big shots couldn't wait."

Just before he leaves after finishing his coffee, he says: "Oh, I almost forgot. Here's a letter for you."

It has Sonja's handwriting on the envelope and I open the envelope with Siegfried watching me. In her letter, she advises me to get some sick leave and to invent some mysterious symptoms so that a medical officer can take me off flying duties for two days. She flew with Siegfried from Berlin, together with some other important people who have to attend to matters in nearby Paris.

"What does my sister tell you, my dear brother-in-law?"

"I am going to report sick and then you are going to take me to my wife. Where is she staying?"

"In a place here in Beauvais. It's described as 'Chambres d'hôte – Clos d'Allonne'. Here is a bottle of Schnapps with which you can bribe a 'Stabsarzt' (medical officer) to book you off sick."

"It won't be possible to fly today, anyway. I'm free. Let's go. And then I can come back and get that sick note from the Stabsarzt."

As a Staffel commander, I am entitled to get a small truck from the vehicle pool and I and Hauptmann Schellenberg leave the air base and enter the town of Beauvais, which lies almost direcly next to the Fliegerhorst.

We find Sonja in her lodgings, an old converted farm house on the outskirts of the town where she is renting a double room. Despite my lack of sleep, I suddenly feel lively and energetic due to the presence of the love of my life and I cannot help but to grab her around her body and pick her up.

Shortly before dinner time, Siegfried and I drive back to the Fliegerhorst where we enjoy a meal in the officers' mess. Thereafter, I take the bottle of Schnapps to the medical section and I get admitted to the surgery of Stabarzt Michael Müller. He listens to my symptoms, hides the bottle of Schnapps in one of his drawers and gets his pen and a printed form. I am to be taken off flying duties for two days because I will have to go into quarantine due to a suspected case of "Turkish Tree Toad Fever" (whatever that is).

Siegried, who waits in the waiting room, promises to take this note to the commander of my Geschwader, Oberst von Wechmar.

After my return to Sonja, we can really talk. She informs me that Siegfried still does not know that she works for the Abwehr and that he is under the impression that she has some sort of a teaching job and that she wanted to visit France to buy some French books.

"I gather that you have been dropping bombs on British cities and towns the past month?"

"Yes. That's my present job description. I am dead tired because we seldom get rest. Every trip is a nightmare, due to all the flack and searchlights and fighters and possible engine failures that we have to endure."

"My Admiral is of the opinion that the bloody bombing of London and other cities is a blooming grave mistake. The Luftwaffe was on the verge of attaining air superiority and wiping the Royal Air Force out when Hitler stopped that campaign and started playing tit for tat with Churchill. He has lost the opportunity of invading Britain because the friggin' RAF has been given an opportunity to bloody-well recover."

"I thought the bombing of London was to intimdate the English so that they would give up the fight when our armies arrive."

"It is not widely known, but that fucking fool of a Hitler already gave the order more than a month ago that 'Unternehmen Seelöwe' (Operation Sea Lion), the plan to invade Engeland, be postponed indefinitely. There is absolutely no flippin' chance that it can be revived because the loony Luftwaffe hasn't beaten the fucking RAF. We also don't have the means to take an army over the Channel to invade England."

"Hell."

"I'm not supposed to be here. I heard unexpectedly that Siegried had to fly here with a bunch of generals and I got permission from Canaris to accompany him on the pretext that I had to do some scouting and to listen to the conversations of those generals while we were flying."

"Hell!"

Beauvais, Monday, 14 October 1940

Since I was still supposed to be in quarantine, it was easy to disappear and spend the day in the presence of my smashing Sonja. The weather has cleared and we listened how the Heinkels at the air base started up and flew away after dark.

It is already Tuesday morning, before daybreak, when we are woken by a few dozen aircraft approaching and getting settled on the airfield.

Sonja: "What do you think? What happened to them this night?"

Me: "They were supposed to start some fires in Manchester. I am sure that quite a few of them bought it, unfortunately."

"Manchester. That's where my aunt lives. I wonder what has happened to her."

"We will only be able to know after the end of the war, unless you are able to slip into England through Spain and Portugal again. As Miss Lizzie Taylor."

"How do you mourn the loss of your colleagues and friends?"

"I don't. I can't. There's no time. My feelings are dead. I just take note of our losses and carry on, regardless. I have no choice. If I start crying about lost colleagues and friends I will simply break apart. So – I just forget about them."

"And you can't even have funerals, because they crashed somewhere on enemy territory?"

"Or at sea. All I can do is send a KIA (killed in action) note to their next of kin. My orderly types the same letter over and over, with only the names changed. In it, the next of kin are assured that the son, brother, husband or whatever, died a heroic death. And then I sign it, without looking at the names."

And suddenly I start to sob. The love of my life gets hold of me and dries my tears and running nose with the sheets on the bed.

Sonja: "Let's hope that I get clean bedding again, because your nose is running in streams."

After I have regained my composure I tell my wife: "Towards you I can be totally honest. Apart from the fact that it actually shakes me when I lose a friend or a colleague, the worst is the fear I feel every time when I take to the air with a load of bombs. I ask myself, will I make it? Will I be able to bring my crew back? All that keeps me awake and disturbs my sleep. I can't eat. I feel despondent the whole time. When I joined the Luftwaffe in 1936 I loved flying. Not anymore. I hate it, actually."

My wife allows my head to rest on her bosom.

I continue: "I don't want to lose you. I've been fortunate because I could see you a few times since the war started. Many of my colleagues didn't have that privilege. Let's hope that life will become more normal once the Brits have seen the folly of resisting the might of Germany and giver up the fight. Then there will be peace again."

"Don't be so sure. The RAF has given the flippin' Luftwaffe a beating. And, apart from that, Hitler, the blooming turd, is due to undertake the folly of attacking Russia. The campaign against France will look like a minor affair compared to our coming fight against the Russian Bear."

"What are you telling me?"

"Prepare yourself for a fucking long war. Hitler wants to drive the Poles and Russians permanently into Siberia so that German settlers can take over the conquored areas. He wants more living space in a greater German Reich. Go and read Mein Kampf, the book he has written. This woozy wacking war is not going to end soon. We're in for shovels full of shit. And you are to stay bloody-well silent about what I've told you."

Beauvais, Tuesday, 19 November 1940

Today, I – as senior Staffelkapitän – became the temporary Gruppenkommandeur of my Gruppe because our Gruppenkommandeur became the temporary Geschwaderkommodore of KG 26.

Our commander, Oberst Karl Freiherr von Wechmar, bought a one-way ticket to the Channel waters. While we were attacking the Thames Estuary yesterday his plane was downed by a fighter. There was no time to bail out and he was classified as KIA.

Our Geschwader has had many losses the last few months and we are down to sixty percent of full strength, despite the arrival of a number of new crews and replacement aircraft.

Aalborg, Saturday, 1 February 1941

Kampgeschwader 26 is back at Aalborg, Denmark. It became clear that Hitler's campaign of bombing British cities did not convince the inhabitants of the British Isles to beg for peace. Although industrial sites were mostly targetted it did not cripple the production of war material. The result was that less and less air raids against British cities took place.

The emphasis shifted back to war against Britain's maritime links for the import of food and raw materials for her industries. KG 26 was back in Denmark from where the North Sea and the Atlantic could be reached more easily. Our Geschwader suffered huge losses during the bombing campaign against Britain. After our Kommodore was lost in action he was replaced by Oberstleutnant Benno Kosch, the previous Kommodore of Kampfgeschwader 1 ("Hindenburg") and a native of Austria.

Immediately after our arrival at Aalborg, I wrote this letter to Sonja:

1 February 1941

My Darling,
You will never gues how I am spending my days since the beginning of this month. I am again selling Danish eels! This is a much better use of my time than swatting at angry birds.

It was horrible spending Christmas and Silvester without you. Let's hope that the coming summer will bring more joy to us all. Send my regards to everybody in Berlin.
As always,
Carolus XXXX

It was again possible to ask a pilot of a transport plane who flew back to Berlin-Gatow to post my letter over there. It won't do to send a letter with a Danish stamp.

I would have liked to tell Sonja about all the near escapes I had over British skies. It happened more than once that the wings of my Heinkel got perforated by machine gun bullts from a British fighter. I am very proud of my crew because they managed to shoot down three RAF Hurricanes.

Because we flew less since the beginning of this year I could get more sleep and my mood improved somewhat, although I will never get used to the fact that I was living an extremely dangerous life. I developed a love-hare relationship with my Heinkel. I loved the machine because she carried me and my crew through flack and the attacks by British fighters. I hated her for not being faster and more agile and because I started shaking after every near escape. Black coffee and a swig of Schnapps usually helped to stop the shaking and the cramps in my stomach.

Every time I took a mouth full of Schnapps I would see the disapproving faces of my pious parents in my mind.

Aalborg, Thursday, 13 February 1941

We have, yet again, a new Geschwaderkommodore, Oberst Alexander Holle.

Since our arrival in Aalborg, we have undertaken a number of sorties over the North Sea to look for maritime targets. We found two convoys coming in from North America and it was possible to send a number of freighters to the bottom of the ocean. In most cases, the crews could be saved by other ships in the convoys.

My mood improved because I felt that I was no longer taking the lives of other people – only destroying equipment that could be used against our cities.

Since we attacked in waves, it was not always possible to pin the sinking of a certain freighter onto a particular crew.

Trondheim, Friday 28 March 1941

It is a strange bed in which I wake up. I look around and discover that I lie in hospital. Nurses are attending to other beds, presumably also filled with patients.

My recollections seep back into my consciousness. I can remember that I and my Staffel patrolled the area north of Scotland in search of enemy ships to attack. We did find a convoy, escorted by a destroyer and a frigate. After I have dropped my bombs and shot up again into the air my Heinkel was hit by shots from one of the war ships. Fortunately, I could keep on flying, but on our way back I discovered that one of my fuel tanks was leaking and that we were losing fuel at an alarming rate.

Werner, my navigator, pointed out that there was a hole in one of the glass panes of our cockpit.

To compound matters, I suddenly had difficulty using my port-side leg.

Werner: "There is blood seeping through your trousers. You must have been wounded. We're not only losing fuel – you're also losing blood."

"That's right. I also see it. I'm sure the pain will register soon. Anyway, Werner, set us on a course to the nearest Fliegerhorst in Norway. We won't be able to make it back to Denmark with our fuel."

"There is a brand new Luftwaffe base on the tip of the Ørlandet Peninsula, west of Trondheim. It is not yet fully operational but we will be able to land on the unfinished runway."

"Men, if you have never prayed in your lives, then now's the time. We need every bit of help from heaven."

I must have passed out on the way to Ørlandet, because I can't remember landing there. It is a mystery how I landed in hospital.

I hear a voice making a remark in Afrikaans next to my bed: "Bliksem! Hierdie outjie lyk bleddie sleg (Bloody thunder! This guy looks bloody bad.)"

I reply in Afrikaans: "En wie de hel is jy? (And who in hell are you?)"

The speaker seems to be an "Arzt" (medical practitioner): "Did I hear correctly? Did you reply in Afrikaans?"

"Ja. I did. And what in hell am I doing in this place? Where am I?"

"You are in the 'Lazarett' (military hospital) in Trondheim. You were pulled from your sinking aircraft by a patrol boat of the Kriegsmarine. You seemed to have tried to make it to Ørlandet, but you didn't get there. According to your navigator, you passed out just at the moment when your fuel ran out – due to blood loss. As you can see, you are linked to a bag of blood to replenish your almost empty blood circulation system."

"What did you do to me?"

"Patched up your left leg."

"So, I didn't lose a leg or something?"

"You're fortunate. I am passing through Trondheim with my unit and while we are waiting to be sent somewhere else, I am helping out in this Lazarett. The men of my unit don't need much medical help and their only complaints are hangovers."

"Who the hell are you?"

"Oh, sorry. I should have introduced myself. I am Oberarzt (medical officer with the rank of Oberleutnant) David Scholtz of the Sixth Mountain Artillery Regiment of the Waffen-SS. I see on your admittance file that you are Oberleutnant Krause. Are you also from South Africa?"

"Yes, from Rustenburg. But I'm actually a German, although I was born in the Transvaal. That's why I can speak Afrikaans – as well as German."

"And how did you manage to become a pilot in the Luftwaffe?"

"I completed an application form."

"Yes, yes, of course. But how did they accept you?"

"My application was approved."

"OK. But how did it come that you applied in the first place?"

"Because I wanted to fly."

"And who introduced you to the Luftwaffe?"

"My brother-in-law, who was an instructor in Berlin."

"And how did he become you brother-in-law?"

"That's a stupid question, really. I married his sister, of course."

"And how did you get to know his sister?"

"You sound just like the guys from the Gestapo – interrogating me like this."

"Although I am with the Waffen-SS, I have no time for the Gestapo. I'm only curious how an Afrikaans-speaking member of the Luftwaffe landed on my operating table."

"Oekee. I competed in the Olympics in thirty-six when I met my wife. She was a member of the German team. And then we got married after I qualified as a pilot. Simple. And how did you become a member of the SS?"

"By accident. I was studying medicine in Berlin when the war broke out. I had to choose between a concentration camp and the SS. I chose the SS. But wait, didn't we meet before the war? In Kufstein?"

"Yes, yes. That's it. I remember now. We became friends then. You were on your honeymoon, you and your brother. Three guys of us were there with our girls."

"Nice to see you again. And, as I told you, you were badly wounded. Fortunately, I am a specialist surgeon and I specialize on legs, feet and hips. That's why the other quacks asked me to take you on. I am going to book you off and send you home to recover. That wound has to heal totally and you will have to learn to walk again."

"Will I be able to ride my bicycle again?"

"Take it easy at first. But that will be excellent exercise to regain the use of your leg."

Berlin, Thursday, 10 April 1941

The crew of the ambulance plane of the Luftwaffe treated me as a very important person since I am also a member of the Luftwaffe with pilot's wings on my uniform. I was loaded onto the plane on a stretcher and a nurse looked after me during the flight.

I was kitted out with all my necessities in Trondheim since I landed there with only a blood-soaked flying suit. My things in Aalborg were already sent to my parents-in-law's address in Berlin-Dahlem.

David Scholtz booked me off for two full months after I have spent twelve days in the Lazarett in Trondheim and I will only have to report back for duty during the second week of June. During my stay in the Lazarett, I had a few conversations with David when he was off-duty. Both of us fellt stuck in the war and both longed to be back in sunny South Africa – instead of in the cold and damp Scandinavia.

The Tante Ju landed with me at Berlin-Gatow where my father-in-law and Sonja came to fetch me. And now I am being nursed by Frau Sonja Krause and Frau Sofia Schellenberg. My sister-in-law, Frau Anja Schellenberg and my borther-in-law, Hauptmann Siegfried Schellenberg, help where they can. They all treat me as a hero.

Although tomorrow is Good Friday, the war keeps going on. And suddenly, I can rest and recuperate. I hope to regain my sanity in the presence of my worried wife.

Berlin, Saturday, 26 April 1941

Sonja has the weekend off and we go on an outing with our racing bikes. We go slowly because I haven't regained the full use of my left leg yet. I had to report at the sick bay at the air base of Berlin-Gatow twice a week to monitor my progress and to receive some physiotherapy. According to the Hauptarzt who looks after me, it is certainly advisable to use my bike.

We have managed to reach the countryside, just outside Berlin and we sit beneath a tree where Sonja takes out our lunch – Brötchen with cheese and ham: "You will have to do without butter, because it is being rationed – just as many other foodstuffs."

We enjoy the pleasant spring weather and we stare at the clouds while lying on our backs. It often happens that a trainer, a fighter or a swarm bombers pass over us. Suddenly, I discover that I miss the sky. I really want to get back into an aircraft's cockpit. During the past four weeks, since my accident, I had enough time to rest, clear up my sleep deficit and get my head clean again. The presence of Sonja has much to do with that, although she often disappears for two or three days without explanation.

Sonja: "It's only a matter of weeks before we invade Russia."

Me: "And how does my spy wife know that? Have you been eavesdropping on the Führer?"

"Not quite. But I was in Switzerland last Monday and Tuesday after I disappeared for a night. With Canaris. I told you that he has a Polish Jewish mistress over there. She has links with the British spies in Switzerland and he passed on the message through her that Britain and America have to put pressure on Hitler to desist from his foolish plan to conquor Russia."

"And you were part of their tête-a-tête?"

"Not all the time. But Canaris needed me as a witness when he told his mistress – her name is Halina Szymanska – about the coming invasion. I slept that night in a hotel room while he stayed with her."

"I suppose that I will be needed to fly a bomber against the Russians."

"That may bloody well be the case. Alternatively, you may be required to aid General Rommel in Africa against the bloody British and the silly South Africans. There is also a chance that you may end up in the Balkans or Greece where we are also fighting. Hitler sent in our troops to invade those parts to keep the Brits out of there and to prevent them from bombing our oil fields in ruddy Romania."

After a long silence, Sonja continues: "Canaris is actually sabotaging the fucking Nazis."

"That's clear. After all, he passes military secrets to the Brits."

"That's not all. The Nazis – especially those retarded turds and trolls in the SS – have started to round up all Jews in conquered countries and sending them to concentration camps. They are used as slave labor and those who are not fit for work are disposed of."

"Disposed of? Killed?"

"In cold blood. Systematically."

"And Canaris tries to stop this barbaric practice?"

"Not too openly. I had to help him by giving a number of Jews in Holland a cursory 'training' of two days' duration to become so-called Abwehr agents. And then they were issued with Abwehr identity cards and passports and sent off to Sweden and Finland, where they can be safe."

"Why are you telling me this?"

"I must talk to somebody. I can't mention these things to my family. They still don't know that I work for Canaris. They think that I merely have some sort of administrative or teaching job in some or other government office where I have to translate documents from English and French to German. You are the only person in whom I can confide.”

"What will happen if I talk in my sleep when I am back with the Luftwaffe?”

"They will think that you’ve been drinking too much.”

"And how does your father and Siegfried feel about this campaign against the Jews?”

"They don’t really know, but it wouldn’t bother them too much. They support every move the fucking Führer and the Nazi pisspot Party make.”

Berlin, Sunday, 8 June 1941

Somebody knocks on the front door, just after dinner. I open the door. Sonja's cousin Walter Schellenberg stands there. After we have greeted, he asks: "May I speak to your wife?"

"I will call her. Please sit down and wait a minute."

Sonja appears: "Walter, what a surprise! How are you?"

After a number of pleasantries and greetings to the other members of the household, Walter asks: "Sonja, may I speak to you in private? Can we go outside? The sun is still shining."

After about twenty minutes, Walter leaves in his motor vehicle without greeting any of us.

Me: "What was all this about?"

Sonja: "Let's go for a walk."

While we are strolling and enjoying the evening dusk, Sonja tells me: "He wants to recruit me for his service, the fucking Sicherheitsdienst of the SS. It sucks. He was recently promoted to the rank of Brigadeführer, which is the equivalent of a Major General. He doesn't dare to come to my office openly and, therefore, he approached me here at home."

"What does he want you to do?"

"To tell him everything about Canaris. He thinks Canaris is busy undermining the war effort and it's important to know about everything he does and says. He seems to know that I am a courier for Canaris."

"What did you tell him?"

"I'm not interested. And, anyway, I told him that Canaris doesn't trust me with any secret stuff. I won't be of much use to him."

"He didn't seem to be satisfied with your response."

"No. But I won't tell him anything I know and what I have told you. The fucking fool is actually after Canaris' job and he wants to use me to reach that goal. He hoped that he could rely on our family ties."

"What did he promise in return for your services?"

"I can keep my job at the Abwehr and he will also pay the same, in addition to my Abwehr salary."

"And you're not interested?"

"That bloody guy gives me the creeps and the cramps."

"I don't know him well, but that also goes for me."

Berlin, Saturday, 14 June 1941

This is the last Saturday of my sick leave and I and Sonja invade the countryside west of Berlin with our racing bikes. By this time, my left leg has healed almost completely and I may be declared fit for active duty again. We rest in a forest where we enjoy the summer weather by getting rid of our clothes.

Sonja: "Operation Barbarossa is to start in a week's time. That's when our boys invade Russia. We are fielding the biggest army in the history of warfare. Millions of men. More or less three million, eight hundred thousand. There will be more than 5 000 aircraft, thousands of tanks, thousands of artillery pieces and thousands of vehicles and horses."

"I have received call-up papers to the first Gruppe of Kampfgeschwader 54. They are stationed in Silesia."

"Then you will certainly bomb the Russians. You won't bomb the Brits and South Africans in North Africa."

Just before we get up to return home, Sonja comes with a bomb shell: "My Admiral pulled a very nasty trick on Stalin, the Russian dictator."

"How?"

"He made him believe that his senior generals were plotting and scheming against him. Stalin made the lot of them take part in parades in front of firing squads. That deprived his Army and Air Force of their most capable generals. He did that only a few weeks ago. Let's hope that will help in our war against Russia."

"What are you telling me? You are walking around with some very dangerous secrets in your head."

"And that's why Cousin Walter wants to recruit me for his slick, slippery, and sucking service."

"He gives me the creeps."

"The same here."

Stubendorf, Monday, 16 June 1941

Fortunately, it was possible to fly from Berlin to the Luftwaffe base of Stubendorf in Silesia, not far from the Polish border. I got a lift on a Junkers Ju 88 bomber with a new crew that had to join KG 54 after having received their flying training.

At Stubendorf, I report to the Geschwaderkommodore, Oberstleutnant Otto Höhne. He's glad to get an experienced Staffelkapitän and he orders the Gruppenkommandeur of the first Gruppe, Hauptmann Richard Linke, to his office so that I can be introduced to him. The Oberstleutnant was a pilot during the previous war and is also a qualified engineer – quite a competent man.

I am told by the Oberstleutnant: "Oberleutnant, you arrived just in time. We leave tomorrow by train for Lublin-Swidnik in Poland. It used to be the biggest air base of the Polish Air Force before our boys took it. We are converting there to the Junkers Ju 88A bombers. Our new aircraft are already waiting for us over there."

Hauptmann Linke: "The Junkers is a much better bomber than the Heinkels we have been using. They are faster and can carry a heavier bomb load."

Me: "That is something to look forward to. I flew here inside one of them as a passenger."

Linke: "You will become Staffelkapitän of the second Staffel. I will take you there so that you can meet the crews. We leave tomorrow morning at six by train."

The Geschwaderkommodore: "I want to remind you of the fact that our Geschwader has the nickname of the "Totenkopf" (Death's Head) Geschwader. That is because our emblem is the skull and crossed bones – almost the sign of the pirates of old. Our mission is to bring destruction and death to our foes."

Me: "So I've heard."

Linke: "You will also see it on our airplanes' cockpits."

Swidnik, Wednesday, 2 July 1941

It took me a fortnight at Swidnik to learn how to fly the Ju 88 well enough. I find it a lovely aircraft, much better than our old Heinkels.

The Ju 88 has a crew of four. After I had qualified on this plane, I started flying with my new crew members so that we could get to know each other. My observer and forward gunner is Oberfeldwebel Ludwig Lohse. The radio operator/rear gunner is Unteroffizier Michael Mommsen. The navigator/ventral gunner is Feldwebel Norbert Niebuhr.

Lohse quipped after we had introduced ourselves to each other: "It is clear that we are the KLMN-Mannschaft – Krause, Lohse, Mommsen and Niebuhr. We are, therefore, an alphabetic crew."

Me: "It would have been a disaster if we were an analphabetic or illiterate crew. I hope all of you can read and write decent German. We must also be a close-knit Mannschaft because we will have to rely on each other."

Operation Barbarossa has already started a fortnight ago when Russia was invaded. We are waiting to become part of this operation.

Swidnik, Thursday, 3 July 1941

KG 54 presently has 70 bombers, of which 64 are serviceable, and we have to support Army Group South in the Ukraine.

Today is my first operational sortie and we are to dive-bomb an airfield. It is easy to identify our target from the height we are flying. My Staffel of twelve bombers is to bomb the ammo stores next to the runway, while the other squadrons have to take out the aircraft on the ground and the control tower.

The only pilot in my Staffel who has had previous experience of bombing with the Ju 88, Leutnant Bock Kapaterski, offers to lead us all in the dive-bombing part. We start our descent as I follow Bock down.

The first step is to adjust the automatic altimeter at 300 meters above ground level. A few seconds before that level is reached, a siren goes off and as soon as the siren stops howling the bombs are to be released.

On the left-side window next to my pilot's seat a number of straight lines are etched, marked with numbers. If one wants to dive down at sixty degrees, for instance, one has to get the line for sixty degrees parallel with the horizon and that's what I do. That ensures that I dive down at the correct angle.

The air brakes under the wings have to be applied simultaneously to stop the aircraft from falling like a rock or a brick onto the target. All these innovations make the Ju 88 a so much better bomber than my old Heinkel 111.

I follow Bock in our dive towards the target and I see how he releases his bombs attached to points under his wings. Two seconds later, that is what I also do. My Junkers shoots up automatically after the bombs have been released and we regroup in the air while we fly back. Our ventral gunners/navigators all exclaim over their radios that the target has exploded as our bombs detonated all the ammo inside the stores.

While we fly back, I find that I can keep my hands and legs still. We encountered zero resistance and our outing was without any danger from flack or Russian fighters. The period of rest while I was training to fly the Ju 88 also helped to calm my nerves.

Swidnik, Thursday, 17 July 1941

We bombed the Russians as they were retreating, fleeing and surrendering to our boys. It became clear that they were rather helpless and that their generals didn't know how to stem the flood of the Wehrmacht.

Our biggest success to date was on 5 July when KG 54, together with KG 55 and KG 51, routed a Soviet counteroffensive and destroyed 220 motor vehicles and 40 tanks near Lviv. We also bombed railway stations, trains, bridges and airfields – wrecking everything with our bombs. We lost three aircraft during a rare clash with Soviet fighters.

Because our forces made such rapid progress, we can't reach the front lines anymore from Swidnik at this stage. We'll have to be relocated to somewhere nearer to the front again.

Hranowka, Friday, 15 August 1941

Hranowka is a small air base with very little infrastructure, situated in southwest Poland. This was our home for the last four weeks. We flew daily sorties against Russian positions. We killed dozens of tanks, destroyed vehicles by their hundreds and neutralized scores of artillery positions. We attacked a number of Russian air fields, destroying hundreds of aircraft on the ground.

I miss my sunny Sonja terrigbly.

Dnjepropetrowsk, Monday, 17 November 1941

During the last three months we moved to four other air bases, deeper into the Ukraine. Dnjepropetrowsk, where we are since October, is a major city in the southern Ukraine on the Dnieper River. The city was taken by our forces during August.

The German advance was so rapid that our troops reached the shores of the Black Sea during August, two months after Operation Barbarossa started on 22 June.

We continued to bomb the same types of targets as before: command centers, armored columns, vehicle convoys, artillery positions, troop concentrations, bridges, railway stations, trains and air fields. To date, our first Gruppe of KG 54 has been credited with 240 aircraft destroyed on the ground, hundreds of artillery pieces and tanks put out of action and thousands of motor vehicles destroyed or damaged. We flew a total of 1,400 sorties and dropped 1,720 tons of bombs on the Russians. Our Gruppenkommandeur, Hauptmann Richard Linke, was credited with 30 tanks destroyed and he was awarded the Knight's Cross of the Iron Cross.

On the other hand, during our group's time in the East, we lost 29 bombers that were destroyed or damaged and a number of men killed, wounded or captured. The other two groups of our Geschwader suffered less.

In order to refit and integrate new crews with their aircraft, we are moving to the Luftwaffe base at Memmingen in Bavaria today.

Memmingen, Thursday, 25 December 1941

While moving around in Poland and the Ukraine, it was impossible to make any contact with Sonja. Here in Memmingen, an old German town south of Ulm, it was possible to phone her at her parents' home and give her the message (in code) that I was back on German soil.

Because part of her job is to work in an office she managed to get some time off during Christmas. She arrived yesterday and today we are taking a long walk through the countryside with our raincoats and umbrellas. Because the weather is not conducive to flying I could slip away from our base this morning and join my wife.

Sonja: "You left Russia just in time before the cold set in. It has already snowed in some parts and our troops are freezing. Many of them don't have winter clothing and they are not used to fighting in the snow. That means that the front line got frozen solid with little prospects of thawing before Spring."

Me: "I believe the Russians will take advantage of the cold weather to harass our positions."

"My Admiral is still adamant that it was a gigantic fucking mistake to tackle Russia. Napoleon tried, but failed, the silly stupid sod. We were able to beat the Russians in 1917 but that was only because a ruddy revolution broke out that unseated the Czar and put a Commie regime in power – and they had to deal with the shit of a long internal struggle to gain control of the country. This time, it's different, damned different. Stalin has an iron grip on the country and the Russians can concentrate all their efforts on beating the Wehrmacht. They can retreat and retreat into the depths of their huge country. They have the space to do so – just as they did when Napoleon attacked them. Our supply lines will get stretched and stretched and may snap, leaving our troops in a hostile country without supplies. That is when the ruthless red Russian Bear will devour the helpless and gullible German Eagle.

"To crown everything, we are losing the bloody battle for Moscow. Our boys reached the outskirts of the city, but they were pushed back. Although the insane Ivans have lost thousands upon thousands of their troops, we were not able to advance into that cockhead city. Stalin even got women to dig deep trenches."

I stay silent because I don't have arguments to counter her insights. We both feel despondent, although most Germans think that we are winning the war. I silently wish that my dear wife's language would become somewhat more civilized.

Later, Sonja resumes her lecture: "And now that fucking fool of a Hitler has decided to declare war on America in an effort to help his friends in jolly Japan."

"But the Japanese will keep the Americans so busy that they won't have time to focus on us."

"That's what you bloody well think. The Yanks have been helping Churchill since the beginning of the war with supplies and war material. They did it initially in secret but now they can do it openly. America has the strongest economy in the world and they will be able to produce tanks, guns, aircraft and ships without any interference from the Luftwaffe or the Kriegsmarine. They are just too far away that we can hurt them, except when we sink some of their ships. But they have the strongest navy in the world. Of course, most of that navy will be used in the Pacific against the Japs, but there will be enough warships and airplanes to give the Kriegsmarine a rough time."

"You and your Admiral are certainly right. But, in the meantime, I'm going to continue bombing the Ivans and the Tommys – and later also the Yankees."

"While the Tommys are bombing Berlin. There was a huge raid with much damage last September and there will be more. But

– let's forget all that for the moment. Let's rather enjoy each other, while we still can."

Catania, Sunday, 28 December 1941

Any hope I had of spending more time with Sonja was dashed when our Gruppe suddenly had to move to Sicily in support of the Afrikakorps of General Erwin Rommel who was fighting British and South African forces in North Africa. We are now based at the airfield of Catania in southeastern Sicily, the most important air base on the island. After our refit at Memmingen we are at full strength again, although I feel rather pessimistic about the new pilots who joined us.. I am afraid they were rushed through their training in an effort to replace all our losses.

We have a new Gruppenkommandeur, Hauptmann Georg Graf von Platen, a nobleman with the title of a 'Graf' (count). He addresses the assembled pilots:

"Meine Herren, you have escaped from the cold of Russia to the heat of the Mediterranean. Our job is to put some more heat on the Allies in Malta and North Africa. Our Führer decided to help his friend, the Italian Duce, Benito Mussolini, when his troops were beaten by the Brits. Hitler wants us to capture the Suez Canal to prevent the Allies' shipping from using that shortcut to resupply the British Isles from Africa and the East.

"Our task will be to bomb the British bases on Malta, Allied shipping on the Mediterranean Sea and Allied troop concentrations and positions in North Africa, including airfields. I ask the more experienced pilots to help our newcomers to find their feet as soon as possible in combat situations.

"We are to start tomorrow morning with our first sorties."

Catania, Tuesday, 27 January 1942

The warning sirens start screaming and shouting and shrieking because a raid by the Royal Air Force is imminent. Administrative and technical personnel dive into bomb shelters. The gunners man their anti-aircraft guns and stack their bombs next to their guns while placing their steel helmets onto their heads. All pilots scramble to get their aircraft into the air to avoid being hit on the ground.

Before I am able to get my Junkers off the ground, she is being riddled by machine gun bullets from a RAF fighter. One of my engines stalls and one of the tires of my right front wheel is damaged while I try to get into the air. My Junkers crashes and I am lucky that no bullet made an entry and exit tunnel through any component of my anatomy.

The raid is over after fifteen minutes. We have been able to shoot down two fighters and two bombers, for the loss of one of our bombers (mine). Damage was done to some of the hangars, other buildings and other equipment.

I feel like crying. This is the second time that I have crashed my plane, albeit both times with the unwelcome help of the RAF. It will take some time before a replacement will be sent out. But, on the other hand, it may just as well happen that one of the other pilots cannot fly for some or other reason and that I will have to replace him. There will, therefore, probably be no rest for me. I am feeling dead tired, just as I felt before my hospitalization in Norway, last year.

Cagliari-Elmas, Tuesday, 10 February 1942

Yesterday, a new Junkers Ju 88A was assigned to me and my crew. I undertook a test flight with my crew and we are very satisfied with the plane. Our skull and bones emblems are already stenciled onto the cockpit.

And now, my Staffel is again on the prowl over the Mediterranean Sea. A convoy has been sighted to the southwest of Sardinia and we are to bomb those ships carrying supplies to Malta and the Allied forces in North Africa. We observe the convoy at the expected point and we perform our dive-bombing routine. I concentrate so much on keeping a big freighter in my visor that I forget about the fears I often feel after having experienced a dangerous situation.

Ludwig, my observer, helps me to loosen my bombs at the right moment and we sweep upwards, less our load of heavy bombs. Flak from an aircraft carrier and two destroyers, escorting the convoy, explode all around my brand-new plane and I decide that I don't like that.

Norbert, in the ventral machine gun position, reports: "I see two explosions on that freighter! Nice!"

A little later Norbert adds: "Two other ships have also been hit. But the plane of Oberfähnrich Schultz has crashed into the sea!"

Ludwig explains: "He has been hit by flak from that aircraft carrier. We have to get away as fast as possible because some fighters are being launched from that carrier!"

As we fly back, Ludwig calls my attention to our fuel level. It is dropping rapidly. Norbert exclaims: "We are leaking fuel from the tank in the starboard wing! The flack must have punctured it."

Me: "We won't make it back to Sicily. Give me a course to somewhere on Sardinia!"

Norbert, who has left his position at the ventral machine gun and takes the role of navigator again, says: "The nearest air field is at Cagliari-Elmas. It's the biggest airfield of the Regia Aeronautica Italiana, next to the prinicpal city on Sardinia, right on the south coast."

I set the right course and we fly into a bank of clouds on my way to Sardinia. Norbert guides me through the clouds and we break through the clouds with the city of Cagliari in front of us. The air base is clearly visible on the western edge of the city, next to a bay with a number of warships and other ships.

As I approach the runway with the last few drops of fuel left in my one intact tank, flack erupts from the defences around the airfield, as well from ships in the bay.

Ludwig: "Are those Ita's blinking blind or something? Or mad? They'll shoot us down! Can't they see we're their German friends?"

I concentrate so much on keeping the Junkers on the correct course to approach the runway that I am unable to respond. I feel very, very angry at these blooming stupid Italians who are trying to ruin my beautiful new plane.

We land safely. After I have parked the plane on a stretch of grass next to the runway and I have switched the engines off, my hands and my legs start to tremble – as so many times in the past. I have been given the biggest fright of my life. The sweat pours over my face. Ludwig passes me a flask with Schapps and I swallow half of the contents in one big gulp.

Just as we get onto solid soil, an Italian truck pulls up alongside my Junkers and an Italian officer gets out and greets me in broken German.

I yell at him: "Why the fuck did your gunners shoot at me while I was making an emergency landing!?"

The officer: "Nein, Herr Kapitän! They didn't shoot at you! They just shot down a Hurricane on your tail!"

Comiso, Sunday, 24 May 1942

Our Gruppe was stationed at Catania since the end of December. Today, towards the end of May, we arrived at the air base of Comiso, the other base on Sicily used by the Luftwaffe. It is situated on the southeastern corner of Sicily and about five kilometers north of the town of Comiso.

During the last five months my Staffel has been quite busy. We got some training in the launching of torpedos from our bombers. We attacked various convoys *en route* to Malta or Egypt and sank a total of ten freighters and one tanker. We helped Rommel in North Africa as his Afrikakorps was hammering the Allied forces in Lybia. We attacked targets on Malta. The bases of the RAF on this island are a constant threat to German convoys carrying supplies from Italy to Lybia for Rommel's boys.

During this time, my Staffel lost four of our twelve aircraft. Four new replacements awaited us as we arrived in Comiso. This is our home for the foreseeable future.

Messina, Monday, 1 June 1942

Yesterday, I got an order to report to the headquarters of II. Fliegerkorps at Messina, the capital of the Italian province of Sicily. After a long wait, I am admitted to the office of General der Flieger (Air Force General) Bruno Loerzer, commander of this corps.

The General addresses me: "Congratulations, Hauptmann Krause. Let me shake your hand."

The only words I can stammer, because something like this comes out of the blue, are: "Thank you, Herr General."

"Go and collect your new rank insignia at the Quartermaster's store. Here is the written confirmation of your promotion to Hauptmann. Your invaluable service and excellent leadership as a Staffelkapitän prompted me to bestow upon you the 'Kriegsorden des Deutschen Kreuzes' (The Order of the German Cross) in Gold. There is no time at this stage of the war to organize a formal parade and, therefore, I want to hang it onto your uniform this very moment."

I stand upright, like a lamp post, as I have been taught at the Police College, nine years ago, while the General pins a shiny trinket onto my uniform. I salute him afterwards. Silently, I think: I've heard some of the guys calling this thing Hitler's "Spiegelei" (Hitler's Fried Egg).

The General continues: "You are, from today, also the Gruppenkommandeur of the first Gruppe of your Geschwader. Your predecessor has been promoted and posted elsewhere. As you certainly know, the other groups of Kampfgeschwader 54 are still deployed on the Russian front."

After this brief ceremony, I drive back to Comiso. At this moment, we have 31 aircraft in the Gruppe, of which 29 are serviceable. We are to continue with our operations in aid of the Afrikakorps.

I wonder how I will be able to continue with my newly increased responsibilities. I need a heavy dose of Schnapps after almost every sortie to calm my runaway nerves, my shaking hands and my tremblng legs. The constant danger I have been subjected to is taking its toll on my health and my head.

It doesn't help that I've got a new golden fried egg pinned onto my jacket and given another pip on my shoulder. I wonder how I will be able to tell Sonja of this.

Tobruk, Friday, 19 June 1942

Being a captive of the Allies was never something I rellished. The possibility always existed, but during the almost three years since the start of the war I have been able to stay out of the clutches of the Brits, the Russians and their friends.

But this morning, my fortunes changed. I am sitting in a makeshift holding area for prisoners of war in Tobruk, a Lybian city held by an Allied force, composed mainly of a South African division under the command of Major General Hendrik Klopper.

I was handed over to a squad of Military Policemen who handled me and my crew members roughly. One of them shouted into my face in English: "You fucking murderer! Your airplane killed some of our mates. We will make you sweat! You will pay for your bloody crimes."

I ignored him and we were locked up in a stinking building, smelling of something very foul. There are already a few other prisoners – ten soldiers of the Afrikakorps and two Italians. The building seems to have been a former shop or an office, but it has since been used as a toilet and a waste dump.

Later, a Military Policeman brings us each a plate of "mieliepap" (maize porridge), a well-known South African staple. I grew up with it, but I must carry on with the pretence that I am only a stupid German who doesn't understand English – let alone, Afrikaans.

In German I tell the Military Police Sergeant, who is in charge of the group of German prisoners: "This looks like pig's fodder. I don't think you will be able to eat it yourself."

The Sergeant turns to his side-kick, a corporal: "Wat sê die bleddie Jerry? Verstaan jy hom?" (What does the bloody Gerry say? Do you inderstand him?)

The Corporal translates for the Sergeant. He turns to me and says in broken German: "I've had some German at school but I have forgotten most of it. That maize porridge is all we can give you at the moment. As you probably know, we are totally surrounded by Rommel's Afrikakorps and we cannot get any supplies through. We drink our coffee black and strong and and bitter. That's, by the way, how I prefer my women."

Me (in German): "You can make this fit for human consumption by adding some honey or syrup if you don't have any sugar. Perhaps some condensed milk will also improve it."

The Corporal translates my words to the Sergeant, who only laughs and walks away. I and my mates have no choice: we have to eat this cold maize porridge, just as it is, if we don't want to starve.

It is, indeed, good news that Tobruk is cut off from the outside world. It will be only a matter of time before Klopper surrenders to Rommel. My Gruppe must have helped to bring this situation about.

During the past three weeks, during which I was the Gruppenkommandeur, we constantly bombed the defences around Tobruk, together with various other units. We also helped to sink cargo ships carrying supplies and reinforcements to the besieged city. From one convoy of six ships, my Gruppe sank four.

It happened more than once that we used the German airfield at Benghazi in Tunisia as a temporary base to refuel and to rebomb before we flew another sortie over Tobruk or the Mediterranean Sea.

My beautiful Junkers was, unfortunately, disabled by flack when her port wing was completely ripped off. We plunged into the Gulf of Bomba, just outside the Tobruk harbour. The Good Lord in Heaven made it possible for all four crew members to leave the sinking wreck and swim ashore with our life jackets, where we surrendered to South African troops.

As we sit in this temporary POW den, I warn the other German prisoners not to talk about the war amongst ourselves.

Nobody knows whether somebody is listening and we don't want to give any secret information away in this manner. The other men accept me as their leader since I'm the most senior officer in this cage.

After dark, I hear the Sergeant, whose name is Sarel van Schalkwyk, say to his side-kick, Corporal Robbie van Rensburg: "Ons beter hierdie Jerries goed behandel. Net môre is ek en jy weer hulle prisoniers" (We had better treat these Gerries well. Just tomorrow, we will again be their prisoners). That gives me hope that Tobruk is about to fall into German and Italian hands and that we will be liberated.

The Corporal: "Moet ons dan nie vir hulle ook'n bietjie 'bully beef' gee nie? Droë mieliepap is darem seker nie baie lekker nie" (Shouldn't we give them some bully beef? Dry maize porridge cannot be very tasty).

The sergeant: "Fok, nee. Hulle verdien niks beters as varkkos nie" (Fuck, no. They don't deserve anything better than pig fodder).

Still later, the Sergeant sighs: "Ek voel lus om daai kapteintjie se 'smile' van sy gevreet af te klap. Hy lyk vir my veels te hans" (I feel like hitting the smile off the mug of that little captain. Hy seems far too arrogant to me).

The corporal: "Moet ek hom vashou terwyl jy hom dônner?" (Must I hold him while you're hitting him?).

The Sergeant: "Los maar. Môre sit ons self weer in die stront" (Leave it. Tomorrow, we sit in the shit ourselves).

The fighting around Tobruk continues throughout the night while we try to sleep on the dirty floor of our prison. We hear bombers of the Luftwaffe – probably also my Gruppe under the temprary command of one of my experienced Staffel captains – diving down and releasing their deadly payloads onto the defenders. The German artillery batteries bark and bang and their projectiles kick up huge amounts of dust and gravel, which also rain upon the roof of our building. Every time when that happens, I and my companions smile at each other.

Tobruk, Sunday, 21 June 1942

Yesterday was a very uncomfortable day. The sun baked and we sweated where we were held in this stuffy and stinking building. Our drinkng water was luke warm and we had to survive on some more maize porridge, despite the fact that the Sergeant of the Military Police thought that we had to be treated better.

During the day, it became clear that the combined German and Italian forces were breaching the defences around Tobruk as the gun shots became louder and louder as the battle shifted in our direction.

This morning, just after daybreak, an Oberleutnant of the German Army and a squad of soldiers enter the place where we are being held. The Sergeant and the Corporal of the Military Police are standing on one side, watching our liberation with sour expressions on their faces. Their pistols have been taken away.

I cannot help to step over to the two men: "Sersantjie, voel jy nog lus om hierdie kapteintjie se bek toe te klap?" (Sergeant, do you still want to hit this little captain's mouth shut?")

The eyes of both men are wide open from shock. Van Schalkwyk exclaims: "Wragtag! Magtag! Jy praat Afrikaans! Wat de hel soek jy hier tussen hierrie blerrie Germane?" (Two untranslateable oaths. You speak Afrikaans! What the hell are you doing between these bloody Germans?)

"Julle sal nooit raai nie" (You will never guess).

I smile: "Manne, dankie dat julle ons op mieliepap en swart koffie aan die lewe gehou het. Julle sal beter kos in 'n Duitse kamp kry" (Men, thank you for keeping us alive on maize porridge and black coffee. You will get beter food in a German camp).

"Ag, sal jy asseblief 'n goeie woordjie vir ons doen?" (Will you please put in a good word for us?)

"Omdat julle ons met groot gasvryheid behandel het? Omdat julle my wou slaan?" (Because you treated us with great hospitality? Because you wante to hit me?)

Both stay silent.

As we are being led away to a waiting truck, the Oberleutnant tells us: "The South African general is busy negotiating with the Germans about his surrender. That will certainly come any time now."

As we are driven out of Tobruk, we pass the vehicle in which Generaloberst Erwin Rommel is standing. I suspect he is waiting for Klopper to come to him to surrender. I cry out: "Stop!" The vehicle stops and I salute the Desert Fox, as he is known. He smiles and returns my salute.

I shout: "Thank you for freeing us!"

Rommel: "Bitte" (Please).

We drive off again. The Oberleutnant, whose name is Klaus Kramer, tells me: "We suspect that about 33 000 men will surrender."

Me: "A huge blow to the Allies."

Comiso, Saturday, 4 July 1942

At last I arrive at my old air base Camiso on Sicily to rejoin my Gruppe.

Since the four of us who were shot down in our Junkers Ju 88 were held in captivity for two days in Tobruk after escaping from an airplane wreck, we were taken to the sick bay at Benghazi, a trip of 400 kilometers to the west. Although we survived the plunge of our broken bomber into the water we still needed medical attention for all the scratches and bruises we had suffered.

After two nights in the sick bay we were discharged and we sought a way to get back to Sicily. We hoped to get lifts in some bombers from Sicily that landed at Benghazi to refuel and get new loads of bombs. Since the remaining British forces were on the run, back towards Egypt, with Rommel's "Panzerarmee Afrika" (Armored Army, Africa) in hot persuit, the focus shifted away from Benghazi and we had to wait more than a week before we could leave African soil.

Directly after I have landed at Camiso I report back to the base commander, Oberst Eugen Kloppenberg. He is very surprised to see me.

"Krause! How did you manage to escape from the grave? You and your crew were reported KIA when your plane was shot down over Tobruk. I can't believe what I'm seeing! Or is it your ghost that comes to haunt me?"

"But here I am, a man of flesh and blood, all in one piece! I never saw the inside of a grave. Me and my crew only sustained a few scratches and bruises. We were captured by the South Africans, but Rommel's boys liberated us two days later when Tobruk was taken."

"Because you were deemed to be dead a new Gruppenkommandeur was apponted in your place. We can't chase him away to give you your old job back. I will have to inform OKL that you are alive and well and that you ready to fly again."

"Did you inform my wife of my death?"

"Of course. That's standard practice. Your adjutant even wrote her a letter of condolence, assuring her that you died a heroic death. I signed it."

"Then I ask your permission to send her a telegramme or something to tell her that the letter she is due to receive contains a false alarm and that I survived the crash."

"I can even organize a telephone call."

"That will be splendid, Herr Oberst."

"And in the meantime, you may lodge in the officers' quarters. You will have to be kitted out anew because we have sent all your effects to your wife, except for your old flying overalls. We argued that she will have no use for that."

"Did you send her all my medals and decorations?"

"Yes. But we can get replacments for you."

"And can you cancel my death certificate, as well as those of my crew members?"

"You will have to write to OKL yourself to have that done. It may, though be a tricky business. For instance, if they started to pay your pension to your grieving widow, that money will have to be recovered. If your name as a fallen hero has been published in a newspaper, all copies of that newspapaer will have to be recalled and re-issued without your name."

"Will the idiotic imbeciles at OKL pay any attention to a letter from a dead person?"

"Perhaps you should include a medical certificate , signed by an Arzt, stating that he has examined you and found that your heart is still beating, that you are awake and that you are not yet ready to be buried. If necessary, I can add a note to confirm that you appeared in my office and that I am convinced that it wasn't your ghost – although I'm not an expert on supernatural matters."

Comiso, Saturday, 11 July 1942

Oberst Kloppenberg sends an Unteroffixier to call me. I am lying on my bed, waiting for a message from OKL about my future deployment. The big shots in the OKL seem to have forgotten about me. It may also be that they don't know how to cancel my death certificate, which has been forwarded to my parents-in-law. I enjoy the company of my old comrades of my Gruppe, but I understand that I can't get my old position back. Since I am not on the strength of any unit at the moment I couldn't take part in any operational flights. I am, therefore, rather bored and glad to be summoned to the Oberst's office.

Upon entering the office, I salute smartly. The Oberst does the same.

Kloppenberg: "Krause, here is a lady from the Abwehr who wants to talk to you. A certain Fräulein Schellenberg. She says that she holds a rank in the Abwehr that is equivalent to that of a Major. I don't want any trouble with the spooks of the Abwehr and, therefore, I immediately sent for you. She was given the last office down the passage. I suppose she wants to talk to you about your experiences as a prisoner of war."

"I'll answer all the questions she may have. I'm also wary of the Abwehr."

As I enter the last office down the passage, I salute again smartly and announce: "Hauptmann Karl Krause reporting, Ma'am. How can I be of service?"

"Hauptmann, lock that door behind you."

I do so.

"And then you are to give your dear wife the best kiss that you have ever given in your life."

After activities of about half-an-hour that left us breathless, I manage to ask: "And what are you doing here?"

"I wanted to be screwed. But only by my first husband."

I am totally taken aback by this straight answer from my civilized wife, but I continue nevertheless: "Is there a second one?"

"No, you fool. And I hope that there will never be one."

"How did you manage to land here?"

"As a passenger in an airplane. How else?"

"And how did you manage that?"

"By pulling some strings."

"What type of strings?"

"Multi-coloured ones. My Admiral gave me some leave of absense. I am entitled to a short holiday, being a grieving widow, and he organized things so that I could get a seat on a Tante Ju from Berlin to this snotty spot. Officially, I'm here to find out how the Italian civilians experience the war. And now we have to get down to serious business. Your Oberst told me that you spent two days as a prisoner of war in Tobruk. Tell me more about that."

Comiso, Sunday, 12 July 1942

After I had spent the night at the Pensione in town where Sonja is staying and enjoyed a late breakfast, we went for a stroll through the streets and alleys of Comiso. It is an unspoilt old town with many buildings from the baroque period, including a beautiful cathedral.

Sonja: "So, you briefly met Erwin Rommel? You surely know that the Führer promoted him to Generalfeldmarschall a day later?"

Me: "Yes."

"Well, Rommel and his armored army, including his Afrikakorps, are inside Egypt now. They got stuck at a pisspot place called El Alamein because their supplies dried up. The Allies are sinking German and Italian ships in the Mediterranean at an alarming rate. The Royal Navy has a strong fleet with bases at Gibraltar, Malta and Alexandria. Also at Port Said. And we don't have the means to neutralize them. The Royal Air Force has a strategic base on Malta, which you Luftwaffe boys couldn't knock out. Their airplanes also send German and Italian supply ships to watery graves. The result is that Rommel is stuck without fuel, food, bullets, bombs, reinforcements and spare parts for his airplanes and tanks and trucks. It is only a matter of time before he is driven out of Egypt."

"Is it so bad?"

"Yes. And, in the end, we will have to write off the whole fucking Afrikakorps. They will be driven back to Tunisia and when the Yankees come messing in it will be tickets for our boys. We don't have the means to evacuate the lot of them and they will end up in a crammy camp for POW's. And to make matters worse, the Italians are not wholeheartedly in the war. They are sick and tired of it and they want to chicken out if they can."

"I thought the Duce and the Führer were big palls."

"They are, yes. Mussolini dreamt of restoring the old Roman Empire by establishing colonies all over Africa and the Balkans, but the fucking fool doesn't have the means to do it. His generals lack balls in their pants and the common soldiers prefer wine and whoring above war. Rommel is stuck with a whole bloody bunch of them in Africa."

"I have been watching the Italians here on Sicily and I came to the conclusion that they are wonderful artists. They can build beautiful buildings, can compose wonderful operas and can make very drinkable wine. Every glass full of wine is a work of art. But they would also have shamed their forefathers, the fearless Roman legionaries."

"Quite so."

"Now tell me more about yourself. What have you been doing since we last saw each other?"

"Sending four poor sods to their deaths. On Operation Pastorius."

"Yes?"

"Yes. Poor guys. I had to help with the training of these four guys by teaching them better American English. Their job is to commit sabotage in New York or somewhere else in America. I delivered them to the Kriegsmarine base at Brest in France where they were taken aboard on U-202. The captain of the submarine, Kapitänleutnant Stefan Strauss, wanted to know what their job was. All I could tell him was that they have to be smuggled into New York.

"By the way: this Strauss is another South African who managed to slip into the Wehrmacht and become an officer."

"How do you know that?"

"Because he swore in Afrikaans and I could understand that. And then we compared notes."

"I know the chap. He rescued me and a dumb new pilot when we lost a plane in the North Sea in July 1939."

"Yes, I remember that you told us about the incident."

"Do you think these saboteurs will achieve anything?"

"Don't know. Probably not. They were supplied with counterfeit dollars and if they are caught with that, it will be good-buy, farewell, cheers, auf Wiedersehen, arrividerci. Since they are running around in civvie clothes they will be deemed to be spies and they can even get shot."

"Do you worry about them?"

"I am sick and tired of my job. I worry the whole time. I can only forget the whole silly stupid sorry affair while you are making love to me. This war is going nowhere. Our boys can't progress any further into ruddy Russia and at some point the Russians have already taken back some parts that we have conquored. And one of these days the Yanks will come and squeeze our balls."

"This war is also giving me the shakes." Silently, I wonder how the Yanks will ever be able to perform this squeezing act on Sonja. I haven't been able to discover any testicles on her anatomy.

"It's called shell-shock."

12 July 1942

"Let's hope that our love affair won't dissipate due to this shell-schock."

Comiso, Monday, 13 July 1942

Sonja: "Do you have any idea where the Luftwaffe may deploy you when they finally remember that you exist?"

Me: "Heaven knows. I may be sent to Greece, or I may stay here in Italy. Or even France or Norway. But the chances are that I will end up in Russia again."

"I think it will be in Russia. That's the focus point of the whole war at the moment. We have more men there than in all other theatres of the war combined."

"But why are we fighting in Russia? Why did we have to invade that country? We had, after all, a non-aggression pact with them."

"If we didn't attack first, they would have attacked us. And it's better to fight on your enemy's territory than on your own, due to all the damage that can be done."

"How do you know that the Russians wanted to attack us?"

"My boss, Canaris, knows all these things. It's his job. That totally treacherous Stalin already wanted to attack us long ago because the Nazis are violently anti-communistic. Stalin wanted to export the Russian revolution to Germany, the home country of Karl Marx, the damned guy who thought communism out in the first place. Fortunately, Canaris played a nasty jolly trick on him by convincing him that a lot of his generals were plotting against him and he had the lot of them shot quite dead – as I've already explained to you. That left the Russian Army and Air Force without leaders, otherwise we would have been fighting them in the streets of Berlin and Hamburg."

"So, Stalin was planning to break the non-aggression pact?"

"That's fucking right. That's why we had to act fast to prevent that. And therefore, we had to take Poland first, in order to get into a position to attack the Ruskies from there. Poland is between us and Russia and, therefre, Poland had to be occupied to get into an attaching position. That's apart from the fact that Hitler wanted more space for German settlers in the east. And that's why Britain and France picked a fight with us.

"The war against blinkin' Britain and fucking France was something different. They declared war on us and we had to defend our borders. But we had no choice but to attack the shits in Russia before they overwhelmed us."

"That's all very intricate and overwhelming. When I was flying with my Staffel over London, I was extremely angry at the Brits for shooting down my friends and colleagues. We only bombed London because they started bombing Berlin, Bremen and other cities."

"And the Brits shot back at your stupid Staffel because you were dropping blooming bombs on them. They had to defend themselves. Just as we have to defend bloody Berlin, Bremen and Bochum."

"This war is crazy, crazy. And it made me crazy as well. I have diagnosed myself with shell shock in a serious degree, an extreme degree. I got the jitters every time I escaped from a dangerous situation. The only thing that keeps me relatively sane is the fact that I have you in my life."

"And the fact that you have a healthy sex life!"

"Which few of my colleagues have, unless they make use of these stinking Italian bordellos."

Tazinskaja, Wednesday, 19 August 1942

By joining the Luftwaffe, I have been able to see much of Europe and the world. I was stationed at various bases in Germany, flew over the Northe Sea and the British Isles, slept in Denmark, Norway, France, Sicily, North Africa, Poland and the Ukraine. And now I step down at Tazinskaja, a primitive airfield in Russia, about 250 kilometers south west from Stalingrad where a battle of gigantic proportions is being fought. This Luftwaffe base is nothing more than a landing strip and a few tents.

Somebody at the OKL suddenly remembered to do something about my lot. At last. I was given command of the second Gruppe of Kampfgeschwader 51 and their emblem is the Edelweiss. I have seen some of their subunits at various places where I previously did duty with KG 26 and KG 54.

It took me more than a week to reach this spot. I flew from Comiso to Rome, to Genoa, to Innsbruck, to Munich, to Berlin, to Warsaw, to Kiev and finally to Tazinskaja. In Berlin I slept over at the Schellenberg home, of course.

In Berlin, Sonja told me that Canaris has lost all confidence in Hitler and his cronies. Hitler is paranoid, psychotic, demented, delusional and a drug addict. Göring is also a drug addict, as well as a glutton, a drunkard and a thief of art treasures. Himmler, the chief of the SS, is an inept scheming sadist. Keitel and Jodl, the two big shots at the OKW (Oberkommando der Wehrmacht – High Command of the Wehrmacht) have the intelligence of earth worms and they are deadly afraid of Hitler with the result that they cringe like worms in his presence.

Canaris knows that he is playing a dangerous game by double-crossing Hitler at times, but he is also thinking about a better Germany after the war – if that is possible.

Sonja: "Speaking of drug addicts: Canaris tells me that Hitler has made drug addicts out of the whole German population. He feeds us methamphetamine that is hidden in our chocolates and coffee in an effort to lift our spirits and to boost morale."

"That sounds dangerous."

"It fucking well is. I have stopped drinking coffee and eating chocolates and I have persuaded my parents and Anja to do the same."

Sonja also told me: "Cousin Walter tried again to recruit me for his service."

"What did you tell him?"

"Thank you, but no thank you. It won't work for family to work together in such a secret set-up. He won't always like what I do and that may lead to unpleasantness and even fights."

"Good for you."

"I also suspect that he wants to lure me into his bed. He has gone through two unhappy marriages and both ended in divorce. He is looking for another woman in his life to screw. I'm not playing along."

I report to the Geschwaderkommodore, Major Wilhelm von Friedeburg, when I arrive at Tazinskaja. He informs me that he only arrived yesterday and that he still has to meet most of the leaders in the Edelweiss Geschwader. We are to help Army Group South and especially the Sixth German Army in and around Stalingrad, a city with strategic value.

Tazinskaja, Saturday, 24 October 1942

The past two months flew by at breakneck speed. There was little time to rest in our primitive tents. We flew daily sorties – whether in the rain, sunshine, dust storms, hail or heat waves. Army Group South got overstretched in its efforts to drive deeper into the Caucasus and capture the Baku oil fields – which failed and was officially abandoned today. That meant that we had to bomb the installations at Baku to deny them to the Russians. Limited success was achieved.

My Gruppe also had to interfere at Stalingrad. The German Sixth Army managed to occupy most of the city but the Volga proved to be an insurmountable barrier to the east. During the night, Soviet fighters slipped over the river to harass our troops. We bombed and bombed Russian positions, but they kept on coming. There are millions of them.

We lost quite a number of planes and my Gruppe is down to twenty-two bombers of which only sixteen are serviceable.

Tazinskaja, Tuesday, 17 November 1942

It is with a huge sigh of relief that I fall down upon my cot in the tent I share with two other officers. Today was horrible. Our Geschwader has been flying non-stop and we lost another aircraft. Our numbers are dwindling, despite the reinforcements occasionally sent to us.

Our birds had to drop explosive eggs on Russian positions on the outskirts of Stalingrad. The Russians have been able to cross the Volga in substantial numbers and they are trying to encircle our boys inside Stalingrad. Transport planes from various airfields drop supplies to the beleaguered footsloggers inside the city.

In addition, we had to help the German Seventeenth Army to clear out of the Taman Peninsula, between the Black Sea and the Caspian Sea. We sank a Russian gunship that was shelling our troops while they were crossing the strait between the Taman Peninsula and the Crimea Peninsula with the Russian hordes in hot pursuit.

I tell one of my tent mates, Hauptmann Rudolf Rahmkatz, commander of a flack battery: "The Russians are getting stronger and stronger by the day. And we don't have the reserves to replace our losses."

Rudolf: "Wait and see. The Führer has promised us some wonderful new weapons. Just wait. One of these days you will be able to fly the most wonderful airplanes. I have heard rumors of huge rockets for the Luftwaffe with which we can bomb New York."

"When will that ever happen?"

I stay silent about what I've heard from Sonja when I last saw her. She mentioned that a team of our scientists was working on a so-called atom bomb. With that, we can wipe a city such as London or Manchester in one blow from the face of the earth. The progress is, though, slow. And worst of all, it seems that the Americans who are also working on a similar weapon, are ahead of us. Sonja was pessimistic about our chances of manufacturing such a bomb in time. She threatened me with execution or castration if I would ever talk about this because the wrong people may hear about it.

Tazinskaja, Sunday, 22 November, 1942

Major Wilhelm von Friedeburg: "Meine Herren, our Geschwader has a new role. We must supply the Sixth Army at Stalingrad from the air. They have been encircled completely by die Red Army. The Führer forbade them to retreat. He also forbade Generalfeldmar-schall von Manstein to help them to break out and they must defend the city at all costs. It is, therefore, our task to fly in ammo, fuel and food so that the poor ground troops can carry on with their defense. There are still four airfields in German hands and we are to land at Pitomnik."

An hour later, my Gruppe takes to the air. We carry tinned food and medicines instead of bombs. En route to Pitomnik we have to contend with Russian flack but we reach our destination without mishap. There are enough helpers to unload our cargoes and we get a number of wounded men to fly out so that they can get better treatment at a Lazarett. I manage to take off with my overloaded Junkers Ju 88, carrying fourteen wounded men.

As we fly back, we are suddenly attacked by Russian fighters. They manage to shoot a few holes through my fuselage, without hurting my engines or other vital parts or instruments. However, two of the wounded soldiers are killed by their machine gun bullets.

I announce that I plan to land at the nearest air strip so as to get my passengers as speedily as possible to medical help. They refuse vehemently and urge me to fly straight to our base at Tazinskaja. They want to get away from the hell of Stalingrad as far as possible.

Tazinskaja and Stalingrad, Monday, 23 November, 1942

We return to Stalingrad today with boxes of tinned food, medicine and ammunition. While eager soldiers download the much-needed supplies, I observe two horrific accidents.

The first accident happens when an overloaded Focke-Wulf FW 200 Condor bomber crashes. This aircraft, the only four-engine bomber in the Luftwaffe's inventory, struggles to take to the air with a heavy load of wounded soldiers. In an effort to gain height as rapidly as possible, the pilot lifts the nose of his aircraft at a steep angle. Suddenly, the aircraft tilts into a vertical position and can't fly any higher. Of course, the Condor falls back to earth, exploding upon impact.

I and my startled crew members speculate that the steep ascent of the bomber caused the heavy load of wounded soldiers to slide down to the back of the plane, upsetting the balance of the aircraft and causing her nose to point straight up in the air.

A few minutes later, an overloaded Tante Ju tries to take off. The runway is, however, too short and she slams with full force into the barrier indicating the end of the runway. She also explodes.

Just before we are ready to take off with a second load of wounded soldiers later in the day, I see one of my Gruppe's planes getting safely off the earth, but she is hit by Russian anti-aircraft fire before she gets very far. Her tail is blown off and she crashes onto some Russian positions, killing all aboard, as well as a number of Russians.

Although I want to take away as many wounded men as possible, I make sure that my Ju-88 isn't overloaded. We are fortunate to reach Tazinskaja safely. One of the wounded soldiers who could still walk, a Hauptfeldwebel, comes to thank me personally for helping him to reach safety. He tells me that he was one of the lucky ones to gain a spot on an airplane.

He had to get past the so-called "Kettenhunde" (chain dogs), the Military Police or Feldgendarmerie whose members are wearing bronze gorgets, hanging from chains around their necks, to distinguish them from other soldiers. They screened the rows of wounded men to weed out malingerers. They also allowed only those men onto the rescue planes when they had, according to them, a chance of survival. Those cases they deemed to be too seriously wounded were left to die in Stalingrad, without a chance to receive adequate medical help.

He adds: "But, Herr Kapitän, was it necessary to fly so high? You very nearly had a heap of frozen corpses in your plane, because it's jolly cold up there in the sky."

Me: "If I flew lower the Russians ground fire would have killed all of us."

When I finally lie down on my cot at Tazinskaja after dark, those horrible scenes haunt me and no amount of Schnapps can put me to sleep. I find it impossible to switch my thoughts off and the horrible accidents of the day continue to be replayed in my mind.

Tomorrow will certainly be a repetition of today.

Tazinskaja, Sunday, 29 November, 1942

After a horrible week, during which my Gruppe had to fly two or even three sorties per day to Stalingrad, weather permitting, we suddenly get another task. We must mine the Volga to prevent supplies from reaching the Russians by boat.

This is another extremely hazardous task. We fly low over the river to make sure that we drop the mines correctly into the water and not onto the adjoining dry land. The mines glide down to the water with parachutes, which are released as soon as the mines hit the water. We continue flying low over the water so that any Russian eyes cannot observe exactly where the mines have been laid.

As we fly low over the river, we are shot at by the infantry on the shores with machine guns and rifles. We lose one bomber.

Tazinskaja, Thursday, 3 December 1942

Just as we are preparing the take to the skies shortly after daybreak, about twenty Russian bombers with red stars on their wings and fuselages attack us. Our anti-aircraft batteries were caught unawares but they react swiftly. Two aircraft are shot down and the rest fly away.

We inspect the damage. Only a few unoccupied tents were blown out of existence, but all our planes and anti-aircraft artillery positions survived unscathed.

Oberst Heinrich Conrady, our new Geschwaderkommodore who joined us two days ago with six new planes and their crews, explains to me: "Those are actually American planes. The A-20 Douglas Havoc Boston light bombers. Franklin Roosevelt donated them to Josef Stalin."

Me: "I saw some of them over North Africa. The Royal Air Force also got some of them."

We drive out to inspect the two Russian wrecks where they fell. They have more machine guns than our Junkers bombers.

Rostov, Tuesday, 8 December 1942

We were being pulled back yesterday because the Russians have started a winter offensive and our troops are losing ground. Our new base is an old Soviet base, Rostov, which was captured last July by our troops. The base is about seven kilometers north west from the centre of this industrial city.

We are told that we will be better off here at Rostov. At our previous bases, we were very far from the nearest railway tracks and supplies and fuel had to be transported by road. Here, at Rostov, we have rail transport available and we will have fewer logistical problems.

Our Geschwader is not yet quite settled, but we have to endure another attack at night by Russian light bombers – probably the same planes that paid us a flying visit last week. This time, they aim much more accurately and they destroy ten planes from various units at this base.

Oberst Conrady: "This cannot go on. We will have to do something about those Ivans and their base."

Rostov, Friday, 8 January 1943

It is clear that these Commie Russians don't have any respect for the Lord's Day. They must all be atheists. A bunch of Russian bombers attacked us again on the first Sunday after Christmas. A total of eleven aircraft of KG 51 were destroyed.

Oberst Conrady again told me: "This has to stop. We have to do something."

And, today we do something. We attack Manychskaya, the base of those Russian bombers. Since the world is covered by snow, we have painted our bombers white to make them invisible against the white fields.

To our dismay, not a single bomber is to be seen at Manychskaya. They must be somewhere else, busy bombing our forces elsewhere. Three of our aircraft crash violently as they are hit by ground fire – including the plane of Oberst Heinrich Conrady.

As we return to Rostov, the Gruppenkommandeur of III./KG 51, Major Egbert von Frankenberg und Proschlitz, assumes temporary command, being the most senior officer left.

8 January 1943

Sleep eludes me and I take a walk outside, despite thick snow covering the fields. I cannot but agree with Sonja's Admiral's pessimism about the outcome of the war. How are we going to prevent these barbarians from Siberia from overrunning our cities and towns in due course? It is certain that they will want to take revenge for all the havoc and destruction and death that we have caused in their country.

I tell myself again that I really must be suffering from something like shell shock. Every time I have to get into my bomber my stomach makes at least six turns inside me. The thoughts running through my mind are as follows every time: Will I make it? Or will I just be another casualty, part of the statistics? Will Sonja find a second husband after I've bought it? Only my stiff self-discipline, instilled by the Police College and the Luftwaffe, keeps me going. I also decide that I can't allow Sonja to become a widow and perhaps another man's wife and for that, I just have to stay alive.

Rostov, Friday, 22 January 1943

The Red Army has taken the last two airfields in German hands at Stalingrad, Pitomnik and Gumrak. The members of our Luftwaffe units still stationed there were taken prisoner since they were forbidden to retreat. It is, therefore, impossible to land there with supplies and evacuate wounded soldiers. All we can do is to drop supplies from the air after having run the gamut of flack and fighters.

The pilots of my Gruppe have flown a few hundred sorties between them in aid of the doomed Sixth Army at Stalingrad. It is only a matter of time now before these poor soldiers will become prisoners of war – those who don't die in the meantime.

Apart from dropping supplies, we also bomb Russian positions as often as possible. We think we are just as tired and burnt-out as the hopeless soldiers of the Sixth Army.

Rostov, Tuesday, 2 February 1943

We get the news that the shivering, starved, scared, sick and scorched members of the Sixth Army in Stalingrad gave up the fight after months of disaster, discomfort, pain, privation and peril. Their commander, Generaloberst Friedrich Paulus, surrendered to the Russian Marshall Voronov after fighting the Russians for six months at this spot.

Hitler forbade him to surrender because it is unthinkable that German soldiers could give up conquored territory. In order to improve the morale of the depleted and defeated Army, Hitler promoted Paulus to Generalfeldmarschall the previous day and showered promotions onto a number of other officers – including a few dead ones. He encouraged the poor soldiers in Stalingrad to hold out with an impassioned speech over the radio and we were forced to listen to it. I could see the contempt on the faces of many men as they were listening to the voice of their Führer.

Ou efforts were, therefore, in vain to help those 270 000 soldiers trapped inside Stalingrad and who were taken captive. Only the day before yesterday, the Edelweiss Geschwader achieved a significant victory by completely destroying the Soviet 51st Army's Headquarters, near Salsk, killing scores of people. That was, however, too late to help our comrades in their dark and hopeless situation.

We console ourselves with the thought that it is not only the Wehrmacht that has suffered a grievous loss. The Russians also paid a high price for their victory at Stalingrad.

Saporoshje, Friday, 5 February 1943

Kampfgeschwader 51 has to retreat again, this time to Saporoshje, about 450 kilometers southeast from Kiev in the Ukraine. We had to evacuate Rostov before the Russian Army overruns us there. As we fly away, we see that somebody is blowing up all the buildings we have been using.

Saporoshje is a fairly large industrial city on the Dnieper and this former airfield of the Soviet Air Force houses quite an assortment of Luftwaffe units – flying units, anti-aircraft units and service units. The headquarters of Luftflotte 4 under the command of my previous commander of Kampfgeschwader 257 at Lüneburg before the war, Generalfeldmarschall Wolfram Freiherr von Richthofen, is situated here.

It is our task to provide the Russians with as many blows and bumps and bangs as we possibly can as they attack our boys still trying to defend Rostov.

Saporoshje, Wednesday, 17 February 1943

Security at Saporoshje is suddenly upgraded. All the ground personnel walk around with side-arms and the gunners sit ready at their 88 millimetre and 20 millimetre anti-aircraft guns around the perimeter of the base. All the fighters at the base, Focke-Wulf Fw 190's, Messerschitt Me 109's and Messerschitt Me 110's, patrol the air space around us in shifts. Our bombers are grounded and dispersed as widely as possible so as not to form a single target if they were bunched together.

Those of us who are not on active duty, such as the bomber crews, are ordered to form a guard of honor. While I proceed to the parade ground with my dress uniform and steel helmet, I happen to bump into von Richthofen. I salute and he does the same.

"Aaah, Krause, are you still with us? Congratulations with your rank as Hauptmann and your decorations."

"Thank you, Herr Generalfeldmarchall."

"Excuse me, but I must run."

I feel honored that he remembers me.

While the lot of us are standing at parade a Tante Ju touches down. Another Generalfeldmarschall exits. Major Harald Hartmann, next to me, murmers: "That's Erich von Manstein, commander of Army Group Don."

We present arms as the Field Marshall comes our way.

A few minutes later, another Tante Ju lands. A SS-officer gets out.

Hartmann: "That's Paul Hausser. Everybody calls him Papa Hausser. Obergruppenführer and General der Waffen-SS. He's the boss of the Second SS Armored corps."

We also present arms for this guy.

Me: "Which big shot will we see next?"

Hartmann: "Don't know Wait and see."

We hear a big aircraft coming nearer and we see a Focke-Wulf Fw 200 Condor land. The two Tante Ju's have been towed away so that the big aircraft can stop right in front of the guard of honor. The door opens and – the Führer himself appears. As he steps down, he is greeted by the assembled Field Marshalls and Generals with von Manstein as the most senior officer greeting him first. Von Richthofen stands next to him. The others salute Hitler with the Nazi salute.

Hartmann: "Doktor Goebbels, our propaganda minister, makes us believe that this chap is the 'Größte Feldherr aller Zeiten' (greatest commander of all times). We have abbreviated it to 'Gröfaz' when we refer to him."

I regard it safer to stay silent, although I know what Canaris thinks of Hitler.

Saporoshje, Monday, 22 February 1943

Hitler stayed three days, till yesterday morning. Security stayed tight, although KG 51 again started to fly out to harass the Russian Army. What Hitler discussed with the Field Marshalls and Generals was, of course, never disclosed to us, the common fighting folks.

After Hitler's departure, things returned to normal – as normal as is possible during war time. However, the Russians thought it best to disturb our sleep late this evening. Perhaps they thought that Hitler was still around and a number of Tupolev Tu-2 bombers tried to conflict some damage on us. Our gunners were, fortunately, still nervous after Hitler's visit and they reacted swiftly, making it impossible for the Russian pilots to achieve anything. The gunners were aided by a bright moon that made the bombers quite visible, apart from our searchlights.

Saporoshje, Tuesday, 23 February 1943

The commander of Luftflotte 4, Generalfeldmarschall von Richthofen, calls a conference of all Geschwaderkommodore, Gruppenkommandeure and other section chiefs under his command. He looks concerned and worried.

"Männer, the Führer isn't satisfied with our performance. The Luftwaffe has been waging an unacceptable gentleman's war in these parts. We must follow the example of the Russians, Waffen-SS, the Allgemene (General) SS and the Army by conducting a scorched-earth approach. Everything belonging to the Russian barbarians must be destroyed. These 'Untermenschen' – according to him – don't deserve anything. Therefore, we are not to feel sorry for them.

"Should it happen that we have to retreat before the onslaughts of these hordes from the plains of Siberia we must destroy everything we leave behind – buildings, equipment, infrastructure, everything. If civilians lose their lives, so be it."

Bagerowo, Friday, 2 April 1943

We operated from Saporoshje more or less two months. The place, however, became overcrowded and we were moved, yet again, to a smaller air field: Bagerowo, next to a village with the same name in the eastern Crimea, fourteen kilometers west from the town of Kerch. This town gives its name to the Kerch Strait that connects the Black Sea with the Caspian Sea.

Bagerovo is no less crowded than Saporoshje. We, together with other units, are called upon to attack targets along the Black Sea coast and further afield.

I haven't heard anything from Sonja since my brief visit to Berlin and I wonder whether she and her family are still alive. We hear rumors of almost daily bombing raids on Berlin by the Allies. This uncertainty intensifies my misery.

Bagerowo, Monday, 5 April 1943

We steal an idea from another Kampfgeschwader. We weld two 400-liter kerosene drums together and fill them with rags, oil and kerosene. On the one end we fit fins and at the front end we attach a mine that will explode upon impact with the water. Two of these crude bombs are attached under my plane and I fly a solo mission against the harbor of the Black Sea port of Sochi, about 400 kilometers from our base, where I drop my two improvised bombs.

The idea is that the exploding mine will rupture the two drums, releasing the highly inflammable mixture upon the water. As I fly back, I can see flames on the water of the harbor, engulfing the ships moored and at anchor there.

Illesheim, Sunday, 9 May 1943

The Edelweiss Kampfgeschwader is back on German soil at the Fliegerhorst Illesheim, 48 kilometers west from Neuremberg in Bavaria. Illesheim is a small village and the air base is separated from the village by a railway line.

The five weeks we spent at Bagerowo were rather uneventful, except for the daily sorties we undertook against Russian targets on the eastern coast of the Black Sea. We left our Junkers Ju 88's at Bagerowo and all the pilots and navigators were taken by transport planes to our new home where we are met by our new Geschwaderkommodore, Major Hannes Heise. The rest of our air crews were left behind and transferred to other units.

Here at Illesheim, we are to refit and convert to the newest fighter-bomber of the Luftwaffe: the Messerschmitt Me 410 "Hornisse" (Hornet). We receive eighty-eight planes for about sixty crews, each consisting of a pilot and a navigator/rear gunner. Twenty-eight new crews, fresh from training schools, join us. I am given command of Gruppe I with a headquarters flight and three squadrons, numbers 1, 2 and 3.

We've heard of fighter-bombers that the Allies use, but these are the first dedicated fighter-bombers of the Luftwaffe. It happened that some Junkers Ju 88's were converted to night fighters, but that was never a great success because they are not fast enough.

My Gruppe with thirty-two planes and thirty-two crews, of which six are novices, like this plane. She is extremely maneuverable, can gain height easily and is much more sophisticated than the Ju 88. The best innovation is a light-weight radar set with which the pilot can detect enemy bombers at a great distance.

The pilot has two forward-firing 20-millimetre canons and two forward-firing machine guns.

The second crew member handles two machine guns from the inside, one on each side of the fuselage. The barrels of these guns can turn in various directions to shoot at enemy planes at any angle.

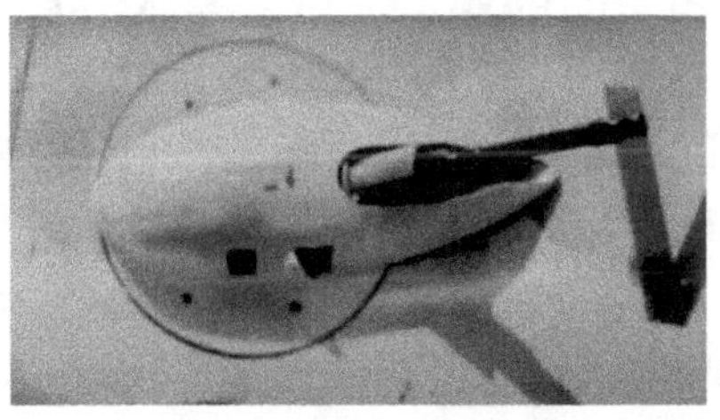

I find my new plane somewhat strange, yet beautiful. The most prominent aspect is that her blunt nose is shorter than her two engines.

Illesheim, Saturday, 22 May 1943

Something is tickling my nose and I sneeze. When I open my eyes I look into the blue eyes of Sonja, lying next to me in a double bed. She is using her long hair to tickle my nose. I take her into my arms and we lie a long time just like that, savoring every moment in each other's presence. This beautiful Spring morning is too precious to be spoilt by talking.

Sonja arrived last night by train from Berlin. Admiral Canaris gave her the weekend off. I did the same for my men in I./KG 51. We all need the rest. As soon as we got settled in Illesheim, I went to the post office across the road from the air base and phoned Sonja. I just gave her the number of that phone and rang off again. A few minutes later she phoned back from a safe phone and I could tell her exactly where I was to be found.

She took the train from Berlin to Nuremburg where she changed onto the local line serving Bad Windesberg and the neighboring Illesheim. I met her at the station next to the air base and we booked into the local hotel in Bahnhofstraße (Railway Street).

After a lazy breakfast, we go for a long walk through the countryside. I would have preferred my racing bike, but the second best is a march through the fields and along a small river.

Sonja: "It happened as I told you when I visited you in Sicily."

"What?"

"The last German and Italian units in North Africa surrendered to the bloody British and the American arseholes a week ago. That means that the Allies have to feed and house more than a hundred thousand hungry and tired prisoners of war."

"I hope they blew up all their equipment and ammo before they surrendered."

"They fucking well did."

We continue walking in silence.

Sonja declares later: "That fucking fool of a Führer is the reason why the Sixth Army suffered such a dramatic defeat at Stalingrad."

Me: "This's what everybody here also thinks."

"Hitler just wouldn't believe that the position of our men In Stalingrad was so bad – even after all the numbers and statistics were given to him. He refused to believe that Russian barbarians were able to defeat German soldiers. Von Manstein begged him more than once to allow Von Paulus to retreat and abandon Stalingrad before his men were encircled, but Hitler was too stinking stupid to listen.

"Hitler was also too pig-headed to take advantage of a wonderful opportunity presented to him in a flowery porcelain pisspot by Stalin."

"How? Tell me more?"

"Stalin secretly sent his ambassador to Sweden, Madame Alexandra Kollontai, to Berlin with an offer to end the war in the east. The victory at Stalingrad cost the Russians millions of casualties. Hitler made her wait because he wanted another victory over the Russians before forcing Stalin to accept his conditions. But, instead, we lost the greatest tank battle in die war, die battle at Kursk, and Stalin recalled Alexandra Kollontai and cancelled his peace offer."

"That was indeed idiotic, insane, imbecilic, irrational of Hitler."

"Yes, indeed. Just remember, you must keep your mumbling mouth securely shut. Do you understand?"

"Of course."

"And the block-headed Brits and those naïve North Americans keep that slick and slimy Stalin in business by sending him massive quantities of hardware."

"Yes, We've been bombed by American bombers flown by the Russians."

"Without all that stuff, Stalin's army would have been annihilated long ago by our boys. Roosevelt and Churchill will become very, very sorry for making the Russians their foolish friends. One can't ever trust these Russian barbarians. They are too damned deceitful and dishonest. It was a grave mistake to boost Uncle Joe as the call that silly Stalin. Just wait and see!"

"That's part of my job to keep these treacherous Ivans out of Europe. But they are pushing us back."

"But only with American and British help!"

After lunch, I ask Sonja: "Would you like to fly with me in my new beautiful Messerschmitt Hornisse?"

"Why not?"

"We are not allowed to take up civilians, actually."

"I'm a member of the Abwehr and, therefore, on the pay role of the Wehrmacht. You may perhaps have noticed that Canaris gave me the rank of Major."

"I will supply you with my old flying overalls and you tie your hair into a knot to fit under a cap."

"Fine. Fortunately, I don't sport blown-up balloons or blimps for boobs and they won't show under your overalls."

"Your boobs are just perfect. But we can hide them under your clothing. I am the only guy who is allowed to admire them."

"Exactly."

I hop over to the barracks to fetch my old overalls with the rank insignia of an Oberleutnant on the sleeves. Sonja gets dressed in them and we saunter over to the spot where my plane is parked. After I have explained that we are to sit back-to-back inside the cockpit and that she will assume the role of rear gunner, she smiles: "Herr Hauptmann, Oberleutnant Schellenberg reports for duty!" We salute each other.

We take to the air and Sonja tells me over the intercom that she enjoys the flight. She thinks that she has even figured out how to handle the two machine guns on both sides of the fuselage by means of the remote control.

Wien-Aspern, Wednesday, 26 May 1943

I have, long ago, lost count of all the airfields where I have been stationed. Today, I and my Gruppe fly onto the Fliegerhorst of Wien-Aspern. This air base is situated just outside the suburb of Aspern on the eastern outskirts of Vienna. I hope that Sonja will be able to visit me here some or other time.

It is expected that our stay here will be somewhat of a holiday because we must train our new crews to become competent with our advanced fighter-bombers before we can be sent on operations.

The check list that I have devised for my first Heinkel squadron has been revised with the Me 410 in mind. I hope to prevent the loss of any of our beautiful aircraft due to careless accidents on account of sloppy inspections before taking to the air.

Wien-Aspern, Tuesday, 20 July 1943

Sonja: "Can you remember why today's date, the 20th of July, is a very important date?"

We are taking a stroll in the Prater, the big park in Vienna on the south western bank of the Danube.

Me: "Not really. I'm sorry."

"You're a bloody barbarian. A stupid shitass. You can't even remember what happened exactly six years ago. Shame on you. I will force you to sleep on the carpet of my hotel room tonight."

"Fortunately, it's Summer."

"Tell me, what happened on the 20th of July, six years ago?"

"Aaah. Yes, I remember, that was when you agreed to become Frau Krause. We were in Kufstein at that time."

"And now we are again in Austria. You are taking me to a decent restaurant tonight so that we can celebrate. I didn't take this long dangerous train trip from Berlin just for the fun of it."

"Then, exactly why did you come?"

"First of all – to get laid. By you, of course. But also, to meet a Russian agent with a message from Canaris."

"Canaris seems to trust you with important messages?"

"Sometimes he delivers them himself. I went to Paris with him last month where he met a certain Colonel Oliver of British Intelligence. He wanted to know which conditions the Brits would pose if we got rid of Hitler."

"Did he get an answer?"

"Oliver came back two days later with the message that Churchill would only be satisfied with unconditional surrender."

"I suppose that didn't satisfy Canaris?"

"Not at all. There is a bunch of Generals who are conspiring to help Hitler into the fires of hell because the maniac of a man is totally mad and he is dragging Germany into the shitty slime. Their leader is actually a Colonel, Claus Graf von Stauffenberg. Their plan is to make Erwin Rommel 'Kanzler' (Prime Minister) of Germany in the place of Hitler. Rommel is highly respected as the wily Desert Fox and people will easily accept him as head of government."

"What type of peace does Canaris wish to get?"

"He wants the bloody Brits and American arseholes to help us drive those goddamn Ivans back into Siberia. But they wouldn't bite."

"You are part of a very dangerous game."

"I know, I know."

"Does your cousin Walter know of this?"

"We don't trust him."

After a long silence, Sonja continues: "You probably know that the Allies are busy chasing the Germans out of Sicily?"

"Yes. That started ten days ago."

"As soon as they have done that they will land in Italy. And then the Italians will just surrender. Leaving our boys to continue the fight on their own."

"You were always correct with your predictions."

"Canaris has his ear very close to the ground. It's his job to know what's going on. I'm often at his side and I also hear things."

"In hotel rooms?"

"Sometimes. But then both of us are fully clothed."

Lechfeld, Friday, 6 August 1943

My Gruppe has barely touched down at our new base of Lechfeld – where I received part of my training many years ago – when we are ordered back into the air to intercept American bombers over Stuttgart.

We hastily refuel and return to the sky. We find an armada of perhaps fifty four-engine bombers flying back from Stuttgart where the Mercedes-Benz plant was bombed. We shoot down seven of them with the loss of two of our aircraft. This is the first time that I fly an interceptor and I find that my Me 410 performs exceptionally well.

After landing again, I discover that the rather relaxed period of conversion to the new fighter-bomber did me well. I didn't experience knots in my stomach, shortcuts in my brain, a funny taste in my mouth, a sweaty forehead, tearful eyes, a runny nose, trembling knees or jittery fingers.

Illesheim, Monday, 6 September 1943

Although I am Gruppenkommandeur of I./KG 51, a bomber wing, my job since the beginning of last month was to shoot down American bombers. In other words: I actually became a fighter pilot.

We suffered losses – mostly of the newest inexperienced pilots who joined my Gruppe from time to time after they had received their training. Their training was much shorter than the training I had received before the war because the Luftwaffe urgently needed replacements for the many pilots who were lost. There also wasn't enough aviation fuel available to give the new chaps enough practice.

Nevertheless, my Gruppe achieved a respectful score of American and British bombers we swept from the skies over Germany. We were only called upon to fly when enemy bombers were sighted on their way to southern Germany. Most bombing raids were, however, targeted against northern Germany – the harbor cities of Hamburg and Bremen, the industrial area along the Ruhr River and Berlin. It, therefore, happened that we only flew three or four sorties per week.

There are no targets within the range of our aircraft to bomb and that meant that we simply became a fighter wing, although we were still officially called a bomber wing.

On this Monday, we are receiving a visit from General der Flakartillerie Emil Zenetti, commander of Luftgau-Kommando VII (Area Command VII). He flies in from Munich.

He is to inspect a parade and distribute a number of decorations. It was possible for Frau Sonja Krause to get leave to attend the ceremony, since she is the wife of the Gruppenkommandeur of I./KG 51, the Edelweiss Geschwader (that's me, of course).

Each of my pilots who has served in Russia receive the Iron Cross, First Class. Other air crews get the Iron Cross, Second Class. The captains of my three squadrons each receive the German Cross in Gold. I am given the the Knight's Cross of the Iron Cross. The Geschwaderkommodore of KG 51, Major Hannes Heise, recommended me for this decoration on account of all the bombing raids in which I successfully participated and the enemy bombers that I have shot down.

The recommendation had to be screened by the Chief of the Personnel Office of the Wehrmacht, approved by the OKW and finaly decided by Hitler himself. These big shots seem to have forgotten that I erroneously claimed to have damaged an aircraft carrier in 1939 and sank a German destroyer in 1940. I hope that it was taken into acount that I helped to damage two heavy cruisers of the Royal Navy.

After the ceremony, while we are enjoying refreshments with the General, Sonja asks: "Karl, are you supposed to sleep with that ruddy ribbon and piece of metal around your neck at night? Or do you have to hang it around your pecker when in bed?"

I ignore her question because I don't know how to handle this awkward situation. The General laughs. The other officers do the same.

That night, Sonja tells me: "The Allies have invaded Italy a few days ago. You probably know that. The Italian generals are secretly talking to the Allies about an armistice and the removal of Mussolini from power. They will certainly succeed. And that means that our Army will have to invade Italy and disarm the fucking Italians and take over the country, otherwise the Allies will march through the Alps into Tyrol next week."

"That sounds grave. When will your Admiral and the other Generals put the Führer away, as the Italians intend doing with the Duce?"

"They have to be damn careful and do everything in secret. Even I don't know how they want to do it. Or when."

"Anyway, will you mind if I put my Ritterkreuz away for the night? It will certainly interfere with what I intend doing with my male ornaments if I allow it to stay hanging somewhere on my anatomy."

Horsching, Saturday, 11 September 1943

Kampfgeschwader 51 moved again, this time to Horsching in northern Austria the day before yesterday. We hardly got settled at this base, a few kilometers' west of the city of Linz, or we receive another high visitor. This time, it's the chief of the Luftwaffe himself, Reichsmarschall Hermann Göring.

A guard of honor is hastily assembled and he is welcomed by the troops presenting arms. He lifts his fancy baton in reply.

There is a meeting in the conference hall in the main building of the Fliegerhorst, attended by Fat Hermann, our Geschwaderkommodore, Major Hannes Heise, the adjutant and the three Gruppenkommandeure. We have to explain our poor record – as the Reichsmarshall calls it – of preventing the Russians of pushing our troops back and for the loss of the Sixth Army at Stalingrad.

According to him, we were afraid, cowardly, lax, undisciplined, lacking in a fighter's spirit and unworthy of the decorations we are sporting.

We can only gape in amazement. He doesn't allow any of us to set the record straight or defend ourselves and while he is leaving his chair, he dismisses Major Heise from his position as

Geschwaderkommodore, without giving any indication of who is to succeed him.

As he leaves the room, we all stand up in the presence of the highest officer of the whole Wehrmacht who is on his feet. He leaves the hall. We hear how the guard of honor outside presents arms again and how his airplane, a Tante Ju, starts up again and departs.

I, as the most senior Gruppenkommandeur, is the first to speak: "Well guys, what do you think of this? I don't think this dismissal is valid because it wasn't given in writing."

Major Heise: "I will stay in command until I'm officially notified by the Personnel Office of OKL that I am dismissed or given another posting."

Me: "But Herr Major, you can only be dismissed if a proper procedure has been followed. A court martial, for instance. Nothing of that sort happened. I vote that you just carry on with your job."

A few voices exclaim: "Hurrah!"

Hauptmann Alphons Albrecht: "If I'm not mistaken, Fat Hermann must have been under the influence of some or other damned drug. I'm sure, tomorrow he will have forgotten what happened today."

Major Heise: "Oekee, Männer. We have work to do. Get on with your jobs."

Me: "I propose that we all write in our logbooks that we have received a visit of Fat Hermann today – and that we failed to feed him a morsel of food because we think he's already fat enough."

Hauptmann Albrecht: "I don't think so. Our esteemed overweight Reichsmarschall might hold it against us that we didn't show him more hospitality."

Horsching, Monday, 20 September 1943

We feel rather bored because we see very little of the war. By this time, I feel confident that all our pilots know how to handle the Me 410.

We are woken at midnight by the siren going off. We run to our aircraft. While we are doing our pre-flight routines, we are informed over the radio that a stream of RAF bombers is on its way, more or less in our direction. Their target is unknown but we must intercept them. Ground control will guide us to them.

There is a crescent Moon rising in the east and that improves visibility.

After flying about forty minutes in a westerly direction, we are told that we must be very near the Lancasters. I detect them on my radar screen and all 25 Me 410's on this sortie follow me. We gain height so that we can pick up speed as we pounce upon them. Searchlights on the ground illuminate the bombers. My rear gunner informs me that the bombers are not accompanied by any fighters.

Two minutes later I have one of the Lancaster bombers in my visor and I fire my canon and machine guns. The tail gunner of the Lancaster also fires in my direction but his aim is poor, especially as I don't offer him a stable target while I swing to and fro. After two seconds of firing, during which about a hundred projectiles in total are shot out, I hit the tail gunner and he falls silent. I also hit one of the engines of the Lancaster and it starts to blow out some smoke.

As I break off, I see that four more bombers are going down in flames. We have lost one of ours.

This is the first time that I have encountered these giant bombers of the RAF and I don't like what I see. The Luftwaffe has nothing like it.

Suddenly, I feel nauseous – again. It could easily have happened that Sonja's husband got a bullet in the chest or the head and I don't want her to experience such a loss. I have written so many letters of condolence to the families of fallen comrades that it became a routine. But I cannot imagine what one of my comrades would write to Sonja should I get shot down and explode on the ground.

2 December 1943

Padua, Thursday, 2 December 1943

While I am looking down on the snow-covered Alps I think back on the strange order that I've received just after lunch today. Our Geschwaderkommodore, Oberstleutnant Hannes Heise (his dismissal by Fat Hermann was never made official and he, instead, got promoted) called me urgently:

"Krause, you are to get a Staffel of ten aircraft ready at short notice. Take only experienced crews and then the lot of you fly off to Italy, to Padua. The commander of Luftflotte 2, which is comprised of all the Luftwaffe units in Italy and the Balkans, specifically asked for you. Get some fuel for your planes and ammo for your guns. You will be bombed up when you arrive at Padua. You seem to be needed for a bombing raid. Get going!"

It is strange, but I actually look forward to the action that awaits us. We had a rather quiet time in Horsching and we didn't fly every day. Bomber raids over Austria didn't occur very frequently and KG 51 was mostly only on standby. By this time, I have managed to shrug off the fright I got from my scrap with the Lancaster. I still enjoy my Me 410 and I and my navigator/rear gunner, Feldwebel Max Moritz, get on very well.

While I am doing my approach to the airfield just outside the Italian town of Padua, I am told by radio that I must report immediately to the Oberbefehlshaber (commander-in-chief) of Luftflotte 2 as soon as I have landed. The aircraft of my Staffel will be taken care of by the ground crews.

I touch down ahead of my Staffel at five o'clock and park almost next to the main building where an Unteroffizier with a flag shows me where to stop. I jump out and run to the building. I am immediately shown into the office of the commander who is none other than my old Geschwaderkommodore of KG 257 at Lüneburg before the war, Generalfeldmarschall Wolfram von Richthofen. He has been transferred here from Russia in June, shortly after KG 51 had been moved back to Germany to refit.

"Ah, here you are, Krause! Thank you for coming immediately. I'm sure you want to know why I need you so urgently."

"Correct, Herr Generalfeldmarschall."

He explains that a reconaissance aircraft flew over the Italian port city of Bari on the "heel" of Italy and discovered that the harbour was full of Allied cargo ships and that there was an absence of anti-aircraft batteries or fighter squadrons in the vicinity. A force of more than one hundred bombers was being assembled from various spots in Italy and the Balkans to make use of this opportunity to sow chaos.

"I discussed this with Kesselring (Generalfeldmarschall Albert Kesselring, the commander-in-chief of all German forces in Italy) and he agrees that we cannot allow this opportunity to slip through our fingers. Your Staffel, comprised of fast fighter-bombers, is to be the spearhead of the attack, the pathfinders for the rest of the bomber force.

"Get your men to get some grub in the mess. You fly off at eighteen hours, sharp. Your Messerschmitts will be fueled and armed by that time."

We arrive over Bari, ahead of the other German planes, at around half-past seven. It isn't difficult to pinpoint the harbour because it is brightly illuminated. My Staffel spreads out over a wide front and we deliver our first load – hundreds of tin foil strips to confuse any radar the Allies may have, as well as illumination flares to provide yet more light for the bombers. We release our bombs.

We get some altitude again and we are followed by dozens of Junkers Ju 88's. They download tons and tons of bombs onto the helpless freighters and tankers in the bay. Some bombs must have damaged fuel storage tanks because huge fires break out, engulfing many ships that have not yet been hit. Two ships containing ammunition blow up and my Me 410 is rocked in the air by the blasts. After the last Junkers have left the scene, my Staffel pounces again and we shoot with our canon and machine guns at targets on land, such as buildings, locomotives and trucks.

Our navigators take as many photos as they can before we fly back. Since the scene is brightly lit, it is easy to take good photos.

Back at Padua, I report to von Richthofen. The exposed films on the cameras of our crew members are rushed to the photographic laboratory. Von Richthofen smiles broadly: "We haven't lost a single aircraft in this operation. The whole affair was planned so hastily that we even had no time to think of a name for the operation. I cannot think of any other operation that was so successful. Thank you for your contribution!"

Evreux, Monday, 6 December 1943

My Gruppe, 1./KG 51, just as most flying units, is being shoved around to hotspots and places where we are needed – again. We are back in France and we have two tasks: we must intercept British and American Bombers on their way to Germany and we have to bomb London.

During our first evening we listen to Radio Berlin while sitting around in the officers' mess. The world is informed that our attack on Bari a few nights ago was a huge success: 28 ships sank and 13 more were seriously damaged, apart from other damage inflicted on the harbor. One of the ammunition ships that exploded released loads of mustard gas, a very poisonous gas, which is prohibited by international law. Most of the dead – it is estimated that more than a thousand people, military personnel, as well as Italian civilians – died of exposure to this deadly gas. The military authorities tried to keep the release of the toxic gas a secret but they could not keep the lid on the news because so many people got affected and medical personnel who treated them, blew their whistles.

My second in command at this stage, Oberleutnant Leopold (Poldi) Lösbeck: "So, those Brits are committing war crimes! Shit! Of course, they wanted to use that gas on us and our children! The swine!"

The Luftwaffe base is situated on the eastern outskirts of Evreux, a town in Normandy and half-way between Paris and the naval base at Le Havre. My Gruppe has 36 crews and 40 Me 410's, of which 32 are serviceable.

Evreux, Sunday, 26 December 1943

Sonja is a bundle of nerves as she lies next to me in her hotel room in the French town of Evreux.

"This war isn't going anywhere. Canaris is very pessimistic. My contacts here in France assure me that the underground Resistance is growing day by day and they are receiving equipment from across the Channel – radios, guns, ammo, explosives, you name it. Everybody expects the Allies to invade Europe somewhere here in France. Hitler and Rommel, who is in charge of the Atlantic coastal defense, both believe it will be in the vicinity of Calais where the Channel is at its narrowest. Canaris thinks it will happen here in Normandy but Hitler distrusts him more and more and won't accept his views."

"Has Canaris spoken to Hitler directly?

"Oh, yes. Only three weeks ago. I was also present at the meeting at Hitler's headquarters where a number of field marshals, generals, admirals and other big shits were present."

"Oh, you saw Hitler himself?"

"I sat about ten meters from him."

"How did you find him?"

"Rude. Uncouth. He yells at his generals and in the process his snotty saliva flies all over the place."

"What do the generals do?"

"They yell back at him. Canaris tells me that these meetings very often degenerate into silly snotty shouting matches. But Hitler usually gets what he wants. He is, after all, the fucking Führer."

After a minute of silence, I ask: "Are you in any danger?"

"Of course. My job is jolly dangerous, fucking dangerous. I meet with secret agents to convey messages or to receive reports. If I'm caught by the Resistance here in France my life won't be worth two blinking 'Groschen' (pennies). And if something happens to Canaris, I won't be able to stay out of the fucking firing line."

"I know that we have lost the bottom half of Italy. It's only a matter of time before the Allies take the whole of Italy – despite the serious blow that we delivered to them at Bari a few months ago."

"And the Russians have recaptured large parts of their country. Our poor frozen boys can't resist all their attacks. We all are stuck in the stinking shit."

"I agree with you. This war is certainly going nowhere. Actually, it's going downhill, faster and faster, into hell, into the fires and flames of 'Götterdämmerung' (Twilight of the Gods)."

"And you will be involved one of these days in some more attacks against England. That pisspot idiot of an Adolf Hitler wants to take revenge for all the attacks by the Brits and the Yanks on Berlin and other German cities. He wants to burn bloody London down, but I won't be friggin' surprised if half of our bombers get burnt out instead. Anyway, throwing a few tons of bombs on London won't really improve our situation. It will only serve to boost that over-inflated ego of Hitler."

"Yes, we've been told that a new bombing campaign is on the cards. We are just waiting for the start of that while training some new crews and assembling enough bombers and fighter-bombers."

"Are there still enough?"

"I doubt it."

"And the worst part is that these bloody Brits know something is brewing because they have noticed that our best bomber units have been concentrated here in France and Belgium. Yours as well. They are much better prepared than in 1940 to

repulse an aerial bombing campaign. And, even worse, you are going to be part of this. There will be huge losses on our side…"
I hold tightly onto my sobbing Sonja.

Evreux, Thursday, 19 January 1944

The commander of the Ninth Fliegerkorps, Generalmajor Dietrich Peltz, addresses all unit commanders in this Corps coming from bases in France, Belgium and Holland. About sixty of us are sitting in the conference hall at Evreux where this Corps has its headquarters and we listen attentatively to the youngest General in the Wehrmacht. He is only 29 years old and well-known for his superb abilities. It is clear why specifically he has been chosen to lead an important operation.

"Männer, our action is to start two nights from now. We are about to launch 'Unternehmen Steinbock' (Operation Capri-corn). I need one last report from each of you regarding your numbers of trained crews, the quantity of aircraft you have and how many are ready to fly. It's the Führer's wish that we take revenge on England for bombing our towns and cities. We must inflict on London and other cities the same treatment – just as we did during 1940."

Evreux, Saturday, 21 January 1944

The weather is clear tonight and there is no moon. There are only the stars to illuminate the world. Every town in France and Engeland is blacked-out – just as in Germany and elsewhere in Europe since September 1939. I am afraid that we have entered another dark age – an age with violence, hate, revenge, destruction and death. I feel as if I am swmming in a fast-flowing river. I am powerless to get out and I just have to accept that the stream is pushing me along. Relentlessly. Faster and faster.

Although I love flying my Hornisse because she is such a beautiful and fast plane, I certainly don't relish the idea of going on yet another bombing raid over London. I have taken my own flask of Schnapps along because there is no observer sitting next to me to hand it to me when I need it. As usual, I make sure that I also take my Bible along.

The target for tonight is the Waterloo area of London. This is our reply to an attack by 800 bombers last night on Berlin. We are to enter British air space in three waves. My Gruppe will be part of the first wave. We have been told that tonight's raid will be performed by about 230 bombers with a total payload of 500 tons. I cannot imagine how much destruction those bombs must cause.

As we reach the English coast, we shoot up to gain height. We stayed low up to now to evade enemy radar. From high above I can see the flares being dropped over the target by the pathfinders and I lead my wave of fast light bombers that way. We are subjected to heavy flack fire but we persist on our course in a shallow dive.

After I have released my bombs over the target area, I and my Gruppe turn around and fly back at a low altitude. We are attacked by at least ten De Haviland Mosquitos but our rear gunners keep them at bay, although we don't manage to shoot one down. I give the order that we break up our formation and that every Hornisse is to do its best to frustrate the aim of a fighter on its tail.

I concentrate so much on weaving around to stay out of the streams of bullets from the Mosquitos that I totally forget about my flask of Schnapps. Only after I have landed safely, I remember to take one big mouthful to stop the trembling and shaking of my limbs.

Evreux, Sunday, 22 January 1944

A post mortem of last nights operation is being held. We are told that we lost 18 aircraft of the first wave for a single one of the RAF that was shot down. Our loss amounts to almost twenty-two percent of the participating aircraft, which is very bad. We have managed to shoot down up to twenty percent of RAF bombers during some of their visits to German skies, which we regarded as superb.

On the other hand, only fifteen bombers of the first wave reached the real target and the rest of us dropped our bombs on empty fields. The Brits were clever enough to shoot up dummy flares to confuse us.

We learn that the second wave also lost 18 bombers and that the third wave lost 6 aircraft. Only 25 reached the intended target but a munitions factory was accidently hit and destroyed.

Evreux, Friday, 28 January 1944

Only a minor opertion is planned for tonight. Sixteen of my Messerschmitt Me 410's, together with ten Focke Wulf Fw 190 bomb-carrying fighters, are flying over the Channel to attack the docks in the Thames.

Bad weather and the failure of our radar stations to guide us correctly cause us to return after daybreak with all our bombs still in position under the bellies of our planes, but without any losses.

Evreux, Saturday, 5 February 1944

My Gruppe participated with 26 aircraft in last night's raid on industrial targets north of London. More than 230 bombers were supposed to have taken off from various airfields, but I hear that only twenty bombers struck the target, while 16 bombers didn't return. It is also suspected that the British managed to jam our radar sets with the result that our navigation was, again, up to maggots.

After all this news I need a good shot of Schnapps to prevent my eyesight from being obscured by sweat from my forehead.

Evreux, Sunday, 6 February 1944

Our sleep is rudely disturbed as the siren on the base starts to scream and screech and shriek. That can only mean one thing: we are about to be visited by enemy bombers.

Before I can get dressed, the first wave already hits us. American B-17 Fortresses. Bombs rain down upon our runways, barracks and other buildings.

I jump into my flying suit and rush out to help the firefighters to douse the blaze. The part of the barracks where I sleep is destroyed shortly afterwards by a second wave of bombers and all my personal belongings are gone, except for the flying overalls in which I ran out when the siren went off.

Miraculously, not a single airplane is hit.

Evreux, Monday, 14 February 1944

Another post mortem is being held after last night's operation. About 230 crews took part but only 15 bombers reached the target area in London. Only ten bombers were lost, which seems to be an improvement.

Generalmajor Peltz looks embarassed and tells us that Göring is very dissatisfied and disappointed.

I feel proud of my Gruppe. Although we also seem to have got lost over England we have only lost one Hornisse so far. I keep my fingers crossed that I won't be the next victim. My Bible in my pocket must help.

Evreux, Saturday, 19 February 1944

During our briefing, we are told that the strategy has been changed. No single target has been chosen and, instead, the operation is to target various RAF and American bases around the greater London area. My Gruppe is to attack the American airfield at Willingale, about thirty kilometers north east of London. It is suspected that this base is home to four squadrons with Martin B–26 Marauder bombers.

We were not expected at Willingale and in the early morning hours my Gruppe strikes. We drop our bombs on a number of buildings and airplanes. We turn around and shoot perforations and pockmarks through some of the remaining aircraft.

The flack batteries only wake up while we are flying away. I think: "Tit for tat, you yellow Yanks!"

Over the Channel a swarm of Mosquitos dive down upon us. Our rear gunners are able to drive them off, but only after my port engine has been hit (despite my best efforts to shrug one of them off), which causes a long tail of smoke to pour out of that engine as I fly on. It is a miracle that I am able to make it to Evreux, shortly after daybreak, although I have to perform a crash landing because the landing gear behind the burning engine won't come out. The Me 410 becomes a write-off as she skids along the runway and overturns. I am also almost a write-off because I break a leg and receive some cuts from broken glass in the process. My rear gunner is unconscious from a bump against the head.

Evreux, Friday, 3 March 1944

With a pair of crutches, I hobble around in the garden outside the sick bay at the Evreux Luftwaffe base. My lower leg on the starboard side is in plaster. The Oberarzt wanted to evacuate me to my home in Berlin, but I resisted. Evreux is a somewhat safer place than Berlin because Berlin experiences frequent bombing raids in comparison with the single raid we were exposed to. I also don't feel like leaving my men on their own and I may, perhaps, give them some encouragement and advice.

I phoned Sonja the day after the accident and she promised to come and visit me here if she can get away, which doesn' t seem likely.

Just after I have found a seat in the late winter sun in the garden, a "Stabsgefreiter" (Lance Corporal) comes to me: "Herr Hauptmann, the Oberst wishes to speak to you. Please come with me. I have a staff car just around the corner.

Because I am in a new uniform that I was issued with after losing my things in the blaze, I try to salute Oberst Thomas von Trauerstein, the base commander. He responds and smiles at my clumsy effort.

"Herr Hauptmann, thank you for coming here swiftly. You seem to be a man in great demand. A 'Kriminalrat' (Criminal Inspector) of the Sicherheitsdienst wants to talk to you. I haven't been told what the reason is, but I was given the assurance that you're not in trouble. You are to be taken by the Stabsgefreiter in the staff car to the Hotel Normandie, here in Evreux, where this person is waiting for you. Ask at the reception for this Kriminalrat."

"Herr Oberst, what exactly is a Kriminalrat? That sounds like a bloody Policeman or something."

"I understand it is a rank equivalent to Sturmbannführer or Major of the SS. Yes, it does sound like a bloody Police or Gestapo official or something."

I feel rather puzzled, but I squeeze myself anyway into the staff vehicle after having left the Oberst's office.

The Hotel Normandie is a very grand place, situated in an old big half-timbered building.

I tell the Stabsgefreiter as I struggle to get out: "Wait here."

I enter the foyer with my crutches and approach an elderly woman behind the counter: "Good day. I'm here to see the Kriminalrat of the SD."

"The Mademoiselle will take you to Suite number 2."

I follow the French girl and we ascend the staircase slowly as I struggle to keep my balance with my crutches. I cannot help but to wonder who this Kriminalrat is and what is expected of me. I cannot think of any criminal act that I may have committed, except for being somewhat untruthful on my application form when I joined the Luftwaffe almost eight years ago. It is also a possibility that somebody has found out about my South African citizenship but, if that is the case, I would have been arrested on the spot.

I am shown into Suite number 2. It is luxurously furnished with antique furniture. A voice calls out: "Come nearer, you moron of a medical wreck!"

I almost stumble over my crutches because it's Sonja's voice!

I turn to the Mademoiselle: "Will you please tell the driver outside in the staff car that he may drive off?"

Sonja sees that I struggle with my clutches and she rushes to me. After a warm embrace she leads me to a comfortable sofa where I can sit tightly next to her.

Me: "What are you doing here?"

"I am performing my duties in my new job as female Kriminalrat."

"How's that?"

"I'm working for Cousin Walter now."

"I thought you told him in no certain terms that you would prefer not to work in his department."

"That was only till three weeks ago. I had to take up on his offer, or get into serious difficulties."

"Yes?"

"The axe has fallen, at last. We expected it some while ago. It happened on the eighth of February."

"What type of axe are you talking about? To chop wood?"

"No, stupid. Hitler decided to get rid of Canaris. He abolished the Abwehr and transferred all the staff members to either the Gestapo, or Walter's 'Sicherheitsdienst (Ausland)' (Secret Service, foreign countries). The Gestapo gives me the fucking heeby jeebies. That's why I chose wily Walter."

"And he feels very satisfied because he got Canaris' job? And you, as well?"

"That's fucking right. To crown everything, Canaris has been placed under bloody house arrest, the day before yesterday. Something like that could have happened to me if I hadn't joined forces with Walter. Walter was nice and he appointed me in the rank of Kriminalrat – the equivalent of a Major, the rank I had with Canaris. I'm part of 'Abteilung B' (Department B), which is tasked with espionage in the West. That's because my English is perfect."

"But you haven't gotten into his bed?"

"Don't be stupid. It won't ever allow that prick's prick into my secret slit. That's reserved for you."

"Do you think that I will be able to perform my matrimonial duties in this condition (while I point to my leg in plaster)?"

"You may lie down and relax while this wily and willing witch will do all the screwing and stinging and squirming."

Evreux, Saturday, 22 April 1944

The plaster on my leg came off three days ago and I am able to use my leg again, although I still feel a little weak in that leg.

Sonja agreed with me that I stay in France. She was afraid what Cousin Walter could do to me if I was with her in Berlin. She promised to visit me regularly in Evreux in the course of her duties, which included visits to Paris. Operation Steinbock carried on without me, although I helped as a staff officer on crutches at headquarters, while wearing the Wound Badge in Silver for having been wounded three times in battle.

The Ninth Fliegerkorps achieved mixed results with a rather high attrition rate. Hitler was adamant, though, that it had to continue, despite the high risks and many losses.

Yesterday, I took to the air again. A new Me 410 was found for me and I tested her. I immediately felt at home again and fell in love with her. The rest period of two months cleared me of any lingering shell shock and I am eager to fly again – although I can't say that I'm very much in the mood to have another look at England from high above.

That is, however, exactly what I and the rest of my Gruppe are supposed to do today. During the late afternoon, we were hastily called and told to intercept a group of American Liberator bombers during their return flight from the Ruhr industrial area in western Germany. When we reach operational height, we are given the exact course to fly to chase these Yanks. Because we are much faster we are confident that we will catch up on them – most likely over British soil where they won't expect us.

We spot the Americans – about forty of them – on our radar screens during dusk, just as we cross the British coast in the vicinity of Brighton. Just as the Liberators are descending to land at their base I give the command to attack. At this point, an aircraft is at its most vulnerbale because it has to fly just above stalling speed while approaching the runway.

It was like shooting ducks on a pond. We shoot down ten aircraft in flames in a few minutes' time, while damaging a few more. We could have downed more if we had more fighter-bombers. Because we are all moving around it is not possible to fire a salvo of more than two seconds at a time. But that is enough to inflict serious damage with our canon and machine guns.

Unfortunately, on our way back, we are harried by Mosquitos. They shoot down two of my planes while our rear gunners send one of them spiralling down. The rest arrive safely back at Evreux

– minus a large quantity of ammo and with much less fuel, but with satisfied smiles on their faces, despite our losses.

Dreux, Sunday, 30 April 1944

The first Gruppe of KG 51 has been shifted again – this time to Dreux, a few kilometers south of Evreux and about 70 kilometers directly west of Paris. It is a fairly small airfield with only a few units based here.

Today, Sunday, a post mortem of last night's sortie is being held. Intelligence was received that a King George V class battleship was docked at Portsmouth harbour and thirty bombers were tasked to bomb the ship. However, bad weather and bad navigation caused us to miss the target totally and we returned with our unused bombs. On the way back, though, one Luftwaffe bomber was shot down by a Spitfire. My rear-gunner was able to damage the engine of another Spitfire with his rear-facing machine guns.

Lechfeld, Tuesday, 23 May 1944

The First Gruppe of KG 51 joins the rest of the Geschwader at Lechfeld today. At the moment, so I've heard, there are three other groups in the Geschwader, numbers II, III and IV. The fourth Gruppe is an experimental unit, testing new aircraft from the nearby Messerschmitt factory.

My Gruppe is very depleted and we hope to receive reinforcements at Lechfeld. At the end of last year, before the start of Operation Steinbock, my Gruppe had a full complement of 40 aircraft with 24 serviceable planes and 36 trained crews. We arrive today with only 22 aircraft and crews.

Operation Steinbock was a failure and Hitler and Göring had to acknowledge to Peltz that the anticipated results haven't been reached. The defenses and counter-measures of the enemy were too strong and the 9th Fliegerkorps lost about sixty percent out of the total of 560 aircraft at its disposal at the beginning. This corps was disbanded and all of its units were distributed to other areas, including my Gruppe.

After having handed our planes over to be serviced by the ground crews, I report to the Geschwaderkommodore. I find my old friend from our training days, Wolfgang Schenck, now an Oberstleutnant, sitting behind the desk. He orders coffee and we start chatting about our experiences since seeing each other the last time in 1937. We change over to Afrikaans, just for the heck of it.

He explains that he has a dual job: Kommodore of KG 51, as well as officer in charge of evaluating the new jet plane, the Messershmitt Me 262. Although he served as a fighter pilot until recently, he was given his present job at a bomber unit because the Me 262 was supposed to be a fighter-bomber. He promises to demonstrate one of those to me as soon as possible.

Lechfeld, Friday, 26 May 1944

Wolfgang Schenck demonstrates his new toy, the Me 262 Schwalbe (Swallow), to me today. Although it is designed to be a single seater, a few double seat trainers were also built and we get into one of those. Wolfgang starts her up and demonstrates to me how fast and agile she is.

Afterwards, he tells me in Afrikaans in order not to be overheard: "The units that have already converted to this aircraft have done some serious damage to the bomber waves from England. We could have won the air war long ago if we had these wonder-weapons a year or more ago. But now, I'm afraid, they came too late to change the outcome of the war."

Me: "That's a pity."

"The development of this beautiful machine was retarded by the constant interference of Hitler and Göring who both have little understanding of modern aerial warfare and the role this plane could and should have played."

I tell him about the failure of Operation Steinbock and that the Luftwaffe's bomber fleet is much smaller as a result.

Lechfeld, Saturday, 27 May 1944

During lunch, I bump onto my old instructor who taught me to fly the Heinkel 111, Werner Baumbach. He's an Oberst now.

He tells me that he is the commander of a special unit here at Lechfeld called Kampfgruppe 200. One of their tasks is to test captured enemy aircraft. After he has heard that I am in command of a Gruppe flying the Me 410, he asks: "I believe you have had quite a few scraps with Mosquitos?"

"We did."

"Are you interested in flying one of them to compare her to your Hornisse?"

"Yes, please. When?"

"Right away. Just allow me to finish lunch and a cup of 'Ersatz Kaffee' (artificial coffee)."

After lunch, I join Baumbach at the hangar of Kampgruppe 200 in my flying suit. The captured Mosquito, painted in the colours of the Luftwaffe, is already being pushed outside. After Baumbach has peformed the preflight procedures and explained what he was doing, we get into the air while I sit in the observer's seat. I watch every move Baumbach makes and after a few minutes he hands me the controls.

I find the Mosquito a wonderful aircraft. I can almost not believe that the fuselage and the wings are made mainly out of wood. I find that my Me 410 and this plane are more or less on the same level. The Me 410 is beter armed, though, with her two rear-facing machine guns that can shoot at pursuers.

Lechfeld, Sunday, 28 May 1944

Sonja: "I want a baby. Or two. Or even three. Or more. You know I love children. That's why I became a teacher."

Me: "Is that why you took this weekend off to ask me to help you in this regard? You know quite well that I understand and mastered the techniques. I've demonstrated that on many occasions."

"No, my treasure. It won't work to start a family right now. It will be a gigantic, grave mistake to make bloody babies in these circumstances, in this shithouse called the Third Reich. Anyone, or both of us, may say good-bye to this sorry, sad, sick world at any time and we cannot allow our children to become orphans."

"The only solution is that we jump off the moving train, get our parachutes and leave the doomed aircraft or get out of the sea before the sharks bite us into tiny bits."

"How the fuck will you manage that?"

"Steal an aircraft and fly somewhere."

"Holy shit! You won't get very far before they send a jet to shoot you down. It's illegal to steal anything, let alone an aircraft. Of course, they can't arrest you while you're in the air but they will make sure that you come back to earth in fucking fiery flames and some stinking slutty smoke."

Silently, I think that my beautiful wife must have picked up a few more dirty and uncouth words while working for the SD.

Lechfeld, Tuesday, 30 June 1944

Both me and Wolfgang are nursing a beer in the officers' mess at Lechfeld. Unfortunately, I have to say good-bye again to my old friend. In Afrikaans. For old times' sake.

"I've just started to rebuild my Gruppe and I think that I've managed a minor miracle with the manpower and tools I have. But the OKL gave me a new job, with promotion."

"Congratulations. So, you're a Major now? You deserved it a long time ago."

"Thanks. I think they held it against me that I sank a destroyer and that's the reason why I had to wait so long for this promotion."

"That's absurd. You deserve a medal for sinking a warship. And a promotion."

"Not if it's one of our own Kriegsmarine."

Wolfgang laughs: "I'm sure you didn't do it on purpose."

"No. A board of inquiry found that the Kriegsmarine was negligent by failing to notify us of the position of a flotilla destroyers."

"When does your promotion take effect?"

"I may only wear my new rank insignia from the day after tomorrow when I assume command of Kampfgeschwader 32."

"Where?"

"Graz."

"What will your job be, exactly?"

"I must take over the whole Geschwader. The Geschwader is known as the Wolf Geschwader because they have a picture of a wolf stencilled on their planes."

"Never heard of them."

"Nether have I. Until yesterday. I understand I will get a number of experienced men in the unit and together with them we must build a credible Geschwader out of a number of young boys, fresh from flying school."

"To do what?"

"To use rockets to sink enemy ships in the Adriatic and enemy bombers hitting our cities."

"I haven't ever seen anybody sinking a bomber over dry land."

"Ach man, you know what I mean."

Graz, Thursday, 20 July 1944

I cannot help but to think about today's date: 20 July. On this day, seven years ago, I announced to Sonja that we are to get engaged – and she agreed. I wonder when we will get another chance to be together again. I am actually very fortunate that my Sonja was able to visit me often – a privilege my colleagues never had.

My new home is the Thalerhof Fliegerhorst, south of the Austrian city of Graz, in the shaddow of the Alpine foothills en next to the village of Feldkirchen. The under-staffed Geschwader has 49 crews and 51 Me 410's. It is my job to help all the pilots to become proficient with a weapon with which I have absolutely no experience: the Werfer.

Four tubes are affixed under the wings of the Hornisse, two on each side. They are loaded with powerful rockets and tilted slightly upwards to compensate for the fact that the rockets tend to lose height as they fly. It has been used with some effect against closely packed bomber streams where one or more hits from a whole

Gruppe is more likely. The advantage of this rocket is that it can be launched out of range of the machine guns in the turrets of the enemy bombers. This rocket is an adaptation from an artillery rocket used by the Army. The tubes can be jetisonned after use to help the plane to become more streamlined.

My squadrons practice regularly with dummy rockets against targets on the Kruckenberg, a hill south west from Graz. We also attack the targets with the canon and machine guns in the noses of our fighter-bombers. It is a matter of urgency that we complete our training because our services are needed in Italy and elsewhere in the Mediterranean theatre of operations against Allied shipping.

Feldkirchen, Friday, 21 July 1944

After dinner, the telephone in my office rings. I hear Sonja's voice: "Wait for me at the Feldkirchen train station just outside your main gate. At eight-fifteen."

Just that. I hear the click as she puts the phone down. Since there is still some time, I get dressed in my best uniform and pack a little bag with necessities for the night. Since I am the Kommodore, I don't need permission from anybody to leave the base and I just inform the base commander of my absence. At eight I drive with my staff vehicle through the gate, cross the railway line and wait outside the station. Because it's summer, the sun is still shining. I see a local train steaming into the station from the direction of Graz and I step onto the platform to look for Sonja. She sees me first and rushes to me with two suitcases in her hands.

After giving me a hug and a kiss, she says: "You look smart in your uniform as a Luftwaffe Major."

"You are no longer my senior. My rank is on the same level as yours now."

"All right, Herr Major, where are you going to take me for a naughty week-end?"

"I don't know. I can't take you to our barracks. We will have to look for accommodation somewhere here in Feldkirchen. Let's hop into my Kübelwagen."

After we have dumped our luggage in a hotel room, Sonja proposes: "Let's go for a walk. It's not dark yet."

I agree since we both know that the walls in hotel rooms have ears. We stroll in an easterly direction to reach the banks of the Mur River.

Sonja: "You told me the other day that you would like to steal a plane and get out of this fucking war."

"But you said it won't work because I will be shot down."

"Yes, that's what I said. But it's very, very, extremely urgent that we get away. Far away. Out of harm's way."

"What do you mean?"

"My life is in goddamn grave danger. And yours as well. Right at this moment, we're living in shit street."

"Of course. Every time I get into the air, there is the danger that I can get shot down."

"Of course. But that's not what I mean. All of a sudden, the Gestapo might turn up and handcuff us, or something."

"Why? How? What have we done? Stealing cookies from the Government's cookie jar?"

"Not that. Please be serious. You will get the news within a few hours. There has been an assassination attempt on Hitler. It failed. Colonel Claus von Stauffenberg placed a bomb in a suitcase under the table at a conference where Hitler was presiding. The bomb went off after Stauffenberg had left, but it wasn't strong enough to kill anybody. Stauffenberg and his co-conspirators were arrested and they will certainly be executed. Canaris is also one of those who has been arrested. It is only a matter of time before I will be rounded up. You, as my husband, will also be regarded as part of the conspiracy."

"Hell! How do you know all that?"

"I phoned Walter last night from my hotel, just to report that I've reached Switzerland safely. And then he told me the story."

"So, Walter heard everything, him being in the security business?"

"Yes. And to complicate matters, I have to confess, I also stole Walter's money before I took the train to come here."

"Sis! That's not nice of you. Small wonder that he's also seeking your blood."

"He doesn't know that I did it. Not yet."

"Hell, and hell again! Tell me more."

"Yes. Walter, who has his ears next to the ground, suspected that the assassination attempt would happen sometime now. He sent me the day before yesterday to Basel in Switzerland with my diplomatic passport to draw some money of his in pounds sterling with which he intended absconding if things got too hot for him. He wanted me to flee with him. Perhaps to Sweden. I agreed to do that, just to get the opportunity to get on my own and to get away from him. Fortunately, he believed me."

"So, you hoodwinked him by promising to become his mistress?"

"Yes, something like that."

"And then you swiped his money from that Swiss bank?"

"That's it. Some of it is in one of my suitcases at the hotel."

"And the rest?"

"Walter gave me a letter to the bank manager, authorizing me to draw money from his bank account. He had to provide his secret bank code in the letter for the bank manager to prove that I had the authority to draw his money. Of course, I made sure that I memorized that secret code. With that, I later almost emptied his account and left him exactly nineteen Swiss Francs. I couldn't get it over my heart to take all of it. I transferred the bulk of it to another account at another bank that I had opened in one of my other assumed names that I used while I still worked for Canaris."

"How much did you take with you?"

"Sixty thousand pounds, Sterling. That's the money I was supposed to deliver to Walter. The rest amounts to more than a million in Sterling, although it is, of course, held in Swiss Francs."

I whistle because I don't have any words.

"I suspect that's mostly stolen money. How he got it, I don't know. But it's most probably the proceeds of crime. He wants to start a new life somewhere else when it becomes too hot for him in Germany. He knows that the Allies plan to prosecute all the important Nazis after the war – him included. But the Gestapo also don't trust him and he had to keep a back door open before they grab him."

"And now we have to disappear? Both of us?"

"That's right. You are involved as my husband and you cannot stay here. How are you going to steal an aircraft?"

"I will have to think of something. There may, perhaps, be something that I can do."

"But first of all, I must be declared dead, somehow or other. Otherwise, my parents and brothers will also be hunted as accomplices of those plotters."

"That's right."

"Nobody knows – except for you – that I took the train through Switzerland into Austria to Graz last night. With all the air raids taking place nowadays with the fucking Allies already comfortably settled in parts of France, it will be easy for me to write a letter to my parents and to Walter, announcing my death. As if I was travelling in a train from blinking Berlin to bloody Basel in swine-filled Switzerland and that this train was shot up by the Americans. Something like that really happened three days ago in the vicinity of Freiburg in the Black Forest. I happened to see the wreck when I was on a later train to Basel. Some of the carriages were totally burnt out."

"You have a good brain for intrigues. Oekee, let's do it that way. It will be easy to forge a letter to me from the Police in Freiburg, informing me as your next of kin of your untimely passing away. And then I can officially disappear during a flying accident or a dogfight with a Mosquito or something."

"Very damn clever."

"You know, when I joined the Luftwaffe, I wrote a letter of resignation to the South African Police Force. Don't you think that we should write letters of resignation to the Luftwaffe and the Sicherheitsdienst before staging our own deaths? That will be much more polite than just to disappear. That, actually, amounts to going AWOL. That will look bad on our service records."

Sonja laughs: "Why worry about our crappy shitty service records at this stage?"

Graz, Sunday, 23 July 1944

Last night, I told Sonja to keep herself ready at any time because KG 32 may be moved on short notice to Italy or somewhere else. That may, perhaps, be our chance to escape. She informed me that she is certain that the hunt for her is already on but that nobody would link her to a girl with the name of Sarah Stilling in a hotel room in Feldkirchen near Graz.

During breakfast, I 'am handed a signal from Generaloberst Hans-Jürgen Stumpff, commander of Luftflotte Reich, the formation that controls all the Luftwaffe units in Greater Germany. He has been requested by Generalfeldmarschall Wolfram von Richthofen, commander of Luftflotte 2, which controls Northern Italy, the Balkans and Greece, to release specifically my Geschwader Me 410's for an operation over the Mediterranean Sea. Luftflotte 2 is too busy fighting the Allies in Italy to undertake this operation. I'm, therefore, to proceed immediately with all available fighter-bombers of my Geschwader to Heraklion in Crete. Refueling has been organized at airfields in northern Italy and mainland Greece.

An appropriate target, a ship coming from Australia en route to Italy with more or less 1 200 troops, has been sighted by a Japanese submarine while she was leaving the harbor of Perth. The submarine's torpedo attack was unsuccessful and the intelligence was passed on to Japan's German allies. It is estimated that she will traverse the Canal on the 28th, five days from now. If she can be sunk, the Canal will be blocked and that will force the Allies to use the Cape of Good Hope route to and from the East – at great additional cost. That will also retard the arrival of the troops in Italy considerably – or even prevent it.

I feel honored that von Richthofen expressed his confidence in me for this operation.

Before I alert my crews, I rush to the hotel in my staff motor car and tell Sonja to get dressed in my old flying suit with the rank insignia of an Oberleutnant and to hide her hair under a cap. I take her and her two suitcases in the car and we go back to the base.

I summon my crews to the conference hall and I introduce my new navigator and rear gunner, Oberleutnant Stephan Steinmann, to the others. Fortunately, Oberleutnant Steinmann stays silent so that nobody can hear her soprano voice. I provide the crews with full details about our planned attack on a troop ship in the Suez Canal. We are to leave for northern Italy in three hours' time and in this time all aircraft have to be ready.

While my crews are busy doing their pre-flight routines, I smuggle Sonja's two suitcases, as well as a bag containing civilian clothes for me, into my Me 410. I pack all that into a water-tight bag.

We are to be accompanied by three Tante Ju's, carrying our rockets and other ammo, as well as our ground crews.

Heraklion and Kabrit, Friday, 28 July 1944

The troop ship that we have to target has been sighted by an agent where she docked at Suez before entering the Canal. It is expected that she will leave within the next hour.

I call my crews together in the conference room at Heraklion: "Meine Herren, our target is due to enter the Suez Canal any moment now. We must blast her a few hours from now. It takes a ship about sixteen hours to pass through the Canal if she sails from south to north. It takes less time the other way round because there is a current or a stream flowing from the Mediterranean Sea to the Red Sea. The best place to intercept this ship with her 1 200 troops is in the narrowest part, just south of the Bitter Lake. She will reach that point in about four hours' time. At that point, she will be at her most vulnerable because she will have to sail slowly and won't be able to maneuver within the rather narrow Canal.

"Our flying time to that point, which is at the outer edge of our range, will be a little more than two hours. We have just enough time to get ready and go through our preparations and routines. Fortunately, our Me 410's have already been refueled and our Werfer rockets have been loaded, just in case we have to fly off in a hurry.

"Any questions?"

One of my Staffel captains ask: "From which side do we attack? East or west?"

"The route that I have worked out is to take us over the coast of the empty Sinai Peninsula and we fly south over the desert until we get into sight of the target. Then we attack with our rockets in waves of four aircraft in a Kette. From the east. After we have flown over the target our rear gunners can use their machine guns to blast the ship further. And then we turn around again to shoot at the ship with our forward-facing guns from the west to cause some more damage and then we disappear again over the Sinai Peninsula to the east and back to the north. You have to aim your rockets and guns at the water line in order to sink the ship."

Somebody else asks: "Any RAF fighters around?"

"Maybe. There is an airfield on a peninsula at the south eastern edge of the Bitter Lake, RAF Station Kabrit. They won't expect us and we will have finished our job before they wake up. I expect, anyway, that this base won't be very active because the Afrikakorps doesn't pose a threat to Egypt anymore."

I show my men some aerial photos of the Canal and the air base at Kabrit, taken during the time the Afrikakorps was still operating in North Africa. The runway of the RAF station is clearly visible and it runs from the north west to the south east.

Two hours later, we fly off in waves. The operation is to be called "Unternehmen Phoenix". By this time, Sonja feels quite at home in my Hornisse and nobody questions her presence. I have hidden two hand grenades, a few tools in a bag, water and enough rations in more watertight bags in the plane before we flew off.

The sun is already approaching the western horizon as we cross into the Sinai Peninsula. I can see the Canal to my right and about fifteen minutes later we see the Bitter Lake. Sonja sits with binoculars and declares: "I can't see a troop ship."

Me: "But I see a much better target. A big fat juicy delicious aircraft carrier just south of the Bitter Lake. She's sailing north, perhaps to go for a refit or something after helping in the war against the Japs in the East."

The other members of the forward Kette confirm that the troop ship hasn't arrived yet, but that the aircraft carrier is a better target. We swoop down on her and launch our rockets. The ship's flack gunners have seen us in time and start shooting at us, but before they can hit us, we have already launched our rockets and turn away for an attack on the ship from the west with the setting sun behind us. We blast her again with our machine guns and canon. I make sure that my Me 410 is the last plane to attack from the west and I see that we managed to inflict some damage on the ship and the aircraft parked on her flight deck because smoke is rising into the air.

Over my radio, I announce: "Auf Wiedersehen, my men. I'm hit. I'm going to crash!" At the same time, I drop one of my hand grenades onto the desert sand after I've pulled the pin to simulate an explosion made by my Me 410 as she "crashes". I drop very low directly over the waterway to become invisible to my comrades as they fly away. Over the radio I hear that the rear gunner in one of the planes exclaims that he has seen the explosion as my plane crashed, which was, actually, only my hand grenade.

I fly very low northwards from the scene of our attack on the aircraft carrier and do a perfect landing in the water of the Bitter Lake after I have turned around to approach the southern coastline from the north. The plane drifts to a spot near the beach on the south side of the lake about three kilometers from the entrance to the Canal and the British air base on the strip of land directly next to the Canal. Sonja and I open the cockpit window and I turn to Sonja: "Are you still alive?"

"Yes. And you?"

I laugh: "Hell, no. You're seeing my ghost."

We step out onto the port wing.

A little later she tells me: "May I remind you: we are both supposed to be dead, squashed or blown to bits, but I don't think I feel dead."

The rest of my Geschwader has already flown away and I listen to their engine sounds growing fainter, although I see that some of them must have received hits from the gunners on the aircraft carrier as they trail smoke. I'm sorry for my men who may crash onto the empty desert somewhere.

I grab the watertight bags with our luggage and tools and Sonja takes our food and water. The shore is nearby and the water is shallow. We wade out and disappear into a grove of olive trees. After we have dumped our burdens, I go back and throw my second-hand grenade into the open cockpit of the Me 410 after pulling the pin. Before it can explode, I get submerged under the water to prevent being hit by any shrapnel. I feel and hear the explosions under the water. As I rise again, I take one last look at my beautiful Hornisse, which isn't so beautiful anymore.

There are a number of houses along the shore of the lake, but before anybody can come to investigate the crashed plane and the bang of the hand grenade, we disappear between the olive trees of the olive grove behind one of the seemingly empty houses.

It rapidly becomes dark and we make ourselves at home deep inside the olive grove. I go back to erase our tracks in the sand on the beach of the lake with a branch full of leaves by the feeble light of a half moon.

There are also many date palms and the vegetation is quite lush. The RAF base is quite near and there has to be British military personnel in the vicinity. I'm not surprised when a motor boat with a searchlight starts combing the area of the lake where the wreck of my Me 410 lies. After a while the crew of the boat seems to have given up their search and they disappear back to the airfield.

From time to time, we hear a vehicle moving somewhere and dogs barking far away, but that's all. I gather that the military personnel at the air base must have assumed that the occupants of the downed and exploded Me 410 must have perished and that nothing can be done about them in the dark.

We get rid of our wet flying suits and dress in civilian clothes. We bury our flying suits in the sand.

Sonja whispers into my ear, although there is nobody who can hear us: "We've done it! Your plan worked!"

I grin in the dusk as I hug my smiling Sonja: "Let's hope we stay undiscovered. We will have to stay undetected for at least two nights before we can do anything. By that time, nobody will expect our next move."

"Are we going to surrender to the Brits?"

"That's the last resort. There are other options."

Kabrit, Saturday, 29 July 1944

During the early morning hours before dawn, I did some scouting. There are some houses and huts on the edge of the Bitter Lake, but there are also buildings further away, along a road running east–west (or west–east, depending upon your perspective) leading to the main gate of the airfield. The property on which we spent the night is a long strip of land between the edge of the lake and the road. I gather that most properties have a narrow lake frontage and that they stretch a few hundred meters away from the lake. Some are overgrown with trees while others have open fields where animals graze.

We cover ourselves with some vegetation and lie completely still, especially when the heat becomes very uncomfortable after the sun has risen high. Somewhere, dogs are barking. We sometimes hear human voices at a distance. There is some vehicle traffic on the west–east road to our south.

Sonja whispers into my ear: "Are those vehicles looking for us?"

Me: "Not the vehicles, but the people travelling in them. The vehicles don't have eyes. But, who knows? Perhaps. Let's hope that's not the case."

We hear some laborer's working on a field to our west.

Sonja: "What will they do if they find us?"

Me: "I've forgotten to bring a pistol along, otherwise I could have blasted them. Sorry. Just lie still. Don't move."

The only intrusion into our den is when a donkey comes sniffing at us, but he loses interest in us soon afterwards.

At about lunch time a British search party appears on the beach of the lake, probably looking for footprints or other signs of our presence. I am glad that I have erased our footprints. Before the search party had arrived, I saw some people moving around on the beach and their tracks must have contaminated the scene considerably.

Later, during the day, we see the aircraft carrier that was attacked yesterday. Two tugs have appeared and they tow the carrier to the south after having turned her around on the lake while we watch through the foliage. I suppose there are repair facilities at Suez on the Red Sea coast in the south. She is listing and it is clear that much damage was done. No aircraft can be launched from her flight deck at that angle.

Me: "This erases my bad record with aircraft carriers."

I believe that my crews will report back that our mission was a bigger success than anticipated because an aircraft carrier was taken out of action. Unfortunately, they will not be able to report that the Canal has been blocked because the carrier didn't sink.

At about four o'clock, we hear an aircraft approaching the nearby air base. It seems to be a Douglas C-47 transport plane. An hour later three aircraft lift off and I see that they are RAF Mosquitos. They circle around the lake and the nearby land and we conclude that a search from the air for us is underway.

We wait in vain for the expected troop ship to appear. She must have docked at Suez for some time before sailing further.

After dusk, I venture towards the water's edge and I see that the wreck of my Me 410 has been towed out of the water and taken to a spot next to the air base. I feel that the RAF may keep that wreck with pleasure because they won't be able to do anything with it. Anyway, the RAF must have retrieved quite a number of wrecks of similar aircraft over England after the failure of Operation Steinbock. We spend a second night in the olive grove. We hear some music and laughter far off. Somebody must be throwing a party.

Before we doze off, I confide in Sonja: "You know that I grew up on a missionary station. I am supposed to be a religious type of person. I always regarded my religion as just a normal part of my life. But since the war started and I had to endure life-threatening and ultra-dangerous situations I started to see things differently."

Sonja: "And then you started to pray again in all earnest?"

"Exactly. I believe that my fervent prayers must be the reason why I am still alive. I even took my Bible along on most flights and I believe that gave me protection."

"That's pure superstition. The Bible isn't a magical object. You must carry the message of the Bible in your heart before the Bible can have any value."

"That makes sense."

"Did you bring your Bible along on this flight?"

"No. I forgot."

Kabrit and Antalya, Tuesday, 1 August 1944

We spent yesterday, our second full day on Egyptian soil, inside another olive grove, nearer to the British air base. We watched as a battleship of the Royal Navy was steaming south, probably to join the fight against the Japanese. We were totally powerless to do anything about her – not even a pot shot at the crew members on her deck.

During the afternoon, a little girl of about ten years old discovered us. We couldn't allow her to sound the alarm and we easily caught her and bound her with pieces of our clothes and a piece of cloth over her mouth to prevent her from calling out.

The little girl got tears in her big eyes. Her body trembled. Sonja, who held her and kept her mouth shut, also got tears in her eyes. After all, she loves children and she must have hated what we were doing. But we had no choice because our survival depended on it. We hoped that her parents would find her later, but only after our departure. She was left lying on the sand under some vegetation. We decided to leave our hiding place and we moved further east, crossing a few properties until we found another spot with dense vegetation.

After dark, we did some more reconnaissance. We walked along the east–west road in the direction of the air base and found that there is a brightly illuminated Police post on the south side of the road. We decided not to venture that way any further.

In the distance, we could hear people calling frantically. We supposed that to be the parents of the little girl, looking for her. We hoped that she would only be found later, otherwise a search for us would certainly start.

We hid at another spot and consume our last consumables. A rather bright three-quarter moon illuminates the white sand and we move nearer to the air base through other plots where we arrive shortly after midnight this morning.

The moon illuminates a big grey passenger ship sailing to the north. That must be the troop ship that was supposed to be our target. There's nothing we can do to stop her and we curse our bad luck in frustration.

We watch for any movement on the base through our binoculars. We see four Mosquitos parked next to the runway, as well as a few C-47's. The only guards we can see are in an illuminated sentry box at the entrance. There are barracks but they are dark with a single outside light burning. We find that only a meshed wire fence separates the base from the outside. With a pair of plyers from my tool set, I cut a hole in the fence through which we slip inside.

Me: "I will have to steal one of those Mosquitoes. Fortunately, I have flown one a few weeks ago. She is also much faster than the available C-47's."

Sonja: "But those other planes are bigger. Won't they be faster?"

"No. They are transport planes, slow transport planes. We will do much better with a Mosquito. And, besides, I don't have any idea how to fly those big ones. My darling, I think you must go and keep those guards busy while I get one of those Mosquitoes ready. Go and flirt with them to draw their attention away from me."

The only response I get is a blow against my head, delivered by my sullen and sour Sonja.

We move towards the parked aircraft. The four Mosquitos stand unguarded. I wriggle into the first one and with the torch from my tool set I inspect the dials of the aircraft. It seems the fuel tank is almost empty. I try the second and the third Mosquitoes with the same calamitous result. I silently think that I will have to take my chances with a C-47 if the tanks of all four Mosquitoes are almost empty.

Just as I hover on the edge of despair, I discover that the fourth Mosquito is actually fueled up. This must be the one that stayed behind when the other three tried to locate us from the air. Sonja helps to lift our luggage into this plane, as silently as possible. We close the entry hatch softly after having pulled the entry ladder up.

Sonja: "How sure are you that this plane is not unserviceable?"

Me: "There's only one way to find out and that's to start her engines and see what happens."

Because I can't quite remember how to conduct a thorough pre-flight routine, I decide to start both engines straight away. They sound all right and I can't detect anything that may point to anything amiss. I do know that one is supposed to fly off only after the engines have been warmed up but I decide against that. There is no time to waste and after I have released the wheel brakes, I take the plane onto the runway.

The runway is more than two kilometers long and there is ample space to build up speed. But just as I get the plane moving with the propellors at maximum revolutions, a siren starts wailing and whining and whistling. All the lights in the base suddenly come on, also in the control tower. Men run around and vehicles switch their lights on and start moving around.

We race off in a south easterly direction along the runway, despite the fact that the engines are still cold, and I manage to lift the Mosquito into the air before we reach the end of the runway. Both of us give a loud shout of relief as we gain height slowly. Two trucks race to cut us off but they are a few seconds too late.

I turn into an easterly direction to get over the Sinai desert. Sonja shouts into my ear: "Those guys have woken up. They will chase us!"

I shout back: "They can't catch us. Those other three fighters don't have enough juice! And the transport planes are too slow and they're also not armed."

Sonja giggles and I laugh.

After a while Sonja discovers how to operate the intercom and we can converse better with each other. We decide that the poor little girl whom we have bound must have been found by her parents and that they have sounded the alarm after hearing from her that she was bound by two foreigners. An alternative is that our flying suits may have been discovered. That may explain the sudden reaction at the airfield, especially after I had started the Mosquito's engines.

Over the desert I turn into a northerly direction to take us to the Mediterranean Sea. We hope to get to Turkey, the only neutral country within reach. We fly low in order not to be detected by any radar stations on land that may be switched on. Sonja discovers a device that registers any radar beams directed in our direction. When we get over the Mediterranean Sea, we register the radar beams of a few ships but that doesn't worry us unduly. In order to conserve fuel, I steadily gain height to fly through thinner air.

I fly at the lowest cruising speed because I don't know how long our fuel will last. I decide that I do like this plane, even if she was built by the engineers at De Haviland in Britain. A beautiful airplane has to be admired, doesn't matter where she came from – just as one has to admire a beautiful horse, doesn't matter who the owner is. Sonja agrees with me.

Since I have plotted our intended route while we were still on Crete, I am confident that we will strike the Turkish coastal city of Antalya, shortly after the sun comes up.

Sonja: "This was almost too easy. Something fucking bad is bound to happen."

Me: "Don't be so superstitious, please. I believe that a very benevolent guardian angel helped us this far. That angel will certainly finish his or her job."

Suddenly I see in the rearward mirror another plane on our tail in the pre-dawn dusk and she is shooting at us. That can't be our guardian angel.

Sonja cries: "That guy has hit our starboard wing!"

Immediately, I take evasive action by diving and turning around. I guess that this plane came from the air base at Port Said and I hope that the pilot is a rookie. The best pilots of the RAF must be busy somewhere in Europe, not in Egypt. The poor guy proves to be a novice because I manage to outfox him and get onto his tail. It is an outdated Hurricane. A short burst from my new Mosquito's machine guns is enough to put him out of action. I am relieved when he gets out with his parachute. I don't want to have yet another life on my conscience.

Sonja: "That guy certainly had no chance against you. Good for you!"

Me: "Please tell me how much damage was done to our wing."

Sonja: "A number of holes in the wooden wing. Nothing serious."

Another Hurricane appears behind us. With my higher speed I simply shoot away from her and she is left behind. As far as I know, the Mosquito's top speed is more than 100 kilometers per hour faster than that of the Hurricane.

I continue along the course we have taken with the hope that we haven't strayed too far off course during the scrap with the first Hurricane. After about forty minutes we see the coast of Turkey in the distance and I am confident that we are flying directly towards our destination. I radio the control tower at Antalya and, fortunately, there is somebody who can speak English. I announce that I intend making an emergency landing and I get permission to set the Mosquito down. The airport is, surprisingly, in the middle of the built-up area on a big open spot, near the coast.

While I'm losing height in my approach, the engines of the Mosquito start to splutter and make unhealthy and ugly hick-ups. The gauge of the fuel tank shows empty. I must have used up more fuel than I could afford in my brush with the two Hurricanes. All I can do is to lift the nose of the Mosquito somewhat so that we can glide the last hundred meters. At the last possible moment, I release the wheels in order to lessen the drag of the air on the aircraft.

With our last bit of momentum, I put the Mosquito down at the very edge of the runway. As in the past, my legs tremble, my hands shake and my eyes can't see due to all the sweat from my forehead. I almost utter a few ugly words because I have forgotten to include a flask of Schnapps in our baggage.

The control tower directs me over the radio to stop at the end of the runway and park on the grass next to the runway. We lose speed steadily but not enough and I manage to swerve the

Mosquito onto the grass next to the runway where she stops after a minute of frantic antics. The wheel brakes won't work because the engines have stopped and they supply the power for the hydraulic brakes. We get out and Sonja holds my shaking hand. Her hand is also shaking, but that may be due to the shaking of my hand.

After about fifteen minutes a Police truck comes racing towards us. We are, of course, regarded as British because we arrived in a RAF plane and we are sure that the Policemen will try to arrest us.

Two armed Policemen get out. They want to handcuff us, but Sonja shows them her German diplomatic passport, which includes me as her travelling companion. She insists on holding onto the passport so that the Policeman cannot confiscate it.

When the Policemen see that we are actually German diplomats – and not English – their attitude becomes somewhat softer. Turkey was, after all, an ally of Germany during the Great War. The biggest ship in the Turkish Navy is a former German battleship from those times, the SMS Goeben. She was renamed the Yavuz Sultan Selim in 1914 when she was transferred to Turkey.

Sonja, the diplomat, insists to be taken to the Police chief of the city. Our two Policemen are only too glad to pass us on to a higher official and they invite us to join them in their truck. We take our luggage with us. Since our bags and suitcases belong to diplomats they may not be opened and searched.

Since we landed before breakfast, we have to wait for the Police chief to finish his breakfast at home before he arrives at nine o' clock. He also knows a little bit of English.

Frau Krause, the diplomat, bends and adjusts the truth in a somewhat diplomatic way and she tells the Police chief that we are diplomatic fugitives. We were abducted from Crete by British commandos who bullied and maltreated us and took us to Alexandria in Egypt in a stuffy submarine. We were thrown into a stinking prison where we were interrogated by some more bullies. She was almost raped in front of her husband but she could defend her honor by biting off part of the ear of one of her tormentors. We were threatened with the death penalty for being spies and because she disfigured one of the guards. A friendly Arab helped us to escape and we stole an aircraft with which we flew to Turkey where we hope to find shelter and, perhaps, asylum.

She concedes that she doesn't know what has to be done about the British airplane and suggests that the Turkish authorities may regard it as a gift.

Fortunately, the Police chief doesn't ask us how we acquired all our luggage.

The Police chief feels sorry for us because we haven't had breakfast and he offers to take us to a nearby café as his guests where we can get something to eat. We accept his offer gracefully because we don't want to insult his generosity and we sit down to a meal with strong coffee and other dishes. The chief explains that we are to consume fried dough (known as pişi), cheese, butter, olives, eggs, muhammara, tomatoes, cucumbers, jam, honey, kaymak, sucuk (a spicy Turkish sausage), pastırma, börek, simit and poğaça. When we cannot understand these words, he writes them down for us.

Sonja mumbles in German: "This is the first decent meal I've had in years. The civilian popilation in Germany is starving because the limited food supplies are earmarked for the Wehrmacht."

Me: "Our meals in the Luftwaffe weren't anything special, either. I'm afraid that all this stuff will give me heartburn or indigestion or something."

After we have explained that we haven't slept all night and that we will have to find some lodgings, he takes us to his home. He commands his wife to take care of us and he returns to his office after promising to inform the German Embassy in Ankara of our presence.

When we are alone in a bedroom with clean white sheets on two beds we can start talking to each other again. We agree that this chief, of course, hopes that these two influential foreign diplomats will bestow some or other favour on him at a later stage. We can speak freely because we are sure that these walls don't have ears.

We agree that we will have to find a hotel to stay during the foreseeable future. Sonja takes out another set of diplomatic passports, according to which we are supposed to be Mister Thomas and Missus Elizabeth Taylor. With those, we can disappear from the Police chief's radar screen. The officials at the German Embassy will certainly scratch their heads in uncertainty about what to do about these two mysterious diplomats who evaporated into thin air.

Me: "Let's pray that all the possible blessings in heaven and on earth be bestowed upon Admiral Wilhelm Canaris and Brigadeführer Walter Schellenberg for providing you with these valuable and useful documents."

Sonja: "Amen! Halleluja! We have to thank them for making it possible to make a new beginning somewhere – away from that whorehouse that Berlin became and the bordello that Germany was turned into. That's what those bloody Nazis made of the country. The lot of them are only good at jumping into a prostitute's bed."

After we have taken a bath and a nap, we dress in clean clothes. We approach our hostess. She doesn't understand a word of English but we convey to her by gestures the idea that we need a taxi. She phones for one and we present her with five British bank notes of twenty pounds each for her hospitality and trouble. She gets tears in her eyes for this great gift.

The taxi arrives and we disappear from the face of the earth as Herr and Frau Krause and we reappear somewhere else as Mister and Missus Taylor, British diplomats. At a later stage, we will become Mister Samuel and Missus Susan Smithson, Canadian diplomats. Or Herr Erich and Frau Doktor Erna Eberhardt, Swiss academics. Or even Herr Gerd and Frau Gerda Grollwitz, German diplomats. Or perhaps Herr Stephan and Frun Sarah Stilling, Swedish citizens. I am disappointed that we cannot turn ourselves into South African diplomats or athletes. I suddenly remember that my South African passport must still be somewhere in the home of my parents-in-law in Berlin. My clothes in which I participated as a member of the South African team at the Olymics, must also still be in their home. Let's hope that the Gestapo won't discover all those items.

Antalya, Wednesday, 2 August 1944

When we wake up in a luxurious hotel room, the sun is already high in the eastern sky. We use the telephone to order breakfast.

Sonja: "With all that money that good and generous Walter unwittingly bestowed upon us we can live as millionaires. I think I like this lifestyle."

Me: "Yes, me likewise."

"You said that we were to take part in Unternehmen Phoenix when we attacked the Suez Canal. Do you agree that this was a very appropriate name for this operation?"

"What do you mean?"

"The Phoenix is an old mythological bird. Herodotus, an ancient Greek historian, wrote that the Egyptians of his time believed that this bird died every so often in a huge flame. He was, however, reborn from his ashes and restored to his old glory. We can compare ourselves to this bird. We simulated an accident with the explosion of your hand grenade that resulted in your official death. But – here we are, as it were, reborn and starting a new life."

"Thanks for that explanation. You do make a very valid point. I think I like the Phoenix better than the Nazi eagle."

After we have been contemplating our fortunate position for a while in silence, I ask: "But do you wish to live the rest of your life in this country? We can't speak the language and sooner or later it will be discovered that we are not really diplomats. Besides, the folks here are Muslims and we are Christians. I don't know how to pray in a mosque. As far as I know, they stay on their knees most of the time. My two silly wounded legs won't stand that. I'm glad that we Christians adopt more comfortable postures when we pray."

Sonja: "I can't say that Turkey is my favorite country. We will have to think of somewhere else. Anywhere. But, please remember, almost the whole of Europe is at war at this moment and that is what we want to avoid at all costs. Fortunately, we have managed to reach a neutral country. If we were caught in Egypt, we both would have been taken prisoner. And I don't relish the idea of rotting in a POW camp, far away from you."

"And we also won't like to go to the English-speaking world – even if both of us speak English well. I can't say that the Brits and the Americans and the Australians and the Canadians are my favorite people. I have fought against them the past four, five years and I still regard them as the enemy. The Brits are also the enemy because they maltreated my grandmother and her two kids during the South African War when they were thrown into a concentration camp. As you say, this place is far better that a POW camp."

"I was also involved in the same war against the same enemies. We've been so busy making plans to escape from the Gestapo and the SS and the SD and the Nazis that we hadn't had any time to really plan our future."

"I would have liked to take you to South Africa, to my folks. They will certainly welcome you with open arms and open hearts and open purses, which we don't really need. I mean, the open purses."

"We can't go back to my parents in Berlin after the war. The place is being bombed almost on a daily basis and everything is in ruins. I would like to raise our children in a sunny and friendly country like South Africa. But you will be treated as a traitor there. You joined their enemies and fought against them. You even bombed the South Africans at Tobruk and probably killed a few."

"True."

"Heaven knows when this war will end. That asshole of a Hitler will be fucking stupid enough to prolong it to the bitter end when everything is smashed to bits – especially after he had survived this damned assassination attempt. Damn! He seems to think that he is bloody well invincible and indestructible and irresistible."

"Let's go for a long walk to clear our heads and get another night's good sleep before we really make definite plans."

"Good idea."

While we are taking a stroll through the streets, Sonja asks: "Why didn't we just escape from Crete and fly directly to this spot? Was it really necessary to take our chances in Egypt? I don't know the geography so well, but I think that it would have been easier if we just stole an aircraft at Heraklion and flew here."

"I've thought about that possibility. Many times. But I had a look at the map while we were in Crete. To reach this spot we would have had to fly over the island of Rhodes."

"Why would that have been a problem?"

"There are two bases of the Luftwaffe on Rhodes – taken over from the Italians when they withdrew from the war last year. I enquired informally at Heraklion and I was told that two fighter squadrons are based at Mandraki and at Maritza on Rhodes. It would have been too dangerous to fly over Rhodes because we would have had to do it clandestinely. We would have been regarded as an unidentified enemy aircraft or German fugitives and

I don't know whether we would have been able to survive a clash with our own fighters. Focke-Wulf Fw 190's."

"I see. That makes sense. I don't know whether I would have had the courage to point my machine guns at German fighters if they attacked us, even if it was in self-defense."

"There are also RAF bases on Cyprus, which could have caused some trouble. I am actually surprised that the RAF on Cyprus didn't try to stop us when we stole a plane in Egypt and flew her off to Turkey."

"I think they just didn't know about us, otherwise there could have been more tubs filled with shit for us. Anyway, thank you for getting us safely out of the fucking clutches of the Gestapo and other Nazis."

"You faced more dangers than I did when you fled from Switzerland to reach me at Graz."

"Look here, I just got a blinking brain wave. Why don't we use our Swedish or Swiss passports to settle in South West Africa? There we can disappear into the German community. But only after this fucking war has ended, of course."

"How are we going to reach the place?"

"We'll find a way."

Antalya, Thursday, 3 August 1944

While we are making plans to leave Turkey for somewhere else, we are having a serious discussion in our luxurious hotel room.

Sonja: "It's actually a pity that those generals weren't able to take that fucking fool of a Hitler out with their bloody bomb."

"But that would have been outright murder. Don't you agree?"

"Look here, Mister. You grew up at a missionary station. You were taught Christian principles. Of course, you respect the lives of other people. The Ten Commandments forbid us to kill people. But I also read in my Bible that a murderer has to be punished."

"And you regard Hitler to be a murderer?"

"Of course. He started this war. Thousands upon thousands of people were killed – soldiers, old people, women, children. It goes without saying that the ruddy Russians, bloody Brits and yellow Yanks also have blood on their hands. But Hitler is the biggest killer of them all and he had to be stopped."

"You know, I almost had a chance of shooting the man myself."

"When was that?"

"When he visited our air base in Russia last year. I was part of a guard of honor with a rifle in my hands with which I had to present arms in salute."

"Why haven't you tried?"

"Never thought of the possibility. But the bloody gun wasn't loaded, in any case."

"When I and Canaris visited his headquarters last year, I thought of shooting the guy between his eyes. But there was no possibility of smuggling a pistol or something into the place."

"The Nazis would have killed you too, on the spot, if you did that."

"And the history books would have declared me to be a hell of a heroine by doing the right thing."

"Yes, that would actually have been the right thing to do. But then I would have lost you. I cannot bear the idea of being without you."

"We have also done the right thing by getting out of the lunacy of this war. We preserved our own lives and we are able to continue to serve mankind. We can carry on doing what is right and good and, perhaps, make a better place of this wounded world."

"Yes, that's what is expected of good Christian folk, like us."

"But will you ever forget the many people whose lives you have taken with your bombs and bullets?"

I look down at my feet on the carpet: "You have diagnosed me as suffering from shell-shock. Of course, those memories will continue to haunt me – even if I defended our country. But they also shot at me and I got wounded more than once."

"Fortunately, your prick stayed intact and fully functional. By making use of that valuable male instrument, you may perhaps get rid of your shell-shock."

Lisbon, Thursday, 10 May 1945

At last! The war in Europe is over. The whole world gives a huge collective sigh of relief that the wholescale carnage, destruction, killing, torture, famine and wrecking of buildings, equipment and people is something of the past in this part of the world, although the Japanese are still holding out against America.

It was reported that Hitler committed suicide in Berlin when the city was surrounded by the Russians and almost no building was left standing. The big shots of the OKW signed a deed of surrender and German soldiers, airmen and seamen are steadily being taken prisoner.

Sonja and I are both in tears. Tears of relief but also tears of sorrow. We don't have the faintest idea what happened to Sonja's family and we didn't dare to write letters to them since we fled because these letters would certainly have been intercepted by the Gestapo. That would have proved that we didn't really die as everybody believed.

During the past nine months, since our miraculous escape from the clutches of the Nazi war machine, we were both often plagued by nightmares and flashbacks about the dangers we had experienced.

We are living in neutral Portugal, after we have managed to get passage on a freighter from Antalya to Barcelona, where we got onto trains from Barcelona to Lisbon. It became safe for neutral and Allied shipping in the Mediterranean at the time of our escape because the Kriegsmarine had no more units left in that part of the world.

We regard our stay in Lisbon as a second honeymoon while we rent a cottage overlooking the Atlantic.

We often got news about the British and American war effort. Horror stories emerged about SS concentration camps where thousands upon thousands of Jews, Gypsies, prisoners of war and other undesirables were systematically exterminated and how occupied countries were systematically stripped of art treasures and other loot. Sonja is convinced that cousin Walter's fortune was amassed in this way.

Me: "The Brits are hypocrites by condemning all the Nazi concentration camps. Of course, those camps and everything that happened there, can never be justified. But the British Army invented concentration camps during the war in South Africa more than forty years ago. My grandmother and her sons almost perished in such a camp. Thousands of women and children died of malnutrition and disease. They never apologized for their crimes in this regard."

Sonja: "These horrible camps ought to make us ashamed of being German."

Me: "The British and the Americans must also be ashamed of themselves. They bombed helpless civilians and killed thousands of Germans."

"Quite right."

"We can be proud of Germany. Not all Germans were Nazis. We fought like heroes and we could have won the war if Hitler and Göring didn't make so many miserable mistakes, as you've often pointed out. You also often mentioned that Germany produced the most wonderful artists and thinkers and scientists. Goethe, Schiller, Beethoven and many others. Don't forget that!"

"And please remember that Germany also produced these two thieves who ran away with Cousin Walter's treasures!" Sonja points her finger at herself and at me: "I did the stealing and you are my accomplice."

"Perhaps we ought to hang our heads in shame for taking his money."

"I don't think so. By robbing him, we prevented him from doing some evil with it. We can use that money to build a new future where we can do good and do the right thing. The best thing would have been if we could have given that money back to the people from whom he stole it, but there is no way that we can ever find them."

All this didn't help us to get rid of the delayed shell shock that both of us are suffering from. It's a terrible condition, characterized by nightmares, anxiety, paralysis, extreme cautiousness and insomnia. We hope to overcome it in a new country.

And today, we are seeking a new future in Africa. We got a cabin on a passenger liner to Luanda in Angola, also known as Portuguese West Africa and we are relieved to get out of war-weary Europe. It is our plan to reach neighboring South West Africa from Luanda, perhaps as Herr and Frun Stilling from Sweden.

Luanda, Monday, 4 June 1945

We reached Luanda a fortnight ago. With the little bit of Portuguese that we had picked up in Lisbon we were able to get along and find lodgings in a guesthouse. Sonja's Portuguese is better than mine because she had Latin in school and Portuguese can be described as pidgin Latin. We decided that our first priority would be to find a way to get into neighboring South West Africa where we want to get settled as German-speaking Swiss citizens, Herr Erich and Frau Doktor Erna Eberhardt.

To our dismay, we find that there is no rail link between Angola and South West Africa and that the dirt roads linking these two countries are in a rather primitive state, to say the least. No busses run between Luanda and Windhoek, the capital of South West (or Windhuk in German). No taxi is prepared to undertake the arduous journey of more than 2 000 kilometers to Windhoek.

After investigating all the possibilities, Sonja proposes: "Let's steal another airplane and fly to Windhoek. We are good at that type of thing."

"Are you serious? Really serious?"

"What else?"

"I can think of two options. First one: we buy an automobile and travel the distance to Windhoek. Second option: we buy an airplane, if we can find one for sale."

"Hell's bells! I love flying. Let's try option number two."

A taxi took us to the primitive airfield outside Luanda and we saunter around between the hangars and airplanes. With our elementary Portuguese we enquire whether there are any airplanes for sale. A grease-covered mechanic, who is working on a rather battered Junkers 52, a Tante Ju, tells us: "Yes, as a matter of fact, there are two planes looking for new owners. The boss of this crate (and his waves in the direction of the Tante Ju) wants to get rid of her. Over there (and he points with his dirty hand) is a Heinkel 70 Blitz in which you may also be interested."

We decide that the Tante Ju might be a little too big for the two of us and we walk over to the Heinkel Blitz.

While I hold my lovely wife's hand, I explain: "This baby might just be the thing. The first civilian types came out in 1933 and they broke several world speed records. Some of them were converted to heavy fighters and sold to Czechoslovakia and other countries."

Sonja: "This is certainly not the most beautiful plane I've ever seen, but she seems oekee enough."

"You know, if we buy her we can start an air service in South West and fly people around. As far as I know, she takes five passengers and two crew members. You can be the radio operator and navigator, while I'm the pilot."

"Let's do it. She can't be too expensive because she already looks old and worn out."

Luanda, Monday, 18 June 1945

It is fairly early in the morning and we are heading to a bank to organize the transfer of money to the owner of the airplane that we are buying. We – that's me, Sonja and Senhor Ferdinand Ferreira, the owner of the aircraft – arrive at the entrance of the BANCO COMERCIAL PORTUGUES shortly before opening time.

A minute after our arrival, three men also arrive at the entrance of the bank. They speak German.

Sonja fires away: "Guten Tag, Herr Kapitänleutnant Strauss!" (Good day, Lieutenant Strauss!).

Mister Strauss almost falls on his back.

Sonja: "We met in 1942 in Brest. I delivered four agents to your U-boat and you had to take them to New York."

One of the older men with Strauss cuts her short: "I don't think we should discuss all these things here in public. Where can we meet in private to have a talk?"

Me: "We are staying in a guest house. We can give you the address. But, by the way, I also know Herr Strauss. He rescued me in July 1939 when my plane fell into the water."

Later, during the afternoon, the three gentlemen join us at our guest house. Korvettenkapitän a.D. (außer Dienst – retired) Stefan Strauss introduces us to his father-in-law, Kapitän zur See a.D. (naval captain, retires) Joachim Graf (count) von Czapiewski, and his father, Herr Septimus Strauss of Walvis Bay.

Sonja: "And what are you gentlemen doing here in Angola? Fleeing from the Nazis?"

The count: "We are here to do banking business, as you saw."

Me: "That's what we were also doing this morning."

Sonja: "What type of banking business? Selling your submarine to the Portuguese? Or the contents of your submarine?"

The count: "Dear lady, my son-on-law told me earlier today that you were with the Abwehr. You, obviously, know a lot. And you also ought to know that there are certain things that ought not to be disclosed because it can bring danger to all those involved."

Sonja laughs: "You may tell us everything. You see, both of us are officially dead. We died in a plane crash almost a year ago. You are actually talking to our spirits!"

The three men laugh and Stefan Strauss says: "I didn't shake the hand of a ghost when I greeted you a little while ago."

Sonja: "Before we carry on discussing military secrets and war crimes, I will ask our landlord to bring us some coffee. He doesn't understand a word of German."

With her cup of coffee in her hand, Sonja continues: "Gentlemen, there is no need for secrecy anymore. The Nazi thugs are on the run, if they haven't been apprehended yet. The only explanation for you presence here in Luanda, instead of being inmates of a prisoner-of-war camp, is that you stole a submarine and fled Europe when everything fell apart. And now you are doing banking business in a Portuguese colony. Stolen Nazi gold, perhaps?"

The count: "We won't admit or deny anything. Please, let's leave it at that. But what are you two doing in this corner of Africa? Did the Abwehr send you to spy on the Portuguese and faked your deaths?"

Me: "No. Our plane really crashed in Egypt during an attack on the Suez Canal. But we survived and stole a British fighter and fled to neutral Turkey. From there we got to Lisbon and now we are buying an airplane here to fly to Windhoek. All above board. We didn't swipe anything from the Nazis. But I imagine that the Nazis were relieved that we are dead."

Stefan Strauus: "But why?"

Sonja: "As a member of the Abwehr, I was indirectly involved in the assassination plot against Hitler. That's why we had to get to neutral Turkey in a hurry."

I am glad that my sly wife doesn't disclose the origin of our money.

After we've swopped a few yarns about our war experiences, our guests leave again.

Sonja confides in me: "Did you see their reaction when I mentioned stolen Nazi gold?"

"Yes. They're guilty as hell. Their shocked faces told us all. Good for them!"

"I'm sure they had to take the gold on a secret mission somewhere and decided to disappear with the loot. That's why they turned up in Luanda, of all places. While I was working for cousin Walter, I heard rumours that some Nazis were planning to smuggle the Reich's gold to South America to prevent the Allies of confiscating it. They wanted to continue a secret war against the Allies. And that's why I guessed that these gentlemen stole some of that gold. I like the fact that those nut-case Nazis won't be able to use that gold for whatever reason. But these guys will always stay fugitives because the remaining Nazis will hunt them down. Poor guys."

"They can't be poor with all that gold…"

Windhoek, Monday, 3 September 1945

Herr and Frau Karl and Sonja Krause are getting settled in their new home in Windhoek. We entered South West Africa legally as German citizens with our original passports and we adopted our old identities, while keeping our military backgrounds secret.

With our treasure trove of money in a Swiss bank we bought the Heinkel Blitz and flew to Windhoek. I registered the plane in my name in this country and started a courier and charter business, flying passengers and freight throughout South West. Sonja is a capable radio operator because it was her first job in the Abwehr to operate a radio to listen to the radio traffic of the Royal Air Force. I taught her the basics of navigation and map reading.

And now we are moving into the first home that we have ever owned.

Sonja: "Do you still know how to make babies? I want a few. This is the place where we are going to start."

It was possible to make contact with our respective families by means of letters after the end of the war. Sonja's parents are both alive and they live in the American sector of Berlin. Circumstances in a devastated Germany are horrible at this stage and we sent them some money. They were overjoyed to learn that their daughter and son-in-law are not dead, after all. Siegfried, who ended the war as an Oberst in the Luftwaffe, was recently released from a POW camp – as was Sepp who became a Korvettenkapitän (Lieutenant Commander) in the Kriegsmarine. My parents-in-law think it's a miracle that all three their children survived.

My parents-in-law informed us that official death certificates were issued for both of us. I was deemed KIA and Sonja was classified as a victim of a bombing raid on the train on which she travelled. They forwarded these death certificates to us, together with my previous death certificate when I was shot down over Tobruk, and we keep them as souvenirs of our miraculous escape. I was also awarded the Knight's Cross with Oak Leaves posthumously for leading the raid on the Suez Canal where an aircraft carrier was seriously damaged. This trinket was also sent to me, together with my other belongings.

Cousin Walter Schellenberg was arrested by British Military Police and was charged with war crimes, just as other Nazi officials. He testified against other SS officers to save his own skin, but he was nevertheless sentenced to five years in prison. Sonja is certain that he has other banking accounts in Switzerland, apart from the one that she has plundered, and that he will live on that money after his release.

My parents in Kroondal were overjoyed when they received their first letter from us. Both are still alive, although my father's health got a knock while he was interned during the war by the South African Government for being born in Germany and having a son who was serving in the Luftwaffe (that's me). During a lull in our business, Sonja and I flew to Rustenburg to surprise my parents.

My charter service is being done in partnership with my old friend, Wolfgang Schenk, who also became a bush pilot in South West Africa after having evaded capture at the end of the war. I bumped into him at the Windhoek airfield shortly after we have entered South West and we decided to become partners. Our services are in rather great demand because this part of the world is badly served by railways and the road system is rather basic.

EPILOGUE

Pretoria, Saturday, 30 August 1975

Today, I put the finishing touches on this story for my children and grandchildren. Yesterday, the last working day of August, a farewell parade was held as I retired as a brigadier of the South African Air Force and senior staff officer at Air Force Headquarters in Pretoria. Earlier this month, I reached the age of sixty, the mandatory retirement age.

When amnesty was given in 1948 to persons who helped the Germans during the war, Sonja and I decided that it became time that we settle in South Africa. Both I and Wolfgang Schenck, who was born in South West Africa, decided to apply to be appointed as officers and pilots in the SAAF because that was the only job we were trained for. I also claimed my old South African citizenship. We both were given the rank of major after receiving some basic training, with the promise of future promotions. We were given conversion training on the DC-3 Dakota transport plane. Both of us had enough of combat aircraft.

I was warned not to wear my German decorations on my South African uniform because that could cause some unpleasantness.

I happened to receive medical treatment at 2 Military Hospital at Wynberg, Cape Town, during December 1957 while being stationed at the nearby Ysterplaat Air Force Base at that time. The surgeon who worked on me was my old acquaintance, Doctor David Scholtz, who was already a full Colonel in the South African Army. He also managed to get into the Medical Service of the Defense Force with his German military background. We spoke alternatively Afrikaans and German.

He told me: "I have a friend who also fought on the German side during the war, while being a South African – Korvettenkapitän Stefan Strauss. He told me that he had saved you shortly before the beginning of the war when your airplane fell into the North Sea next to his submarine."

"Yes, I remember him. And I've bumped into him in Luanda shortly after the end of the war. I also visited him in Walvis Bay where he has a shipping business when I landed there with my plane."

I didn't disclose that I and Sonja suspected that he financed his business with the proceeds of the sale of stolen Nazi gold.

After that conversation, which I reported to Sonja, both of us struggled to sleep that night. All our old fears, anxieties, worries, and insecurities surfaced again and we were afraid that we would experience old nightmares again while asleep.

We felt guilty about all the pain and death that we had caused. Of course, we had to defend our people and our loved ones against the attacks of the enemy, but that didn't take away our own feelings of guilt. And, the worst of all, there is no way in which we can compensate those whose lives we have taken or to whom we brought pain and suffering. We also felt guilty because we both survived the war, despite the dangers and risks we encountered. We often asked ourselves: what did we do to deserve the fact that we were still alive while so many friends and colleagues paid with their lives? These dead people often visit us in our dreams and they stare at us with accusing eyes.

Serious, grave, painful lingering shell-shock, together with depression, anxiety, despair, sadness, and unhappiness, was our sad lot. Fortunately, we have each other and our children and we understand each other completely. That helps. As time went on, the lingering shell-shock dissipated and our shell-shocked love affair blossomed.

Pretoria, Tuesday, 9 September 1975

It is our plan to go on a long holiday after my retirement a week ago. While I'm preparing our motor car for a trip to the Kruger National Park tomorrow, stunning Sonja comes to me with a worried expression on her lovely face: "Siegfried just phoned from Berlin. He gave me a very bad message. I almost don't know how to tell you."

"What does your brother say?"

Sonja starts sobbing and I put my arms protectively over her shoulders and I pat her on her back. I plant a kiss on the top of her head.

Sonja regains her voice after a while: "I must tell you what Siegfried said. It has to do with what happened in 1944."

"My love, there's no need to feel bad about the war anymore. That's ancient history. I'm sure that both of us have been able to get rid of the horrible shell-shock of those days.

Sonja stays silent for a whole minute before speaking again: "The executors of the estate of my late cousin, Walter Schellenberg, want to take both of us to court for stealing his money. They want to force us to pay back the money. And with interest!"

"Ha-ha! That application can't succeed. You can't sue dead people! Both of us don't exist. We officially died in July 1944! We can always show our death certificates to the judge to prove that we're not alive anymore. I personally have not only one but actually two official death certificates, both with signatures and date stamps. I would very much like to see the judge's face when he sees both of them!"

GLOSSARY

The greatest part of this story is situated in Germany or in a German environment. Therefore, many German words and terms are used. They are given their English equivalents the first time they occur, but for the benefit of the reader a list of such words, terms and abbreviations that are used repeatedly is given here:

Abitur	Matriculation
Abwehr	The Wehrmacht's Intelligence Service
Außer Dienst	Retired
Bande	Gang
Brigadeführer	Major General of the SS
Brötchen	Bread rolls
Du	You
Ersatz	Replacement
Ersatz Kaffee	Artificial coffee
Fahnenjunker	Flight cadet
Fahnenjunker-Feldwebel	Flight Cadet-Sergeant
Fahnenjunker-Unterfeldwebel	Flight Cadet-Senior Corporal
Fähnrich	Ensign
Fallschirmjäger	Paratrooper
Feldwebel	Sergeant
Flieger	Airman
Fliegerhorst	Air base
Fliegerkorps	Air corps
Frau	Missus
Freiherr	Baron
Führer	Leader
Gefreiter	Airman, First Class
General der Flieger	Air Force General
Generalfeldmarshall	Field Marshall

Generalleutnant	Lieutenant General
Generalmajor	Major General
Generaloberst	Colonel General
Gestapo (Geheime Staatspolizei)	Secret State Police
Gruppe	Group
Gruppenkommandeur	Group Commander
Hals-und-Beinbruch	Break your neck and leg! – the German way of wishing somebody a pleasant outing
Hauptbahnhof	Main station
Hauptgefreiter	Lance corporal
Hauptmann	Captain
Hausfrau	House wife
Heiligabend	Christmas Eve
Herr	Mister
Jagdgeschwader	Fighter wing
Kaiserliche Marine	Imperial Navy
Kampffliegerschule	Bomber School
Kampfgeschwader	Bomber Wing
Karfreitag	Good Friday
Kette	Flight (of aircraft)
Kommodore	Commander of a wing
Kriegsmarine	German Navy
Lazarett	Military hospital
Lehrgang	Curriculum
Leutnant	Second Lieutenant
Leutnantzur See	Naval Ensign
Luftflotte	Air fleet
Luftkriegakademie	Air Warfare Academy
Luftkriegschule	Air Warfare School
Luftwaffe	Air Force
Mannschaft	Team
Oberfähnrich	Senior Ensign

Oberfeldwebel — Flight Seargeant

Oberleutnant — Lieutenant

Oberst — Colonel

Oberstleutnant — Lieutenant Colonel

Oekee — The way the Germans pronounce OK

Offiziersanwärter — Officer candidate

OKL (Oberkommando der Luftwaffe) — High Command of the Luftwaffe

OKW (Oberkommando der Wehrmacht) — High Command of the Wehrmacht

Pension — Guest house

Reich — Empire

Reichsmarschall — Marshall of the Reich

Schützstaffel (SS) — Protection Squadron

Sekt — Sparkling wine

Sie — You (formal address)

Sicherheitsdienst — Security Service

Spiegelei — Fried egg

Stabsartzt — Medical officer

Stabsgefreiter — Lance Corporal

Staffel — Squadron

Staffelkapitän — Squadron Captain

Standartenführer — Colonel of the SS

Sturmbannführer — Major of the SS

Tante Ju — Aunty Ju (the Junkers Ju 52 transport plane)

Tintenkuli — Fountain pen

Verstanden? — Do you understand?

U-boot — Submarine

Untermensch — Subhuman

Unteroffizier — Corporal

Vati — Daddy

Waffen-SS	Armed SS
Wehrmacht	Defence Force

RANK STRUCTURE OF THE LUFTWAFFE 1935-1945

It is necessary to explain the rank structure of the Luftwaffe and give the English equivalents since most of these are used in this story:

General Officers

Collar	Shoulder Strap	Sleeve on Flying Jacket	Rank
			Reichsmarschall (Marshall of the Reich)
			Generalfeldmarschall (Field Marshall)
			Generaloberst (Colonel General)
			General der Flieger General der Fallschirmtruppe General der Luftnachrichten-truppe General der Flakartillerie

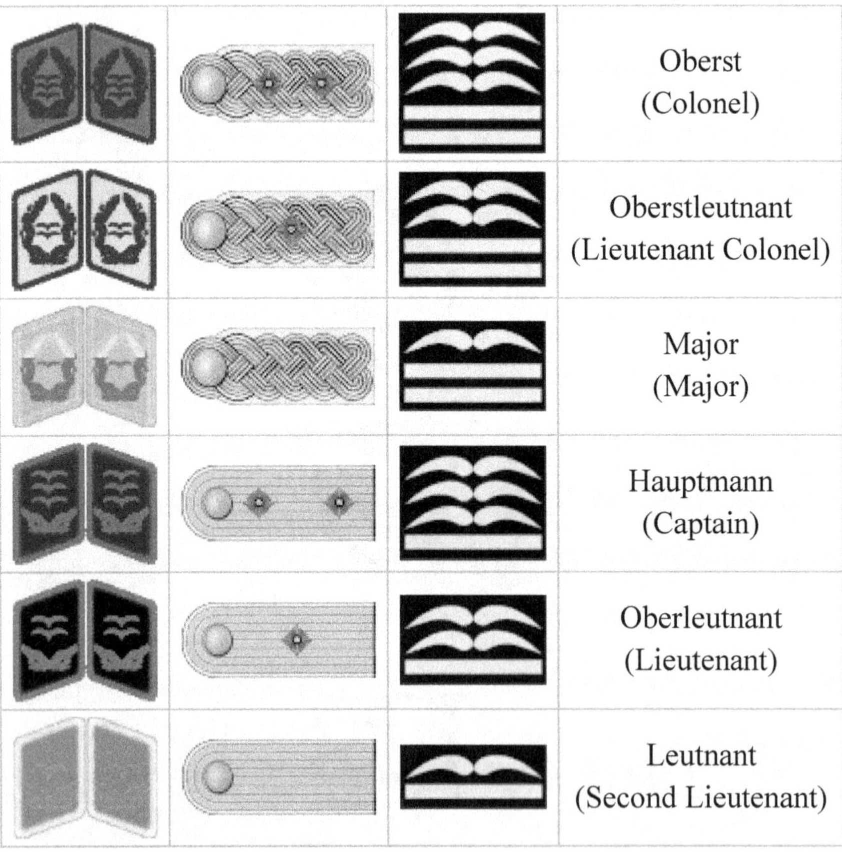

			(General)
			Generalleutnant (Lieutenant General)
			Generalmajor (Major General)

Officers

			Oberst (Colonel)
			Oberstleutnant (Lieutenant Colonel)
			Major (Major)
			Hauptmann (Captain)
			Oberleutnant (Lieutenant)
			Leutnant (Second Lieutenant)

Candidate Officers and Senior NCO's

			Oberfähnrich/ Stabsfeldwebel (Senior Ensign/Sergeant Major)
			Fähnrich/ Oberfeldwebel (Ensign/Flight Sergeant)
			Fahnenjunker/ Feldwebel (Flight Cadet/Sergeant)
			Fahnenjunker/ Unterfeldwebel (Flight Cadet/Sergeant)
			Unterfeldwebel (Sergeant)
			Fahnenjunker/ Unteroffizier (Flight Cadet/Corporal) Unteroffizier (Corporal)

Enlisted Personnel

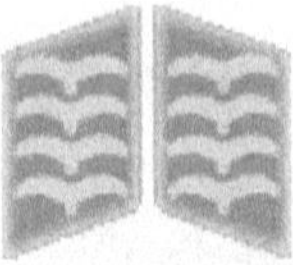			Stabsgefreiter (Lance corporal)
			Hauptgefreiter (Lance corporal)
			Obergefreiter (Lance Corporal)
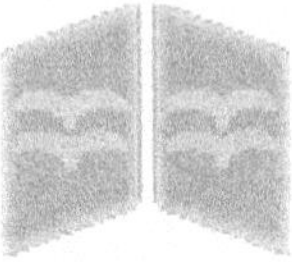			Gefreiter (Private, Class 1)
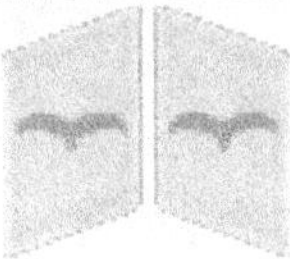			Flieger (Private/Airman)

PICTURE CREDITS

Outside cover
Messerschmitt Me 410 trailing smoke
https://www.youtube.com/watch?v=elqE5MjXcw8

Prologue
Bicycle
https://za.pinterest.com/pin/145804106661448582/

Berlin, Friday, 17 July 1936
SS Usambara
https://i.pinimg.com/originals/47/5a/2e/475a2ea87429a0b1a8947b87e1e
60d3f.jpg

Unter den Linden, Berlin, with swastika flags
https://en.wikipedia.org/wiki/File:Unter_den_Linden,_jobbra_a_Staatsbi
bliothek,_h%C3%A1tt%C3%A9rben_a_Brandenburgi_kapu._Fortepan_
17439.jpg

Berlin, Sunday, 26 July 1936
Arado 66 Trainer
http://aviadejavu.ru/Site/Crafts/Craft22183.htm

Berlin, Saturday, 1 August 1936
Olympic stadium with athletes marching in
https://en.wikipedia.org/wiki/File:Bundesarchiv_B_145_Bild-
P017045,_Berlin,_Er%C3%B6ffnung_der_XI._Olympischen_Spiele.jpg

Olympic Emblem, 1936
https://en.wikipedia.org/wiki/File:1936_berlin_logo.jpg

Adolf Hitler with a few German athletes
https://www.normandyamericanheroes.com/blog/germany-hitler-1936-
olympics

Berlin, Monday, 17 August 1939

Barracks at Berlin-Gatwo Fliegerhorst
http://www.daedalus-berlin.de/gatow%20geschichte%201.htm

Berlin, Friday, 13 November 1936
Hitler and Nazi officials with an aeroplane
https://www.thesun.co.uk/news/2442990/germany-largest-refugee-camp-
tempelhof-airport-berlin-attack-lorry-driver-navid-b/

Berlin, Friday, 19 February 1937
Luftwaffe parade at Berlin-Gatow, 1935
file:///C:/Users/User/Downloads/kriegswichtig_luftkriegsakademie%20(
2).pdf

Berlin, Monday, 22 February 1937
Focke-Wulf 44 Stieglitz taking off
https://airandspace.si.edu/collection-objects/focke-wulf-fw-44-stieglitz-
goldfinch-photograph-0

Berlin, Tuesday, 1 June 1937
Focke-Wulf 44 Stieglitz in the air
https://en.wikipedia.org/wiki/Focke-
Wulf_Fw_44_Stieglitz#/media/File:Stieglitzc_2008.jpg

Berlin, Friday, 16 June 1937
Focke-Wulf 44 Stieglitz in formation
https://www.ww2-weapons.com/pilot-training-of-the-luftwaffe/

Berlin, Friday, 9 July 1937
Luftwaffe parade, 1937
file:///C:/Users/User/Downloads/kriegswichtig_luftkriegsakademie%20(
2).pdf

Pilot's badge, Luftwaffe
https://upload.wikimedia.org/wikipedia/commons/a/af/Flugzeugf%C3%
BChrerabzeichen.jpg

Kufstein, Tuesday, 13 July 1937
Pension in Kufstein
https://www.kufstein.com/en/book/kufstein/inn/gasthof-pension-kienbergklamm.html

Lechfeld, Tuesday, 3 August 1937
Heinkel He 111 taking off
https://www.mcmahanphoto.com/rs070--german-wwii-heinkel-he-111-bomber-take-off-photo.html

Lechfeld, Wednesday, 4 August 1937
Oberleutnant Werner Baumbach
https://upload.wikimedia.org/wikipedia/en/6/6d/Werner_Baumbach.jpg

Interior of He 111 cockpit
https://forum.warthunder.com/index.php?/topic/31373-bomber-cockpit/

Berlin, Wednesday, 22 December 1937
Old church in Berlin-Dahlem
https://upload.wikimedia.org/wikipedia/commons/d/d6/DK_Gatow_Mau
erwerk_des_Turmbereichs.jpg

Walter Schellenberg as SS Major
https://deutschesoldaten.fandom.com/wiki/Schellenberg

Lüneburg, Monday, 3 January 1938
Wolfram Freiherr (Baron) von Richthofen.
https://www.pinterest.se/pin/292171094573265395/visual-search/

Lüneburg, Tuesday, 4 January 1938
Heinkel He 111 cockpit
https://www.justflight.com/product/aeroplane-heaven-heinkel-he-111-bundle

Lüneburg, Thursday, 6 January 1938
Heinkel He 111 in the air

https://www.justflight.com/product/aeroplane-heaven-heinkel-he-111-bundle

Berlin, Tuesday, 1 March 1938
Luftwaffe Day in Berlin, 1938
https://ww2db.com/image.php?image_id=12737

Lüneburg, Thursday, 1 September 1938
Heinkel He 11 releasing a bomb
http://luftwaffesim.com/wp-content/uploads/2014/07/He-111-IL-21.png

Lüneburg, Monday, 1 May 1939
Oberst Hans Siburg
https://www.ima-usa.com/products/original-german-wwii-general-der-flieger-hans-siburg-7x50-dienstglas-binoculars-with-1939-dated-case?variant=19632628334661

Lüneburg and North Sea, Monday, 3 July 1939
U-30
https://www.wikiwand.com/en/German_submarine_U-30_(1936)

Berlin, Sunday, 16 July 1939
Wilhelm Canaris
https://www.tracesofwar.com/articles/3007/Canaris-Wilhelm.htm

Lüneburg, Monday, 31 July 1939
Emblem of KG 26
https://en.wikipedia.org/wiki/Kampfgeschwader_26

Lüneburg, Friday, 1 September 1939
Two Heinkel He 111's flying in formation
https://www.youtube.com/watch?v=8WmyR6Mjj98

Schleswig, Monday, 25 September 1939
Squadron of parked Heinkel He 111's

http://www.daveswarbirds.com/bob/pics/aircraft/111s/P151_HE-
111s_inspected_by_generals.jpg

Schleswig, Tuesday, 26 September 1939
HMS Ark Royal being bombed
https://upload.wikimedia.org/wikipedia/commons/7/7a/HMS_Ark_Royal
_attack.jpg

Schleswig, Tuesday, 17 October 1939
Formation of Heinkel He 111's
https://www.youtube.com/watch?v=O3LRKegCdRI

Schleswig, Saturday, 28 October 1939
Spitfire shooting at a Heinkel He 111
https://www.spitfireassociation.com/spitfiredevelopment.php

Schleswig, Saturday, 7 December 1939
Heinkel He 111
https://www.justflight.com/product/aeroplane-heaven-heinkel-he-111-
bundle

Schleswig, Thursday, 22 February 1940
German destroyer Leberecht Maass
https://i.pinimg.com/736x/c6/38/1c/c6381ced8c65fa1fad246ba616800d3
1.jpg

Schleswig, Saturday, 16 March 1940
HMS Norfolk
https://forum.worldofwarships.com/topic/91663-color-pics-of-hms-
norfolk-york-and-exeter-image-heavy/

Schleswig, Tuesday, 9 April 1940
Heavy gun on the island of Drøbak, Oslo Fjord
Photo taken by the author

Schleswig, Wednesday, 10 April 1940
Heinkel He 111 with torpedoes
https://twitter.com/TeamFusionSim/status/12249696924622 11072/photo/
1

Aalborg, Wednesday, 17 April 1940
HMS Suffolk after being hit
https://za.pinterest.com/pin/474496510716946775/

Trondheim, Tuesday, 30 April 1940
Værnes airfield near Trondheim
https://upload.wikimedia.org/wikipedia/commons/3/3c/V%C3%A6rnesm
oen_1936.jpg

Thon Hotel Nidaros, Trondheim, Norway
https://www.booking.com/hotel/no/thon-
gildevangen.html?aid=303948&label=trondheim-

Trondheim, Friday, 7 June 1940
HMS Glorious sinking
https://www.facebook.com/Schiffposting/photos/a.1010691879138573/1
191467267727699/

Trondheim, Monday, 24 June 1940
Generaloberst Erhard Milch inpcting a parade in Norway
https://en.wikipedia.org/wiki/Trondheim_Airport,_V%C3%A6rnes#/med
ia/File:Bundesarchiv_Bild_101I-760-0165N-
26,_Norwegen,_Erhard_Milch_bei_Stuka-Staffel.jpg

Stavanger, Tuesday, 13 August 1940
Golden Luftwaffe Eagle with Swastika
https://www.epicmilitaria.com/luftwaffe-generals-gold-metal-tunic-
eagle.html

North Sea and London, Wednesday, 28 August 1940
Searchlights and London skyline

https://www.military-history.org/feature/world-war-2/blitz-ww2.htm

Beauvais, Sunday, 13 October 1940
Chambres d'hôte – Clos d'Allonne
https://www.booking.com/hotel/fr/clos-d-39-allonne.en-gb.html

Aalborg, Saturday, 1 February 1941
Oberstleutnant Benno Kosch
https://www.alexautographs.com/auction-lot/benno-kosch_EF8449EAEE

Aalborg, Thursday, 13 February 1941
Oberst Alexander Holle
https://en.wikipedia.org/wiki/Alexander_Holle#/media/File:Bundesarchiv_Bild_146-2008-0286,_Alexander_Holle.jpg

Berlin, Thursday, 10 April 1941
Junkers Ju 52 ambulance aeroplane
http://bennosfiguresforum.com/viewtopic.php?p=211204

Berlin, Sunday, 8 June 1941
Walter Schellenberg
https://en.wikipedia.org/wiki/Walter_Schellenberg

Stubendorf, Monday, 16 June 1941
Oberstleutnant Otto Höhne
https://upload.wikimedia.org/wikipedia/commons/c/c5/GMHoehne.jpg

Emblem of KG 54
https://en.wikipedia.org/wiki/Kampfgeschwader_54

Swidnik, Wednesday, 2 July 1941
Junkers Ju 88 of KG 54 in flight
https://www.facebook.com/photo.php?fbid=2761236123889885&set=p.2761236123889885&type=3

Swidnik, Thursday, 3 July 1941

Junkers Ju 88 dive-bombing a target
https://www.youtube.com/watch?v=kLTwRymkTVc

Hranowka, Friday, 15 August 1941
Junkjers Ju 88 with bombs
https://en.topwar.ru/164863-boevye-samolety-junkers-ju-88-universalnyj-ubijca.html
th-a-Torpedo-Grosseto-Italy-01.html

Catania, Tuesday, 27 January 1942
Crashed Junkers Ju 88
https://www.worldwarphotos.info/gallery/germany/aircrafts-2/junkers_ju88/crashed-ju88-of-kg-1/

Cagliari-Elmas, Tuesday, 10 February 1942
Junkers Ju 88 of KG 54
https://en.wikipedia.org/wiki/Kampfgeschwader_54#/media/File:Bundes
archiv_Bild_101I-405-0593-36,_Flugzeug_Junkers_Ju_88.jpg

Comiso, Sunday, 24 May 1942
Junkers Ju 88 with torpedoes
https://en.topwar.ru/164863-boevye-samolety-junkers-ju-88-universalnyj-ubijca.html

Messina, Monday, 1 June 1942
General der Flieger (Air Force General) Bruno Loerzer
https://www.findagrave.com/memorial/144394916/bruno-loerzer

Kriegsorden des Deutschen Kreuzes
https://en.wikipedia.org/wiki/German_Cross

Tobruk, Sunday, 21 June 1942
General Erwin Rommel
https://www.pinterest.co.uk/pin/316237205081100619/

Comiso, Sunday,12 July 1942

Cathedral in Comiso
https://www.accommodation-sicily.com/val-di-noto/comiso

Tazinskaja, Wednesday, 19 August 1942
Emblem of KG 51
https://en.wikipedia.org/wiki/Kampfgeschwader_51

Tazinskaja, Saturday, 24 October 1942
Junkers Ju 88 of KG 51

Tazinskaja, Tuesday, 17 November 1942
Junkers JU 88 in flight
https://www.youtube.com/watch?v=vrkiKI6zE-Q

Tazinskaja and Stalingrad, Monday, 23 November, 1942
Military Policeman
https://radindustries.wordpress.com/2019/06/04/feldgendarmerie/

Tazinskaja, Thursday, 3 December 1942
A-20 Douglas Havoc Boston light bomber of the Soviet Air Force
https://www.reddit.com/r/WWIIplanes/comments/l0vzvx/soviet_lendleas
e_b25_link_in_comments_about_these/

Rostov, Friday, 8 January 1943
Junkers Ju 88 painted white
https://www.youtube.com/watch?v=kLTwRymkTVc

Saporoshje, Wednesday, 17 February 1943
Hitler being greeted by Generalfeldmarschall Erich von Manstein
https://en.wikipedia.org/wiki/Erich_von_Manstein#/media/File:Bundesar
chiv_Bild_146-1995-041-
23A,_Ostfront,_Adolf_Hitler,_Erich_v._Manstein.jpg

Saporoshje, Monday, 22 February 1943
Tupolev Tu-2 bomber

https://crewdaily.com/interesting-facts-about-the-tupolev-tu-2-bat/

Saporoshje, Tuesday, 23 February 1943
Generalfeldmarschall Wolfram von Richthofen
https://en.wikipedia.org/wiki/Wolfram_Freiherr_von_Richthofen#/media
/File:Bundesarchiv_Bild_101I-452-0985-
36,_Russland,_Gener%C3%A4le_L%C3%B6hr_und_W._v._Richthofen
_(cropped).jpg

Bagerowo, Monday, 5 April 1943
Bomb made of two welded kerosene drums
Brüting, Georg: Das waren die deutschen Kampfflieger-Ase, 1939-1945.
Motorbuch Verlag, Stuttgart, 1983, p 73.

Illesheim, Sunday, 9 May 1943
Messerschmitt Me 410 fighter-bomber
http://www.hyperscale.com/features/2000/me410a1ir_2.htm

Rear-facing machine gun of the Me 410
https://www.youtube.com/watch?v=Je5ySCoUrvY

Illesheim, Saturday, 22 May 1943
Messerschmitt Me 410 in the sky
https://lcka.com.au/product/messerschmitt-me-410-hornise-short-kit-
plans-dr/

Wien-Aspern, Wednesday, 26 May 1943
Messerschmitt Me 410
http://www.warbirdphotographs.com/LCBW8/Me410-21f.jpg

Lechfeld, Friday, 6 August 1943
Messerschmitt Me 410 in flight
https://www.youtube.com/watch?v=Jufr9eu2wqQ

Illesheim, Monday, 6 September 1943

General der Flakartillerie Emil Zenetti
https://ww2gravestone.com/people/zenetti-emil/

Ritterkreuz des Eisernen Kreuzes
https://en.wikipedia.org/wiki/Knight%27s_Cross_of_the_Iron_Cross

Horsching, Saturday, 11 September 1943
Reichsmarschall Hermann Göring
https://za.pinterest.com/edisohasso/hermann/

Major Hanns Heise
https://sylviolassance.blogspot.com/2014/07/heise-hanns-horst-
0102191318051992.html

Horsching, Monday, 20 September 1943
Lancaster bomber of the RAF in flight
https://www.youtube.com/watch?v=ojLjMkaaios

Horsching, Monday, 27 September 1943
Messerschmitt Me 410 from below
https://www.youtube.com/watch?v=ojLjMkaaios

Padua, Thursday, 2 December 1943
Attack on the harbour of Bari
https://worldwartwointheair.weebly.com/air-raid-on-bari---december-
1943.html

Evreux, Thursday, 19 January 1944
Generalmajor Dietrich Peltz
https://alchetron.com/Dietrich-Peltz

Evreux, Saturday, 21 January 1944
Messerschmitt Me 410 from below
https://www.youtube.com/watch?v=elqE5MjXcw8

Evreux, Monday, 14 February 1944

Messerschmitt Me 410 in flight
https://i.pinimg.com/originals/1a/b1/48/1ab148af21ca2ac7ebe9b04bf2f4
3fed.jpg

Evreux, Friday, 28 January 1944
Messerschmitt Me 410, showing bomb load
https://www.youtube.com/watch?v=Jufr9eu2wqQ

Evreux, Saturday, 19 February 1944
Messerschmitt Me 410 with one engine on fire
https://www.youtube.com/watch?v=elqE5MjXcw8

Evreux, Friday, 3 March 1944
Hotel Normandie, Evreux
https://www.booking.com/hotel/fr/logis-normandy.en-gb.html

Evreux, Saturday, 22 April 1944
German Wound Badge in Silver
https://www.historybunker.com/product/ww2-german-medal-wound-
badge/

Messerschmitt Me 410 shooting at a bomber
https://www.youtube.com/watch?v=ojLjMkaaios

Lechfeld, Tuesday, 23 May 1944
Oberstleutnant Wolfgang Schenck
https://en.wikipedia.org/wiki/Wolfgang_Schenck_(pilot)

Lechfeld, Friday, 26 May 1944
Messerschmitt Me 262 jet trainer
https://za.pinterest.com/pin/64809682111666203/

Lechfeld, Saturday, 27 May 1944
De Haviland Mosquito in Luftwaffe colours
https://kampfgruppe144.blogspot.com/2018/11/1144-de-havilland-
mosquito-priv-biv.html

Lechfeld, Tuesday, 30 June 1944
Heraldic shield with a wolf's head
https://za.pinterest.com/pin/720153796636516064/

Graz, Thursday, 20 July 1944
Werfer-rockets being loaded onto a Messerschmitt Me 410
https://forum.il2sturmovik.com/topic/36435-bf-110-rockets/

Graz, Sunday, 23 July 1944
Squadron Meserschmitt Me 410's
https://simhq.com/forum/ubbthreads.php/topics/4499633/last-build-for-
the-year-mengs-1-48-me410-heavy-fighter

Heraklion, Sunday, 28 July 1944
Suez Canal
https://face2faceafrica.com/article/a-history-of-the-suez-canal-and-how-
it-impacts-you

Kabrit, Monday, 29 July 1944
Aircraft carrier that was attacked
https://imgur.com/Vt9GjLd

Kabrit and Antalya, Wednesday, 31 July 1944
Battleship of the Royal Navy in the Suez Canal
https://en.wikipedia.org/wiki/HMS_Howe_(32)

Passanger ship (troop ship) in the Suez Canal
https://acidhistory.wordpress.com/2012/05/14/royal-signals-19461947-
in-pictures-part-6-ships-in-the-suez/

De Haviland Mosquito
https://www.memorialflightclub.com/blog/win-mosquito-experience-day

Hawker Hurricane
https://www.autoevolution.com/news/this-1940-hawker-hurricane-was-
shot-down-and-lost-for-50-years-back-in-the-air-152250.html#agal_0

Antalya, Thursday, 1 August 1944
The Phoenix
https://www.crystalinks.com/phoenix.html

Luanda, Monday, 4 June 1945
Heinkel He 70 Blitz
http://www.aviastar.org/air/germany/he-70.php

Pretoria, Saturday, 30 August 1975
Dakota DC 3
https://www.aviationcentral.co.za/tag/saaf100/

Rank Structure of the Luftwaffe, 1935-1945
https://military.wikia.org/wiki/Ranks_and_insignia_of_the_Luftwaffe_(1
935%E2%80%931945)

9 781666 746709